ALL IS FAIR

All is Fair

DEE GARRETSON

Swoon READS

SWOON READS · NEW YORK

A SWOON READS BOOK

An imprint of Feiwel and Friends and Macmillan Publishing Group, LLC
175 Fifth Avenue, New York, NY 10010

Our books may be purchased in bulk for promotional, educational, or business
use. Please contact your local bookseller or the Macmillan Corporate and
Premium Sales Department at (800) 221-7945 ext. 5442 or by email at
MacmillanSpecialMarkets@macmillan.com.

Library of Congress Control Number: 2018944892
ISBN 978-1-250-16869-6 (hardcover) / ISBN 978-1-250-16868-9 (ebook)

Book design by Liz Dresner

First edition, 2019

10 9 8 7 6 5 4 3 2 1

swoonreads.com

To Ann Braithwaite

Always a good friend

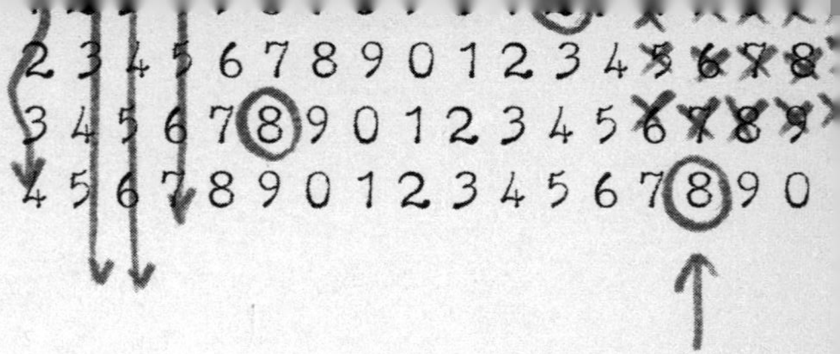
2 3 4 5 6 7 8 9 0 1 2 3 4 5 6 7 8
3 4 5 6 7 8 9 0 1 2 3 4 5 6 7 8 9
4 5 6 7 8 9 0 1 2 3 4 5 6 7 8 9 0

ALL IS FAIR

CHAPTER
ONE

I SHOULD HAVE heard the creaking of the floorboards out-side the old silver pantry, but I was too busy pretending to be a Romanian prince disguised as the school's gardener. My friends, some of the other girls in the fifth form, were choking with laugh-ter at my accent, so they didn't hear the approach either.

I struck a dramatic pose and said my last line to the prince's true love, whose part I had also played. "We will go to my castle and grow turnips together happily ever after."

Bowing, I waited for the laughs. None came. Instead, looks

of horror spread across my friends' faces. I turned to see the heavy door opening with a groan.

Miss Climpson, the overlord of Winterbourne Academy, stood in the doorway. I braced myself for the wrath about to fall upon us, sentencing us to the perpetual writing of lines for our offense, but instead she just said, "Thomasina, I need to see you in my office. The rest of you girls, go to bed."

Dorothy, her eyes wide, gave me a look that meant either *Run for your life!* or *I'll cry at your funeral.* Pretending not to notice, I raised my chin and walked out of the pantry, not wanting the others to think I was a spineless ninny.

But as I followed Miss Climpson down the long central hall of the academy, I became a spineless ninny. My feet dragged more and more as we approached her office. Her door, the portal of despair, was open. Miss Climpson's dark lair with the grim portraits struck terror in the hearts of all the students at the school and I was no exception, though at sixteen I shouldn't have been scared of one tiny old woman who barely came up to my shoulder.

I knew she was going to lecture me about being a poor role model. She'd done it many times before, and it always started the same way: *Now, Thomasina, the girls follow your lead; therefore, you should be a good leader. You should want to make your parents proud of you, even if your marks are not as good as they should be.* Many more "shoulds" would follow, and I would be sufficiently contrite, until the next time.

"Come in and sit down," she said. Her voice was warm and gentle, a tone we usually heard only when Miss Climpson spoke to parents. At those times, her grandmotherly charm was as sudden and shocking to us girls as a gramophone turned on in a quiet room.

I felt chilled as soon as I walked in. Miss Climpson never had a fire lit, even on the most frigid of days. Girls said it was so cold that dust motes froze in midair. With the shortage of housemaids since the Great War had begun, I could imagine dust accumulating until it would eventually look as if a snowfall had struck the office.

War with Germany was giving the former housemaids a choice to have far more exciting lives as nurses and ambulance drivers. If I were a housemaid with a choice between being stuck at Winterbourne cleaning under Miss Climpson's thumb or dodging shells while speeding around in an ambulance, I would have chosen ambulance driving too. The danger would have been worth it in return for doing something to help the war effort.

The headmistress had a strange expression on her face, one I couldn't place. It took me a moment to realize the woman was at a loss for words. When Miss Climpson motioned for me to come farther into the room, I saw it. A telegram envelope lay in the center of the desk, the pale yellow of the paper stark against the almost black wood.

I felt sick. It hadn't occurred to me that it would be a telegram. My brother, Crispin, had been missing for months now, and I'd mostly stopped expecting he'd be found, except when I'd pass too close to the old looking glass in the dark corner of the hall. Then time would stop in the wavy light, my heart would skip, and I could almost see Crispin making faces back at me. He loved practicing his silly voices in looking glasses before reading aloud to us. In one of his letters at the beginning of the war, he'd written that he read to his men from *Alice's Adventures in Wonderland* to keep their spirits up. I supposed that Crispin playing the Mad Hatter in a dugout made as much sense as anything else in the war.

I made myself move to the desk and reach for the telegram, but then drew back my hand. What if it wasn't Crispin? What if it was my father? It wasn't as if each family could make one sacrifice and then be safe from having to make any more. If something had happened to my father, would such news come by telegram, or would someone in the Foreign Office come in person? Winterbourne didn't have a telephone.

I felt a buzzing in my head and then the desk in front of me shrank as if it were moving far away, growing smaller and smaller. I wondered why the room had grown so hot and begun swaying back and forth like a cabin on a ship.

"Thomasina!" The headmistress took my arm, leading me over to a chair and practically pushing me down into it. "Put your head in your lap so you don't faint." I did as I was told, feeling Miss Climpson's hand on my hair. It reminded me of my mother comforting me when I was a child, and that gave me the strength to sit up as soon as the buzzing stopped. The desk was back to its normal size, the telegram still there.

"Take all the time you need, dear. It may not be as bad as you fear."

I wanted to believe her, but it still took all my willpower to pick it up and open it.

2 April 1918

Thomasina,

Your old father has a request. A friend has written that your cousin is ill. She needs you to come home to Hallington right away. Have your things sent as well. Get help from Mrs. Brommers if you need it. She will be glad to give it. To communicate with me, wire the Foreign Office if the situation worsens. Best you don't tell your cousin you are coming. We're at Thornhill but don't know for how long. Once home, let us know of your safe arrival. Give my best to Julius. Remember, two are often better than one.

Father

I tried to clear my mind of the fear the sight of the telegram had given me so I could concentrate, but I was confused. This telegram was far longer than most, and it read like a joke. First of all, even though I had a cousin, Eugenia, she didn't live with us. She lived in Scotland. It was also impossible to imagine Eugenia ill. The woman walked miles a day on her "nature rambles," her storklike figure a common sight for everyone for miles around her home. She never took to her bed for any reason.

Second, I didn't know a Mrs. Brommers, nor had I ever heard of a place called Thornhill. And who was the "we"? My mother was in America helping my uncle, whose wife was ill. My sister, Margaret, was in London.

Third, my father would never refer to himself as an "old

father." People often commented on how Reese Tretheway still looked much as he had in the days he was a valued secret agent for the British government, tracking spies across Europe.

And last, the only Julius I had ever heard of was Julius Caesar, because my father had read all his writings and subjected us to many of the man's sayings. There were so many of them, I thought the man must have spent half his time sitting about thinking up pithy quotes to outlast him.

"Is it bad news, dear?" Miss Climpson asked gently.

I handed the telegram to her.

"I'm sorry your cousin is ill," the headmistress said after she read it. "This is most irregular, but I suppose we should follow Lord Tretheway's instructions. I'll make arrangements to get you home as soon as possible."

I was barely listening, still thinking about the strangeness of the telegram. A memory of my father's voice tugged at me. He was sitting beside my bed, trying to get me to look at him. I was facing the wall, angry that he was insisting I stay in my room to recover from scarlet fever. *It's like a game,* he coaxed. *All spies must know ciphers and codes. Don't you want to learn some? You're a clever girl. Perhaps someday you can be a code breaker in the Foreign Office—the first girl ever to have such an important job.*

A thrill of excitement ran through me. The telegram was strange because it was a cipher, and I knew just how to decipher it. I needed to get to my room to read it in private.

"Yes, I have to go home," I said to Miss Climpson. "Right away."

CHAPTER
TWO

SINCE JULIUS CAESAR was long dead, I couldn't give him my father's best, but I knew that wasn't what my father had meant. The name was a clue. I couldn't believe I hadn't remembered right away. My father, trying to impress upon me that ancient history was worth studying, had taught me that Julius Caesar was one of the first people to use a secret code. Later, when my father was abroad, he would mention Julius in his letters so I'd know they contained a cipher. The key to deciphering this message lay in the telegram's last sentence, just as it had in his letters: *Two are* *often better than one.* That meant I needed to take the second word of each sentence and read the result.

I wasn't going to explain it all to Miss Climpson, though. She'd think I'd come down with a case of brain fever. "May I go pack?" I asked. "I'd like to take a train in the morning."

"Of course, dear." Miss Climpson hesitated, as if she was going to say something else.

But I wanted to get out of there before she could ask questions. "Thank you, Miss Climpson." I darted out of the office, knowing she wouldn't dash after me. Miss Climpson didn't dash.

Dorothy was waiting for me when I got back to our room. "What is it?" she cried, grabbing my hands. "You look strange. You're so pale. Are you ill? What did she say? Tell me!"

"I need a pencil." I pulled away and rummaged around in the clutter on my desk, knocking some books to the floor. My hands felt shaky. "I got a telegram from my father that has a secret message in it. I need to write it out." I knew I was talking too fast, but I couldn't help it.

Dorothy clapped her hands and then practically danced over to her own desk. "This is so exciting! You're so lucky to have a father who was a spy!" She took a pencil from her own desk. "Sit at my desk. Yours doesn't have any room to write on it."

I sat down and opened the telegram, underlining as I read it again. *Your* OLD *father has a request.* A FRIEND *has written that your cousin is ill. She* NEEDS *you to come home to Hallington right away. Have* YOUR *things sent as well. Get* HELP *from Mrs. Brommers if you need it. She* WILL *be glad to give it. To* COMMUNICATE *with me, wire the Foreign Office if the situation worsens.*

Best YOU *don't tell your cousin you are coming. We're* AT *Thornhill but don't know for how long. Once* HOME, *let us know of your safe arrival. Give my best to Julius. Remember, two are often better than one.*

Dorothy was hovering over me. "What is the message? Let me see or read it out loud."

I took a deep breath so I could calm down. "It says 'Old friend needs your help will communicate you at home.'" I read it again, trying to make sense of it.

"An actual mysterious message!" Dorothy squealed. "I can't believe it!"

Dorothy's excitement made my own suddenly change to apprehension. This wasn't a game. My father was a very serious man even in normal times. Something had to be very wrong for him to contact me with a cipher telegram when he had the whole Foreign Office at his disposal. "I can't think of any of his old friends I could help. I can't do anything special."

Dorothy snapped her fingers. "It could be because of your languages! An old friend needs something translated. You are better at languages than anyone here at school, and you know all those ones most people here don't speak."

I did have an odd knack for languages, just like my father, but that couldn't be the reason behind the telegram. "I doubt it. My father could translate everything I could. The country is full of people who know all sorts of languages."

Folding the telegram, I got up and looked around the room. I had to concentrate. One step at a time. First, I had to get home. "I need to pack. I don't know when I'm coming back. I don't know what to take."

Dorothy picked my geometry textbook up off the floor. "You should take your schoolbooks. You can keep up with some of the work at home."

I shuddered. "No, you know I won't open them." Unlike Dorothy, I was fairly hopeless at most school subjects, mainly because I couldn't get myself to study. I'd be even less likely to at home, with the garden calling to me. Besides languages, gardening was my only other talent. Mr. Applewhite, the gardener at Hallington, acknowledged that I could coax any flower to bloom, though no one but the two of us seemed to think it was much of an accomplishment. But whatever was behind my father's telegram, it wouldn't involve gardening.

By the time I'd finished packing it was very late, but morning still took forever to arrive. Either the bed had gotten lumpier or I really was coming down with brain fever. I spent most of the night running through all our acquaintances in my head, trying to think of old friends I could help. None came to mind.

Dorothy had begged Miss Climpson to accompany us to the railway station and Miss Climpson had agreed, surprising us both. Once we were there, Miss Climpson bustled about. "We'll attempt to find you a compartment without soldiers in it," she said as we scanned the carriages for an empty seat. The train was so packed with men in uniform, I doubted that would be possible. I just wanted to sit somewhere, anywhere, so I could be on my way.

Dorothy linked her arm through mine and whispered in my ear, "Maybe you'll be lucky and get stuck in a compartment full of very handsome soldiers."

"I don't usually have that kind of luck," I whispered back. "I'll be stuck with some gossipy ladies or a family with a fretful baby." Even if there were handsome soldiers, I wouldn't know what to say to them. Since the war, I'd mostly been at home or at school, not going anywhere where one might stumble upon a handsome man. The only one I actually knew was my brother's friend Andrew, my first crush, whom I had followed around for so many years that it had become something of a family joke.

"Here's a spot!" Miss Climpson called as an entire family exited a compartment. She gestured for me to get in. "Now, if soldiers join you and they become impertinent, you know what to do—get up and ask the conductor to find you a different seat."

"Yes, Miss Climpson," I said, not intending to do any such thing. Sadly, I couldn't imagine any soldier would even notice me in my unsophisticated school uniform and coat, with my hair in a plait and my shoes so sensible and ugly they would make any girl want to weep. My sister, Margaret, always said it was a pity my hair was neither straight nor curly, just wavy, and the color neither here nor there, just brown to match my eyes. I hadn't inherited my siblings' striking looks of black hair and blue eyes. When I was a little girl, Margaret had teased that I was a change-ling baby brought by the autumn fairies in a basket full of oak leaves and acorns.

"You'll write, won't you?" pleaded Dorothy "It will just be beastly here without you. Here, I was saving these, but I want you to have them." She pushed a packet of pear drops into my hand. "I know they aren't your favorite, but they are better than nothing." She gave a sniffle and wiped a tear from her cheek. I knew she loved pear drops, and her gift was very sweet, I thought.

"Dorothy, you are being much too dramatic," Miss Climpson

scolded. "It's not like Thomasina is being sent off to the Far East. Lincolnshire is not the ends of the Earth." The train's whistle blew and the headmistress added, "We should get back to school. Do you have everything, Thomasina?"

"I'll be fine, Miss Climpson. Thank you for coming to the station." I hugged Dorothy. "You have to write too. No excuses."

"I will." The whistle blew again.

"Come along, Dorothy. Goodbye, Thomasina. Safe journey."

I settled in, happy that I still had the compartment to myself so I could have one of Dorothy's pear drops. Miss Climpson always lectured that ladies didn't eat in train compartments, which I interpreted to mean that they didn't eat in front of strangers. Someday I'd travel by train as a regular person, not caring whether anyone thought I was a "proper lady" or not, and then I could eat as much as I wanted in front of everyone.

I quickly popped a pear drop into my mouth, knowing the compartment wouldn't be empty for long. Ever since the war had started, the trains were always full, and the smell of soldiers' uniforms lingered everywhere, a mix of damp wool, boot polish, and cigarette smoke. Every soldier smoked, and the air in the trains and stations was thick with it.

I supposed I'd be tempted to take up smoking too, if I had to face the trenches. In Crispin's last letters before he disappeared, he had written of the nightmare of mud and stink and death. It was a letter addressed to my father, one that Father wouldn't let me read, though I had gone into his study when he was out riding and read it anyway. The despair in the words bled from the page until I dropped the paper back on the desk, feeling a chill in my fingers. If I hadn't recognized the handwriting, I wouldn't have believed Crispin had written it.

Trying not to think about him, I looked out the window to wave at Dorothy. The whistle sounded and Dorothy's face grew even more woebegone. I knew what would make her more cheerful. I opened the window and leaned out. "We will go to my castle and grow turnips together happily ever after!"

Miss Climpson looked first shocked and then disapproving, but Dorothy at least broke into laughter.

I closed the window and sat back down, only then realizing there was a young man standing in the doorway grinning at me. My ears turned hot. They always did when I was embarrassed. I knew they would be red too, which made it all the worse, so there was no way I could pretend I hadn't been yelling ridiculous things out the window. I dropped my gaze, but not before I noticed his eyes. They were somewhere between blue and green, and lovely. His hair was too long, though, and unruly, sandy blond and waving every which way.

"You have a castle?" he asked with an American accent. That explained the longish hair and the fact that his skin didn't have the winter paleness still cloaking everyone else.

"No. It was a line from a play," I said, as if it was perfectly normal to yell lines out train windows.

"That's too bad. I'd like to see some castles while I'm here." He motioned to the seat opposite me. "Is this seat taken?"

"No."

He came in and sat down, looking around the compartment as if he'd never been in one before. I wondered if he was even supposed to be in first class. His jacket was old, and I could see his sleeves were frayed at the cuffs. He had traces of grease on his hands, as if he'd been working on some machinery. I found myself staring at his odd boots, well-worn leather with a swirling design. I recognized them—they were actual cowboy boots. My American uncle had a pair like them. What was a cowboy doing on a train in Oxfordshire? In general, Americans were rare outside England's cities, but American *cowboys* were as rare as hens' teeth, as our cook would say. I looked out the window so I wouldn't keep staring.

A woman pushing a man in a wheelchair came to a stop on the platform right outside the compartment. I couldn't help but look. The man's head and face were completely covered with a linen cloth so his features were hidden. He wore his soldier's cap on top of the cloth. I wondered if the cloth hid some terrible mustard gas burns to his face, or if he no longer wanted to see the world. My father had told me some of the shell-shocked couldn't stop seeing horrors in even ordinary things.

The woman leaned down and spoke to the man before walking over to talk to a porter. The man's head turned toward my window, and though I couldn't see his eyes, I was afraid he saw me staring. I didn't know what to do. Waving would have been ridiculous. I placed my hand on the window, hoping he hadn't seen me acting so foolish before. I knew being at school allowed us more time than most had to push the war away when we wanted. Others never could. I felt ashamed that I'd spent my time thinking how exciting it would be to drive an ambulance, not even considering who I'd be transporting.

"Do you mind?" A deep voice startled me. I turned to see two officers standing in the compartment's doorway, one of them motioning to the empty seats.

"No," I said, trying to act as though I traveled by myself all the time. The American just shook his head.

I knew by their uniforms that the men were naval aviators, probably stationed at the military base at Cranwell, near my home. The older aviator had a solid country-gentleman air about him, but the younger officer was handsome in a way my mother would describe as "sleek as an otter" with his small black mustache, oiled black hair, and smooth skin. I thought the man had overdone the hair oil, however. He looked positively wet.

When they had seated themselves, the younger man held out a silver cigarette case engraved with a coat of arms and asked, "Would you like a cigarette?"

His voice sounded familiar. I looked at him again, but couldn't place him. I knew the correct way to answer his question. Dorothy instructed all the girls in what to say to men, should we ever have a chance to converse with any. Having two brothers who talked freely gave Dorothy copious amounts of information that she passed on to the more sheltered of us at Winterbourne. According to Dorothy, if I took one, men would assume I was fast, because nice girls either didn't smoke or only smoked in private.

"No thank you, I don't smoke." As soon as I added the last part, I wished I hadn't. It made me sound like a prim schoolgirl.

I glanced over at the American to find him contemplating me with amusement, as if he didn't quite believe my words.

The men purposely ignored the American, and the rudeness

puzzled me. They should have offered him a cigarette as well. Perhaps they thought he looked out of place in first class too. When the two aviators began to talk to each other, I realized they were showing off a bit.

"I'd like another little jaunt like the last one," the older one said. "Watching the fireworks when that ammunition shed blew was quite a show."

"That was a first-rate stunt," the other said. "More of it to come, I expect, though I'd like a new bus before we go up again. My old wreck has one too many bullet holes in it. I half expect it to fall to bits around me."

I couldn't help but look at the American again. He still appeared amused, like he was watching a performance. When he caught me watching him, he had the nerve to wink. I willed my ears not to turn red again, pretending I was actually staring over his right shoulder, thinking lofty thoughts about . . . something other than the way one curl on his forehead looked as if someone should brush it back. Since I couldn't think of a single actual lofty thought and I felt the telltale warmth in my earlobes, I forced myself to open my book and pretended to read.

When I heard one of the officers say the word "Hallington," I looked up. His next words made me think he was talking about my house.

"Smith's group is going to be housed in the new huts there," the younger one said. "Lucky fellows. Beautiful place, much better than our flatlands, and close to Cranwell."

"Have you met him—Smith?" the other asked.

"Yes. He is more of a regular chap than I thought he would

be. One certainly can't call him a shirker. I was surprised he had such a noticeable stutter. At least, being who he is, the boys won't give him a rough time for it."

"Excuse me," I said, closing the book. I knew it was impolite to break into a conversation, but was unable to stop myself. "Are you talking about Hallington Manor? In Lincolnshire?"

"Yes, it's near our base," the younger one said. He leaned forward. "Say, I thought I knew you. You're Lord Tretheway's daughter, aren't you? Lady Thomasina? Hallington is Lord Tretheway's place," he explained to his friend. "I'm Harold Rigall, Captain Rigall." He held out his hand to me. "I met you with your family at my sister's wedding years ago. I danced with your sister, Margaret, though I think she was just taking pity on me. And this is Squadron Leader MacElvoy."

"How do you do?" I replied. I couldn't remember Harold. I remembered all the lovely food because it was before the shortages got so severe, and I remembered how happy my parents had looked dancing, though my mother wasn't very good at it. She had never been a good dancer, but my father didn't care.

Crispin had been there too—the last time I had seen him. It occurred to me that it was the last time all five of the family were together, but of course we hadn't known that then. We hadn't known that our world would suddenly turn upside down, though we'd be expected to carry on as if nothing could defeat us. Some days all I wanted to do was go outside and scream as loudly as I could about how unfair it all was. Crispin should have been at Oxford studying literature, putting on theatricals, and going to fabulous parties. He and Andrew would both have been at

Oxford, and on holidays they would have come home and livened up the whole house with their presence.

One of the men coughed, and I realized they were waiting for me to say something. "I haven't been home recently. Do you mean to say there will be men in the park at Hallington?" I tried to picture the grounds full of buildings for military quarters. There had been talk of it for over a year, but I hadn't known the plan had turned into reality.

"They are already there. About a hundred fellows just starting flight training. Any word of your brother?"

I shook my head just as the whistle blew and the train began to slow for the stop at Northhampton. I could feel myself closing up; I didn't want to talk about Crispin with strangers.

"Chin up and all that," Captain Rigall said, "though I expect you get tired of hearing such advice." I was relieved when he switched topics. "And is your sister at Hallington? I was so sorry to hear about her husband's death." His question was casual, but his eyes betrayed a keen interest in my answer. I wasn't surprised. Margaret had always cut a wide swath through crowds of adoring men, even as a widow.

"No," I said. "She's in London."

The man's shoulders sagged a bit. "Oh. Pity. When you speak to her, give her my regards, would you?"

"Of course."

"Good enough." The two men stood up. "Very nice to have a word with you. Makes me remember some pleasant times." They left without even acknowledging the American.

I felt like I had to apologize for them, but before I could, the

American stood up too. "I'm off as well," he said. "Goodbye. I suspect we will meet again very soon. In fact, you may be surprised by exactly how soon." He grinned again as he left the compartment. I heard him start to whistle and recognized the melody from a popular tune. *So send me away with a smile, little girl, brush the tears from eyes of brown.*

I watched through the window as he got off the train. He looked back and motioned for me to lower the window. When I did, he called out, "Don't you have any lines you want to yell at me?"

I don't know what came over me, but another line from the play popped into my head. The prince's true love had tried to send him away, sacrificing their happiness. "I'll give you up because your homeland needs you!" I shouted.

People turned to look at me, and I realized what I had done. I sank back down in the seat, out of view. I could hear Miss Climpson's voice in my head: *Thomasina, you know why you never get good marks in Deportment. I do wish you would try harder to control yourself.* Since the headmistress wasn't with me, I gave myself a failing mark for the day.

The whistle sounded. The compartment seemed very empty now. I should have been glad the American had gotten off the train—he probably winked at every girl he met. He looked like trouble, and that was one thing I didn't need, not with some important war work ahead of me, whatever it was. Nevertheless, I told myself I'd have something to tell Dorothy in the first letter I wrote her. It would make an interesting story.

As the train pulled away, I noticed an elderly man selling

newspapers was waving one about, trying to drum up business. "German arrested in Lincoln!" he shouted. "Spy cut telegraph wires! Read all about it!" I wished I'd noticed him before and been able to buy a paper. We girls had smuggled newspapers into school whenever we could after Dorothy told us Miss Climpson was keeping news from us about all the spies that were infiltrating Britain.

Even though my father had told me most of it was nonsense and people were just looking for reasons to be frightened, I wasn't so sure. That's what he would tell me, after all, because he would think I wasn't old enough to know the truth. Maybe the telegram proved he'd changed his mind about me. I would show him that I too could do my part. Too fidgety to sit still, I got up and stuck my head out the window, as if that would make the train go faster, though I knew I had several more hours until I got home.

CHAPTER THREE

MISS CLIMPSON HAD sent a wire to the house with the arrival time of the train, which meant Lettie, one of the housemaids, would be there to meet me with the pony cart. Since my father was living at our London house to be closer to his work, he had the motorcar with him, and the household relied on Lettie and the cart. Lettie had started out as a scullery maid before moving up to housemaid and sometimes lady's maid, but once the men joined up, she had taken over many of their jobs. She had grown up on a farm, so she knew how to do all sorts of marvelous things I wished I could do.

I spotted Lettie's bright blue tam-o'-shanter first. My mother had given her the hat and Lettie loved it, so she wore it every chance she got. It looked good on her too, contrasting against her black curls.

She waved when she saw me getting off the train and came forward to take my bag, chattering away. Mrs. Brickles, the cook, grumbled that Lettie was as talkative as a magpie and she couldn't get a thing done when Lettie was gossiping in her kitchen. I suspected Mrs. Brickles couldn't get anything done because she was too busy gossiping back. No one was sure who would win in a contest between the two.

I took a moment to give the pony, Sunny, a pat, waking him from a doze, and then climbed into the cart. As we drove, Lettie told me all the doings of the neighborhood. I admit I was only half listening because my thoughts kept straying to the American. I wondered where he was at the moment. Probably winking at some other girl—some girl who didn't have important war work ahead of her. I doubted the mysterious old friend from the telegram was already at Hallington waiting for me, but I had to ask Lettie anyway. "Do we have any guests at the house?"

"No," Lettie said, sounding confused. "Are there supposed to be guests?"

"No, I was just curious." In all the flurry of the telegram and packing and getting home, I hadn't thought about why the telegram directed me to go to Hallington instead of meeting my father in London. Why would someone come to the country instead of somewhere more convenient? "Has my father been home recently?" I asked. I realized I didn't know if he was even in England.

"About a month ago, just for a day and a night," Lettie said, flicking the reins. Sunny snorted but didn't pick up his pace. "Very secret meeting that night. The drive was lined with motorcars. Mr. Norris came with your father and acted as footman, and he was the only one allowed in the Tapestry Room to serve. Lady Margaret and her friend weren't even invited. They had trays in Lady Margaret's room, though they dressed up like they were at dinner. Such pretty clothes! We were all asked to stay in the servants' hall."

The news that my sister had been home was surprising, but not as surprising as the news about Mr. Norris. "Mr. Norris hasn't acted as footman for years!" Mr. Norris was my father's valet, and had been with him for as long as I could remember. Before the war, only young men were footmen, so it was difficult for me to envision the middle-aged Mr. Norris in the role.

"He acted as one that night, livery and all, and he wouldn't tell us a thing," Lettie said. "He kept his lips buttoned up like he'd been sworn to secrecy. Mrs. Brickles couldn't get a useful word out of him, though she tried her best. She was in a right temper with him."

"Who came to the meeting?" I asked.

"No one told us," Lettie said. "They tried to be very secret, but Mrs. Brickles and I worked it out. First of all, the chauffeurs wouldn't come in for a cup of tea. They stayed outside by the cars. I've never heard of that before. And there were soldiers stationed at all the doors."

"Soldiers! So someone important was in the house." Just my luck that I had missed being at home. Even though I knew my father would never give away details about a secret meeting, being there while it was happening would have been exciting.

Lettie dropped her voice, glancing up and down the road as if it were teeming with listeners. "I think one of them was the prime minister. Imagine that! Of course, we haven't told anyone. Not for us to give away state secrets. We've never said a word outside the household about any of the meetings your father has. My brother says there are some down at the White Bull who have tried to pry information out of him, thinking I'd tell him and he'd pass it on!" She flicked the reins again. "Get on there, you old dobbin!"

Sunny turned his head and glared at her exactly the way a person would, but he didn't go any faster. Lettie didn't seem to notice. "Those motorcars driving through the village draw a bit of notice. I tell anyone who asks that they're just letting their imagination run away. It won't be me who gives it away. Too much gossip in the neighborhood as it is."

I knew my father's work with the government was the only reason the house hadn't been turned into a convalescent home or a hospital. Most of the other large homes had long since been put to use. Though my father had never told me, I had figured out that the meetings at Hallington occurred when someone in the government needed a place outside London where they wouldn't draw attention.

"I wish they'd come to meetings more often," Lettie said.

"Isn't that a lot more work for you?"

"Yes, but then the house isn't so empty. When I hear a noise, I know it's a guest. If no one is there and I hear a noise . . ." Her voice trailed off.

"What kind of noises have you been hearing? There are all sorts of creaks and pipe clangs in such an old house."

"I know, miss, but sometimes the noises don't sound right. Hannah, the new housemaid, says it must be ghosts, but she does go on so. I'm not sure I believe her, though sometimes I do feel like there is a presence in the house that shouldn't be there."

I'd never heard Lettie be so fanciful before. "Don't worry, Lettie. I've never heard tales of ghosts at the house." I didn't add that I'd always wished we had at least one ghost. It didn't seem fair to live in a big house and not have one mysterious lady in white or a spirit who dragged around a chain. "At least now that I'm home, it won't be so empty," I told her. "And if there are any strange noises, I'll find out what is causing them. I'm sure there is a simple explanation."

A distant roar came from above. I looked up to see a squadron of aeroplanes in the distance. "You'll get used to that," Lettie said as she turned the cart into the drive. "They go by all the time from Cranwell. They've also built an encampment in the park, so you'll see lights all night."

I felt a pang of jealousy at the sight of the aeroplanes. Even if my father would ever allow me to fly, with the war on, there were no aeroplanes or opportunities available for teaching girls. Someday I would learn, though. The war couldn't last forever.

When we were almost to the front door, I saw a curtain move in an upstairs window, in what had been Crispin's room. But Crispin's room, along with most of the other rooms in the house, had been closed off. I wondered if someone had gone in to air out the room and forgotten to make sure the window was shut tight, making the wind move the curtain. I'd ask Miss Tanner, the housekeeper, to check it.

I didn't like going into Crispin's room. I didn't like seeing the old hourglass that sat on his desk. He'd found it in the attic and declared it a perfect prop for his Father Time character in one of our Christmas theatricals. We'd all laughed as he crept about the makeshift stage wrapped in an old sheet, carrying it and croaking, *Gather ye rosebuds while ye may, Old Time is still a-flying; and this same flower that smiles today tomorrow will be dying.*

I didn't realize that Lettie had brought the cart to a stop at the front door until the pony stamped his hooves and blew air out of his nose.

"I'm sorry, Lettie. I was woolgathering," I said, jumping down, "and I'm keeping Sunny from his stall."

As they drove away, I walked up the steps and into the hall, immediately aware of how quiet it was. I'd known the staff would be in the lower part of the house and the upstairs would be empty, but I'd expected some sound. Then I realized what was missing: Someone had forgotten to wind the hall clock.

A noise from the morning room almost made me drop my bag. Before I could react, my sister, Margaret, walked into the hall. "Mina? What are you doing home? Is something wrong?"

I was just as surprised as she was. She was supposed to be in

London. "I've come home from school," I said, as if it was perfectly normal. "Didn't Miss Tanner tell you?"

"You didn't get expelled, did you?" she asked.

"No, of course I didn't get expelled." Leave it to Margaret to assume the worst.

"So why are you here? Does Father know you've left school?" She sounded almost angry.

"Yes." I had to think of a reason fast, so I said the first thing that popped into my head. "There was a measles outbreak and classes have been suspended temporarily. Some girls stayed on, but I'm sure I can make myself more useful here. It's obvious Mr. Applewhite needs help. The gardens look abandoned." I had noticed as we came up the drive how unkempt the gardens had become with only elderly Mr. Applewhite to care for them. Both of the undergardeners had been called up the previous year.

"You'd rather muck about in the garden than have fun with your friends away from all this war nonsense?"

I didn't understand why she still seemed angry. "Yes, I would." I tried to sound as if I meant it. "What are *you* doing here?" I couldn't imagine a reason for my sister to leave London. Margaret avoided Lincolnshire at all costs, saying it was too deadly dull for words. I noticed that she didn't look herself. My sister had always been thin, but now her thinness seemed brittle, and there were shadows under her eyes. "Have you been ill?"

"No, I couldn't bear the city any longer. I came home for a few days about a month ago and when I went back to London, I realized I couldn't stay." She walked over to one of the tables that edged the walls and moved the vase on it a few inches. "London is nothing like it used to be. Knowing there could be a zeppelin raid at any time set my nerves on edge. You can't imagine the horror of them overhead." She turned back to me. "And I've found I'm terrible at nursing. There, I've said it. I can't bear to see people in pain. Poor souls are better off without me. I thought I could be of more use here." Her eyes dropped away from mine and she became very intent upon examining her nails.

I knew that gesture meant she was lying, at least about being of more use here. She never realized how easily she gave herself away. I'd find out the truth eventually. Margaret was not only bad at telling lies, but also bad at keeping secrets, and I was very, very good at discovering them. Once I'd learned my father had been a spy, I'd wanted to be one too, and practiced by tracking my subjects throughout the house and grounds. It had always driven my older siblings mad.

Margaret patted her hair. "And I'm in desperate need of a new lady's maid. I can't believe how awful I look! I thought while I was here I might hire one from among the local girls, even if I have to train her. I couldn't find anyone in London after mine quit to work at a munitions factory. I don't know what came over that woman."

I didn't comment on this, but I wasn't surprised. My sister never kept maids for long. When Margaret was a child, my mother had always described her as the "just so" child—everything had to be in order and as she expected, or a flood of tears followed. Since Margaret had lost her husband, her desire for order had only grown. Even though she annoyed me at times, I felt awful for her. The world Margaret wanted to live in had never existed, except maybe in books. I suspected that's why her room still held her collection of Mrs. Molesworth's stories, her childhood favorites of happy families and happy places.

I wondered if Margaret's return had anything to do with my telegram. Would my father involve her too? "Does Father know you are home?"

"I mentioned it, but he is so busy, he may not have paid attention," she said. Once again she examined her nails. She was lying again, which meant she hadn't actually told him she was coming home, although I couldn't think of a reason why.

The door to the lower level opened and Miss Tanner, the housekeeper, came into the hall. "I'm sorry I wasn't in the hall to meet you, Lady Thomasina."

"Hello, Miss Tanner," I said. "It's quite all right." It still jarred me to see her, because Miss Tanner was so unlike every other housekeeper I'd met. The woman was far younger than most for such a senior position at a large house, though it was hard to tell exactly how old she was, because she wore her hair pulled back in a severe bun and dressed in dark, old-fashioned clothes. The first time I'd met her, I decided she would make a wonderful character in a gothic novel—the sinister housekeeper hoarding her secrets.

At least the woman was extremely efficient. I had to give her that. I didn't know where my father had found someone in the middle of a war who was so frighteningly unflappable, but with the family scattered, the house needed a Miss Tanner to keep it running.

"Did you know Mina was coming home?" Margaret asked her. "Why didn't you tell me?"

Miss Tanner's mouth twitched, but her expression didn't

change. "I'm sorry, Lady Margaret. I assumed you knew. Yes, I received a telegram this morning."

"Well, I didn't." Margaret put a hand to her forehead. "I've got such a headache. I'm going upstairs for the rest of the afternoon. I'll have a tray in my room for dinner, Miss Tanner. Oh, and please talk to the new maid. The girl talks too much. If she brings up my tray, I don't want to engage in a long conversation with her."

"Yes, Lady Margaret," Miss Tanner said. "I'll speak to Hannah. May I take your bag up to your room?" she asked me.

"Thank you, no. I can carry it," I said, following Margaret up the stairs. She disappeared into her own room without another word, and I went into mine. I noticed the chill first, and then the fine layer of dust that covered everything. The room had never been dusty. I set my bag down, took out a handkerchief, and wiped off the dressing table and the top of my bookcase. The silence upstairs was even worse than it had been downstairs. It was as if time had stopped at the house, or gathered into itself to shut out the war.

I didn't want to stay in my room, but I couldn't make the staff set up the dining room just for me if Margaret was having a tray in her room. I'd have one too. If I could have, I would have just eaten something simple in the kitchen, but I knew Miss Tanner would never allow it.

I took a tour of the gardens to see how much work needed to be done. It was as bad as I feared. I vowed to start first thing in the morning.

When it grew dark, I went back inside and read until Lettie brought up the tray. She was quiet and I noticed that she looked very tired, so we didn't talk much. I suspected she wanted to get back downstairs and finish whatever chores Miss Tanner had set for her so she could go to bed.

After dinner, I paced around my room on pins and needles, hoping someone would appear, someone who I could help. I reread the telegram to see if I had been too quick to think I'd deciphered it correctly. But no matter how many other ways I tried to find a different message, there was nothing else there.

As I was getting ready for bed, a noise from the hallway startled me. I opened the door to find Jove, my father's old retriever. When I let him in, he immediately heaved himself up on my bed, turning around a few times before curling up. I wrinkled my nose. "You don't smell very good," I said to him. He ignored me and gave a contented little dog sigh. I knew he was lonely without my father, and since I was lonely too, I decided we could keep each other company. I missed my own little terrier, Bella. She'd been gone over a year, but I still sometimes thought I could hear her trotting down the hall.

Another noise came from outside my window, a faint noise I couldn't identify. I went to the window, but couldn't see anything in the moon's glow except the distant lights from the camp in the park.

As I was about to go back to bed, a movement below caught my eye. Someone was running away from the house, heading to the woods on the east side. I couldn't see clearly enough to tell anything about the person, beyond that it looked like a man, and a young man at that, moving quickly. There shouldn't have been a young man here. We no longer had any men on the staff except old Mr. Applewhite and Mr. Norris, who was only here when my father was home.

I pulled my wrap around me more tightly. Had Miss Tanner checked all the doors and windows? It had been the butler's job, but it hadn't occurred to me to wonder who had taken over the task. There were so many doors and windows, and so many unused rooms. The man was gone now, but what if he came back? What if it was someone who had tried to break in to steal something, someone who knew how little staff we had now? What if he was the source of Lettie's strange noises? I tried to think what to do, knowing I'd feel ridiculous waking Miss Tanner if it turned out to be nothing. I decided I could check myself.

Jove lumbered off the bed and came over to me, wagging his tail. "What do you think, boy?" I said to him. The dog nudged my hand so I would pet him. That little motion and the dog's presence made me feel better. "Come along, Jove. We're going to investigate."

As I went out into the hall, the dog walked next to me, wagging his tail. I figured that even as old as he was, if there was something strange about the house, he'd know and react. Or at least I hoped he would.

The stillness of the house wrapped around me and made me creep down the stairs as if I had to be quiet. It struck me that there was something else odd about the house. The scent of lavender that normally filled the place was gone. My mother grew a border of lavender to make into potpourri, and it was a tradition for us to spend a day picking it and hanging it to dry. The scent had disappeared, and the house just smelled of stale air.

Downstairs, there was no sound at all, except Jove's wheezy breathing. I told myself everything was fine. I stood for a moment listening, and when I heard nothing, I decided to check the terrace door first.

The door was secure and there was no movement outside, not even a breeze stirring the leaves. "Nothing to worry about here, Jove," I said, knowing I was talking to the dog for my sake, not his. "Let's go check the library." Then the moon came out from behind a cloud and I caught sight of a glint from something lying on the terrace.

I had to know what it was, so I opened the door and walked outside. Jove came with me. He reached it first, sniffing it. Before he could drool all over it, I picked it up. It was a battered wristlet with a broken leather band. My first thought was that it must be Crispin's. The other men on the estate all used pocket watches.

Crispin had been one of the first men I knew to take up the new military wristlet, a band for the wrist that held his pocket watch. He said he'd quickly learned it was too hard to get out a pocket watch while in a trench under fire. But he would have been wearing it when he disappeared.

An owl hooted. I looked out into the dark and decided I'd rather examine the wristlet inside. I shoved it in my pocket and went back into the drawing room, running right into a solid figure. I let out a shriek and stumbled backward.

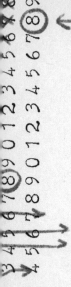

CHAPTER
FOUR

"LADY THOMASINA!" It was Miss Tanner's voice. I would have expected the housekeeper to be in bed hours ago, but she was still wearing one of her standard black dresses.

"I-I didn't realize it was you," I stuttered, my heart pounding.

"Is anything wrong?" Miss Tanner asked. "It's very late."

I had never realized how narrow Miss Tanner's eyes were behind her wire spectacles, narrow and dark and a little frightening. "I saw a man running away from the house," I said, taking a step back, "and I wanted to make sure all the doors and windows were locked." For some reason, I didn't want to tell her about the wristlet.

The housekeeper stood very still for a moment and then asked, "When? Where did you see him?"

"I saw him from my window. He was running across the east lawn and into the woods, just a few moments ago."

"Are you sure it wasn't just a trick of the moonlight?"

"No, I'm sure I saw someone." Miss Tanner didn't look like she believed me, so I added, "He was wearing some sort of cap," as if that detail would make him more real.

The housekeeper clasped her hands. "You shouldn't worry. I check all the doors and windows each evening. It may have been someone hoping to find a way into the kitchen to steal food. Some of the soldiers who have been invalided out of the army can't seem to settle back into normal life at regular jobs, and I've heard many just roam the countryside. I'll make sure the constable knows so he can warn the neighbors. Men like that won't stop at trying the doors of just one house."

"That's terrible," I said. "I mean, it's terrible that former soldiers are going hungry. I thought there were organizations trying to help them."

"There are, but there aren't enough for all the ones in need. Now, if there's nothing else, would you please excuse me?"

"Of course." I felt a yawn stealing over me. The housekeeper disappeared into the gloom and I made my way upstairs, Jove next to me. I put my hand on his head. "He won't come back, will he, boy? And I'm sorry I said you were smelly earlier. You can stay with me every night."

Back in my room, I took the watch out of my pocket and held it under the light. The glass on the front of the case was so scratched, I didn't know how anyone could easily tell time with it. The band had a peculiar odor. I brought it closer to my nose. It smelled of cucumbers for some reason, and reminded me of the lovely soup Mrs. Brickles made on hot days.

Something tugged at my memory, but I couldn't think of exactly what it was. I tried to read the name of the manufacturer. It was just barely visible: *Helma Wasserdicht*. I knew what "wasserdicht" meant—it was German for "waterproof." It wasn't Crispin's. The pocket watch he'd put in his wristlet had said *Harrods* on it. I took the watch off the band and turned it over, wondering if it had an inscription on it. There was nothing there, so I put it back in place.

I couldn't help but think about what the man selling newspapers at the train station had yelled about a German spy in Lincoln. But Lincoln was miles away, and a German wristlet meant nothing. My father had a German pocket watch. Germany was renowned for its watches. I didn't want to be someone who overreacted. Maybe the hungry soldier had taken it off a dead German, though the thought of that brought bile to my throat.

I hadn't known soldiers did that until I overheard Crispin telling my father that he'd had to reprimand one of his men for taking a cigarette case off a body they'd stumbled across. My father's quiet response had been that Crispin should overlook it as much as possible. "Not every rule has to be enforced in the middle of combat," he'd said. The soldiers' world was so far from mine, I couldn't even begin to put myself in their place.

I went back to the window. It had begun to rain, a light rain, the kind that Mr. Applewhite called a mizzle. It was so dark that I couldn't see anything. I closed the curtain, something I never normally did. It made the room feel safer. I lay down, listening to Jove's snuffly breathing. It was a little strange that the housekeeper had been walking through the house so late at night. Perhaps the woman just didn't need much sleep. I could imagine Miss Tanner deciding to sleep only a certain number of hours and to do it efficiently as well. No insomnia for her.

The next thing I knew, a knock on the door woke me. A maid carrying a tea tray entered. I was so groggy that it took me a moment to realize it was morning. I didn't recognize the maid, so I knew it must be the new girl, Hannah. Jove slipped out the door like he'd been waiting for it to open.

"Good morning, Lady Thomasina." Hannah set the tray down on the table by my bed. I was surprised to see it. My mother had decided that before-breakfast tea trays were unnecessary for the duration of the war, since it was just more work for the servants.

As if the girl could read my mind, she said, "Mrs. Brickles thought you'd like a tea tray this morning as a special treat since you had such a long traveling day yesterday." The girl looked younger than me at first glance, with her small stature, the wisps of blond curls escaping from her cap, and her heart-shaped face. When I studied her more closely, however, I realized she might have been older, perhaps eighteen or nineteen.

"Please thank Mrs. Brickles for me." I noticed a small nosegay of violets on the tray. "Did you pick these flowers?" I picked them up and held them to my nose so I could catch their delicate scent. Mr. Applewhite and I had decided that the violets at Hallington gave off a far better scent than other violets.

"Yes, miss," the girl said. "The house seems so empty, and I just thought it would give more life to your room if there were flowers about. I like them too. My mum has a little garden of her own, and I've always been one for pretty flowers. She grows sweet peas that fill the whole house with the nicest scent. I would have gotten you some real flowers from the garden, but I'm scared of that old gardener. He guards those flowers like a dragon guarding his treasure."

It was a good description of Mr. Applewhite's attitude toward the flowers, though I'd never thought of him as fierce. He was a tiny man, wrinkled from years of outdoor work, given to talking to his favorite plants to coax them to grow. I'd learned everything I knew about plants from him.

Hannah went over to the window and opened the curtains. "My mum says flowers belong inside as much as they do outside. Someday I'm going to have a garden and a house so I can bring flowers inside too." The girl was as chatty as Margaret had said. If the housekeeper had taken her to task for talking too much, it didn't seem to have made much of an impact.

"Wait until June when the gardens are in full bloom," I told her. "We'll make sure we sneak lots of bouquets inside when Mr. Applewhite isn't looking."

"That would be nice." Hannah gave a little squeak and pointed at the clock on the mantel. "I should go now. I have to start dusting before Miss Tanner complains. She's very persnickety."

The woman was persnickety, but I didn't think it would be

appropriate for me to agree with Hannah. "Thank you again for the flowers."

After she left, I gulped down my tea, wanting to get outside to see if there were more clues to the identity of the person I'd seen last night. When I went to the wardrobe to find something to wear, it held nothing except some old frocks of Margaret's. Apparently my mother had carried through on her plan to get rid of items that were too small for me, but had not replaced them with anything new.

Margaret's castoffs were all of the garden party variety, not suitable for anything except standing about wishing one could eat the whole tray of muffins rather than just the one that it was polite to take. And none of them suited me. Margaret had excellent taste for what looked good on her, but none of her clothes were right for me in style or color. I grabbed one anyway. My choices were that, one of my school uniforms, or a dress meant for funerals. I put it on, catching sight of myself in the looking glass. Yes, definitely not suited for wielding a trowel, but it would have to do.

As I was trying to get my hair under control, I heard barking outside. Jove never barked except when someone or something who didn't belong came onto the property, which usually meant the occasional lost hiker. Few people had the time to hike with the war on. I felt a little twinge of unease. What if the intruder was back?

The barking increased. I hurried outside just in time to see Jove running across the front lawn, ears flattened and tail down. He was too old and too wheezy to run that fast. It couldn't be good for him. I ran after him, calling for him to stop. As I drew close to the road, I wasn't watching the ground, so I didn't see the muddy spot where the grass thinned. My feet went out from under me and I sat down hard on the ground. It hurt, and a few words I wasn't supposed to use slipped out of my mouth.

When cold water seeped up around me, I realized I was in a shallow puddle. I tried to get back up but slipped again, managing to get the front of my dress muddy to match the back. More bad words. They didn't make me feel better. I was a wet, muddy mess.

Scrambling back up, I saw that Jove was near the edge of the property. Whoever or whatever he'd been chasing was not in sight. I yelled for the dog to stop, knowing he was near the road, but a squadron of planes coming from Cranwell drowned out my voice. Jove crossed the road and continued into the field on the other side of it.

I ran into the road, still calling for him to stop. Then, to my horror, an automobile, an open roadster, came around a sharp curve only feet away. The driver slammed on the brakes and swerved off the road, barely missing a tree.

I skidded to a stop, nearly falling down again. My throat tightened until I saw both people in the car were still upright and moving their heads. "I'm so sorry!" I yelled.

A man in a uniform got out. His hair was short and he looked tired, so much more tired than when I had last seen him, but I knew him. "Andrew!" I flung myself at him and hugged him, forgetting I was covered in mud.

"Mina?" he said. Putting his hands on my shoulders, he moved me a bit away from him. He stared at my face. "I didn't recognize you at first," he said. "You've grown."

Someone laughed behind him and I turned my attention to the young man still in the car. He grinned. My heart did an odd little skip. It was the American from the train.

"Yes, the young lady is quite grown," the young man said, hopping easily over and out of the car, not bothering to open the door. He was dressed in a suit now, though he still wore the cowboy boots.

As he stood there staring at me, I realized that I must look a fright with all the water and mud on me. I could feel my ears turning hot, which meant red too. Just what I needed—bright red ears to go with the gray-brown mud. "I fell when I was chasing Jove. It rained and it was slippery and then I fell again trying to get up." I didn't know why I was going into such detail. The American was smiling as if it was funny I'd fallen. I saw then that I'd gotten mud on Andrew's uniform.

"Why is he with you?" I asked Andrew. I knew it was rude of me to be so blunt, but I couldn't get over my shock. I hadn't expected to ever see the American again.

"Mina, this is Lucas Miller," Andrew said. "He's over from America. Lucas, Lady Thomasina Tretheway."

"We've met," Lucas said. "In a way. I know the young lady doesn't smoke and she wishes she could grow turnips and she doesn't live in a castle. Back in Oklahoma, that would be enough to call ourselves friends."

"I don't understand. You've met?" Andrew sounded completely confused. "How?"

"We shared a compartment on the train, though we weren't properly introduced," I said, not even attempting to explain about the turnips and the other nonsense. I looked at Lucas. "In England, asking someone to yell out the window at them isn't considered an introduction. I was just being polite when I responded. Etiquette lessons, you know: Always yell at people when asked."

While I was speaking, Jove came back and immediately went to Lucas, wagging his tail as if greeting a long-lost friend. What was wrong with the dog? He was supposed to be suspicious of strangers, especially cheeky Americans.

"Very polite of you," Lucas drawled as he petted the dog. "So we have been introduced now, haven't we? How do you do, your ladyshipness?"

I was about to tell him he didn't need to call me that when the creaking of a cart's wheels warned me someone else was coming along the road. I looked toward the sound and spotted the county gossip, Mrs. Underdown, in her pony cart. As usual, the woman sat bolt upright, dressed in one of her vaguely nautical ensembles in homage to her late husband, the admiral. She lived in the village but found reasons to drive her cart everywhere on various missions of goodwill, guiding her little shaggy black pony as if commanding a battleship. Thank heavens she hadn't seen me hugging Andrew. It would have been all over the neighborhood by nightfall.

"Lady Thomasina! I heard you were back," Mrs. Underdown said as she pulled up. "Good heavens! Is everything all right?" she asked, looking me up and down and then glaring at Andrew. Her expression changed when she recognized him. "Lord Andrew, forgive me. I didn't realize it was you."

"How are you, Mrs. Underdown?" Andrew asked.

"Fine, very fine. Quite busy, in fact." She was staring at the American, and I could see the curiosity in her eyes.

"Let me introduce you. Mrs. Underdown, this is Lucas Miller," Andrew said.

"How do you do?" she said. I knew she was waiting for more information. I was too.

Andrew didn't give it. "It's very nice to see you again," he said instead. "I'm sorry we can't stay to talk, but we must get on our way. War work, you understand." That was the polite way of saying she shouldn't ask any more questions.

Mrs. Underdown mimed zipping her lips. "Oh, war work. Hush, hush. I understand. Of course you're on your way to Cranwell. Where else would you be going? I didn't know you were an aviator, Lord Andrew. And you, young man, are you an aviator too? I didn't know there were any American aviators at Cranwell."

So much for not asking any more questions. Both Andrew and the American looked at a loss for words, and guilty too, for some reason.

"Lucas designs aeroplanes," Andrew said suddenly. "He's quite a genius at it," he added, stumbling over the words and blinking several times as he said them. I stared at him. He wasn't telling the truth. Andrew had always been nearly as bad at lying as Margaret. When he and Crispin were in trouble, Crispin had been the one to try to talk their way out it, because Andrew couldn't keep his voice steady when he told an untruth. Lucas didn't look much older than me and he didn't look like a genius, though I confess I'd never met one. So which part was the untruth? Designing aeroplanes? Being a genius? Or both?

Of course Mrs. Underdown didn't question Andrew. She would believe anything he said, no matter how absurd, because he was the son of a marquis. Rank had many privileges. "Are you staying at Cranwell or at Hallington?" she asked.

"Hallington," Andrew said. "Cranwell is short on space. It's wonderful that Lord Tretheway is always so welcoming to old friends." His eyes were fixed on mine.

Old friend needs your help. Andrew was the old friend in the telegram. I don't know why it hadn't occurred to me that it would be him, except that the phrasing "old friend" made me think it was someone we hadn't seen for a long time, or someone who was actually old. The fact that it was Andrew was wonderful.

Mrs. Underdown smiled like she'd been given a present. "How lovely," she said. "Lady Thomasina, I'm so delighted you and your sister are both home. So unexpected! But it's turned out to be very convenient timing. Now that you are both home, I'll call later today to discuss something very important with the both of you."

"Margaret is here?" Andrew sounded horrified at the news. I didn't understand why. He and Margaret had never been great friends, but they had tolerated each other.

"Yes," I said. "It was unexpected, from what I understand." I wanted to take back the words as soon as I saw Mrs. Underdown's eyes narrow and her mouth twitch. I knew that look. I'd seen it many times, whenever Mrs. Underdown realized she hadn't been told everything. The woman would want to know why Margaret's arrival had been unexpected, and she'd stop at nothing to find out. She was ruthless at ferreting out information.

I really wanted to know why Andrew and Lucas had come to Hallington, and I needed to get rid of Mrs. Underdown so I could ask. "I think I'm catching a chill," I said, adding in a shudder for effect. "I need to get back to the house to change."

But my ploy didn't exactly work as I had hoped. "Of course, Lady Thomasina!" Mrs. Underdown said. "How thoughtless of me to keep you standing here. Climb in the cart and I'll take you right to your front door while Lord Andrew and Mr. Miller deal with the automobile."

I'd completely forgotten about the vehicle. "It isn't damaged, is it?" I asked, feeling guilty.

Andrew surveyed the automobile. "I don't think so." He motioned to Lucas. "Let's see if we can get it back on the road."

I climbed into the cart as the two of them went back to the automobile. Jove stayed with them, sticking close to Lucas as if the American was his new owner. Ungrateful animal. If Jove had been chasing the intruder, he'd completely forgotten about him, or decided he'd properly secured the grounds by chasing the man off.

On the short ride up the driveway, Mrs. Underdown chatted away, but I could hardly force myself to listen. I looked back and saw Andrew's car turn into the drive. I wanted to jump down from the cart and run, just to get rid of some of the excitement that was filling me up. Andrew was here, and the American too, and I'd finally be part of something important.

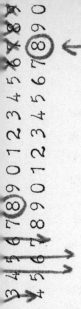

CHAPTER
FIVE

I THANKED MRS. UNDERDOWN when she let me off and she drove away, waving as Andrew and Lucas came up the drive in the opposite direction, Jove trotting behind the car.

They stopped at the bottom of the steps, but before I could demand some explanations, Margaret opened the door and came out in a hurry, as if she had been waiting for someone. From the look on her face, I knew it wasn't Andrew.

Lucas and Andrew got out. This time Lucas used the door instead of hopping over it. Jove caught up and sat down at

Lucas's feet with what could only be described as a worshipful expression.

"Hello, Margaret," Andrew said. He took out his cigarette case and opened it, but then closed it again without taking a cigarette. When he went to put it back in his pocket, he dropped it. "I didn't realize you'd be here," he said as he picked it back up. "Lord Tretheway suggested we stay while we are in the area. I hope it's not an inconvenience."

"Not at all," Margaret replied. It was clear she didn't mean it.

Andrew gestured at Lucas. "This is Lucas Miller from America. Lucas, this is Lady Margaret Babington." He made a motion as if he was going to get his cigarette case back out, but stopped himself before he did. It wasn't like him to be so jittery.

"Pleased to meet you," Lucas said.

Margaret nodded to him. "How do you do?" Her tone was as chilly as I had claimed to be.

Hannah practically skipped out the front door. She stopped short when she saw Lucas. Her eyes widened and her mouth curved into a smile. He smiled back. I half expected him to wink at her.

"Yes, Hannah?" Margaret snapped.

Hannah gave a tiny bob and said, "Miss Tanner asked to see you about dinner."

"I'll be in shortly. Go tell Miss Tanner she needs to get two rooms ready for our guests." Hannah smiled again at Lucas, but I noticed he was too busy looking up at the house to catch her expression. Her mouth turned down and she went back inside.

"I'm afraid things aren't quite as they should be since we have so little help," Margaret said to Andrew. "We're not set up for houseguests."

"Don't apologize. We'll just drop off the bags inside," Andrew said. "And there's no need to give us lunch. We need to get to Cranwell. We're running late."

Lucas didn't seem in too much of a hurry to leave. I saw Jove had brought him a stick. Lucas reached down and took it from the dog, then lobbed it off into the grass. Jove loped after it.

"Fine," Margaret said. "If you'll excuse me, I must see Miss Tanner." As she hurried back inside, I realized that she hadn't noticed I was covered in mud.

Jove brought the stick back. "Nice dog," Lucas said to me. "Nice house too. It's almost a castle. I can see I'll have to mind my manners here." He smiled at me. "I'm sure no one yells out windows or anything like that."

"If you yell properly, you're allowed," I said. "Lines from plays are acceptable. Random greetings and such are not."

"I have no idea what you two are talking about," Andrew shook his head as if he was trying to clear it. "Lucas, we need to go."

"I'll show you where to put the bags," I took them inside, to the small anteroom where the footman used to sit. "You can leave them here. Someone will take them upstairs later."

I followed them back outside, expecting Andrew to tell me why they were there and how I could help.

Instead, he said, "We'll be off, then."

"But, but . . ." I started to say something about the telegram and then I realized I shouldn't. Not until I knew more. Maybe the American wasn't part of it.

I watched them drive away. When they were halfway down the drive, Lucas turned around and waved. Jove lay down at the bottom of the steps, the stick beside him, looking as dejected as I felt. So much for an exciting day. I picked up the stick and threw it for him, but he didn't get up. He just stared down the drive as if he was going to stay put until Lucas returned.

"Fine," I told him. "Go ahead and forget who used to play hours of fetch with you." My stomach rumbled, reminding me that I hadn't eaten breakfast. I went up to my room, changed into another of Margaret's old dresses, and then went down to the breakfast room.

Hannah came in almost immediately after I did, carrying a toast rack. She put the toast on the sideboard and said, "Cook says if you want more jam, just ring. She knows you are very fond of the strawberry. I have to say I'm fond of it too, that and plum as well. Oh, and pear. I don't like quince jam at all, though."

"I don't like quince either," I said.

"Mrs. Brickles is happy you're home. She said she has a good excuse to make some more jam tarts now. She's cranky when there is no one here to cook for. Last time your father was home, she was in a good mood for two whole days." Hannah checked the chafing dish with the eggs in it. "Do you think your father will come back soon? It's very exciting when he comes here with all the important people."

"I don't know when he'll be back," I said. "It must be extra work for you when guests are here. I know there isn't enough staff."

"I don't mind. I'm used to hard work. I don't like it when it's too quiet. I was hoping your sister would bring her sweetheart to dinner."

I choked on my toast. "My sister's sweetheart?"

"Oh yes, didn't you know? Last time Lady Margaret was home, I opened my window one night to get some air and I saw her and a man kissing on the terrace."

I didn't know how to respond, but Hannah must have seen the stunned look on my face because she said, "Oh, I don't gossip about it. Miss Tanner wouldn't like that. I asked Lettie who it was and she didn't know. He is a tall, thin man." She stopped talking, looking at me as if waiting to see if I might provide an answer. I had no idea. It was probably someone stationed at Cranwell.

When I didn't offer up any possibilities, Hannah said, "Lady Margaret seems terribly burdened with worry, though. I can sense worry in people. Mother claims it's a gift I have."

"I think everyone is very worried these days," I managed to say, preoccupied with who my sister had been kissing. She'd been a widow for years, ever since her husband was killed at the Battle of Ypres, but I hadn't known there was anyone special in her life. Whoever it was, I knew I probably shouldn't encourage Hannah to talk more about it. If Miss Tanner overheard her gossiping about one of the family, she'd be very angry with the girl. I'd have to find out from Margaret.

Hannah chattered some more and then said something about dusting. After I finished eating, it occurred to me that if Margaret was meeting someone at the house, it might explain Lettie's belief that there was a "presence" roaming around. It didn't explain the night before, however. I couldn't imagine anyone who had been there to see Margaret running off into the woods.

It occurred to me that if there were hungry soldiers in the neighborhood, Mrs. Brickles might know about it. Even before the war, we'd occasionally had a person stop at the back door and ask for a bit of bread. She'd always send them on their way with far more than that.

I decided to ask her and use that as an excuse to visit the kitchen as well. It had long been my favorite place in the house— ever since I was old enough to tag after Crispin and Andrew. The boys had usually stopped in at some point in the day to beg Mrs. Brickles for jam and bread, though it didn't take much begging; Mrs. Brickles doted on Crispin. And when Crispin was at school, I'd still go there, happy to sit and listen to everyone talk.

As I went in, Mrs. Brickles came in from the scullery carrying a large stockpot. "How are you, Mrs. Brickles?" I asked.

"Fair to middling, Lady Thomasina," she said, setting the pot on the stove. "How nice to see you!" She studied me. "You are a mite pale, if you don't mind my saying. Some good fresh air will put the roses back in your cheeks now that you're away from that air down south." Mrs. Brickles was convinced that anyplace outside of Lincolnshire had an unhealthy climate that would eventually lead to illness and decline.

"It's nice to be home," I said. "I hope it's not too much work for you with both Margaret and me home at the same time, and now the two guests as well. I know you are very short-staffed." I looked around. It was odd to see the kitchen so empty. Something besides people was missing, but I couldn't pinpoint the change.

"Of course it's not too much work! We manage, some days better than others, though I wish some of the old staff was still here." She picked up what looked like a bunch of weeds. "Look what that girl Hannah brought me—weeds! I sent her out to get parsnips and she brought me back these. The girl doesn't seem to know a cabbage from a carrot," she grumbled.

She tossed the weeds in a bucket and took an onion from a basket on the table. "I am as prepared as I can be for whatever guests may arrive. Lord Tretheway doesn't have to say it, but we all know he brings important guests here. We'll do our part. It's little enough." She motioned to the shelf behind the table, which held the canisters and the spices. "Though with the sugar rationing, and the new butter rationing starting soon, I don't know how I'll give them a decent pudding."

I realized then what was different about the kitchen. Mrs. Brickles was renowned for her lemon tarts, and normally the kitchen smelled of lemon.

"You're too modest, Mrs. Brickles," I said. "Everything you send up is delicious, even with all the shortages. It's too bad there are so many." It seemed like a good opening for my question. "I hear there are even hungry soldiers about here in the county, not just in the cities. In fact, I think Jove might have spotted one this morning on the grounds. Have you seen any?"

She frowned. "I haven't heard anything like that, and I'd be the one to know. People should be taking care of them that served, those who are trying to keep us safe. Even if they can't go back to the fighting, work could be found for them. Guarding places against spies and such should be something they could manage. Just yesterday I heard they've caught a spy in Lincoln! That's far too close to home! Who knows how many people he might have murdered in their beds before he was found out!" She sliced into the onion with sudden ferocity. "Gives me the horrors to think of someone like that sneaking around after dark."

I hadn't realized that Miss Tanner had come into the room until she spoke. "You could have rung for me if you needed something, Lady Thomasina."

"I just came to say hello." I felt a little defensive because Miss Tanner seemed irritated whenever she found me in the kitchen.

"Now, Mrs. Brickles, we don't yet know any details," Miss Tanner said, disapproval clear in her voice. "They are investigating the man to see if he actually is a spy."

"Where there's smoke, there's fire," Mrs. Brickles muttered as she diced the onion.

I saw a frown cross Miss Tanner's face. She cleared her throat. "Excuse me, Lady Thomasina. May I speak to you? Perhaps in your mother's sitting room?"

That seemed an odd place to have a conversation. It was on the other side of the house and up two flights of stairs. Then I realized it was where housekeepers had always discussed household matters with my mother.

"Of course." I smiled and tried to sound as if there was nothing I'd rather do than talk to the housekeeper, quelling the impulse to make up an urgent need to write a letter or knit a sock for a soldier. "We could talk in your office instead," I suggested. "I may go out to the kitchen garden when we are finished."

"Very well," she said, though I could tell she didn't approve.

Inside her office, I sat in the chair in front of the housekeeper's worktable, feeling like a maid about to be scolded. Miss Tanner kept the room free of decoration, except for a strange little pewter curio of the "speak no evil, see no evil, hear no evil" monkeys on the table. I wondered if Miss Tanner kept it as a silent reminder to the staff of her expectations for their behavior.

Miss Tanner sat down, brushed an invisible speck of dust off the table, and then peered at me over the tops of her spectacles, which she wore pushed down on her nose. As usual, she didn't blink. I didn't know how she managed that. "I should perhaps speak to Lady Margaret as well, in light of your mother's absence, but I don't want to upset your sister unnecessarily." That was code for needing to maintain the facade that everything was "just so" to keep Margaret happy. "We have some girls coming in during the day to help Mrs. Brickles when we need them," she continued, "but as for the meals, the new girl, Hannah, will have to serve. Lettie has too many other chores and can be clumsy, though Hannah has her own flaws. She has not adapted to her new situation as well as I had hoped. I've given her extensive instructions, but it appears to go in one ear and out the other."

"It's fine," I said. "Everyone has grown used to the change in standards everywhere." It felt silly to be worrying about the standards of the house when our soldiers in France were sitting in the mud, eating cold tinned beef while shells landed all around them.

Miss Tanner sighed. "I do feel I'm letting down Lord Tretheway. I interviewed the girl and hired her myself. I'm afraid I've slipped up, but I thought since she has a local connection, she would do. She was quite eager for a job since her mother is ill." The housekeeper frowned and flicked another speck of invisible dust off the desk before she continued. "There's another problem. She's also far too talkative, as Lady Margaret indicated. I've had to speak to her already. When Lord Tretheway was last home, I caught her telling your father about her mother's neighbor! Some trifling gossip. It's unheard of!"

I had to hide a smile over the scandalized tone of Miss Tanner's voice. I wished I had been there to watch that scene. Most servants were too intimidated to utter a word in my father's presence, though if they did, he was perfectly polite to them.

"Let's give her a chance," I said, feeling like it was what my mother would say. I stood up, wanting to get outside.

Miss Tanner stood up as well. "Very well. I hope you will be so good as to let me know if you notice any of the servants behaving oddly or remarking upon anything unusual. I had to confiscate one of the more lurid newspapers from one of the scullery maids who came in from the village to help out for a few days. She read bits of it to the others and it inflamed their fears. I've found it's best to put a stop to such nonsense as soon as possible. This spy news will just add to their fear if we don't keep it under control."

I didn't answer. I had no intention of reporting on the servants like I was some kind of household snitch. I made some excuse about the garden and went outside.

It occurred to me then that I should look for footprints. Surely there'd be some with the wet ground. But I combed the lawn and didn't find any, except what were probably Mr. Applewhite's because they were so small. He was a very small man, and while I'd never actually paid attention to his feet, I was sure they fit the rest of him. It was frustrating to find nothing. I had seen *someone*. The wristlet proved a stranger had been there.

I went in search of Mr. Applewhite. If anyone had seen anything unusual, it would be him. I found him right beyond the terrace, inspecting one of the Lady Banks roses. It was among his favorites, and we'd nearly lost it the year before.

"Good morning, Mr. Applewhite. It's looking better." I touched one of the tiny yellow flowers.

"That she is, Lady Thomasina. Can I help you with something?"

"I wondered if you'd seen any strangers about. I think Jove tried to chase someone off the property this morning."

"Oh, I don't think so. I haven't noticed anyone about. Jove used to have quite an interest in rabbits when he was a pup. Maybe the interest came back."

I didn't remember that, but Jove was only a few years younger than I was. "If you see anything unusual, will you let me know?" I asked.

"Of course. I'll keep a sharp eye out."

"Thank you." I left him and wandered around the garden, trying to decide what should be done first. I was about to go get some gardening tools when I heard the sound of an aeroplane. Shading my eyes from the sun, I could see one coming from the direction of Cranwell, flying very low. As I watched, the front of it tipped even lower. It was coming down, and it was coming down in the pasture behind the gardens.

CHAPTER
SIX

I RAN TO the pasture as fast as I could, horrified that the plane might crash. But as it dropped even farther, I realized it didn't look completely out of control. Someone was landing in the pasture on purpose.

It came down fast and hard, hitting the ground and bumping back up in the air, then down again in a series of strange little hops, turning to one side before finally coming to a stop. The pilot cut the engine, jumped out, and pulled off his helmet and goggles. It was Lucas.

Andrew climbed down from the rear seat of the aeroplane more slowly. Neither of them saw me. By the time I reached them, I could hear Andrew taking Lucas to task. "Why didn't you listen when I said you were coming in too fast? You're going to have to listen to my instructions if you want to survive this, and we don't have much time for practice."

That stopped me. Survive what?

"I didn't think I was going too fast," Lucas said. "And better too fast than too slow. I don't want to drop out of the sky like a lead weight."

Though I wanted to know more, I didn't want Andrew to think I was eavesdropping. "Hello," I called.

Lucas spun around. "Hello, your ladyshipness." He grinned and did an absurdly exaggerated bow, nearly losing his balance. "Want to go for a ride?"

"No," I said. "And please call me Mina. I think I'd rather learn to fly myself and be the one in the pilot's seat. It would be safer that way."

Lucas laughed. "I could teach you, and you'd learn fast. It's fantastic being up in the air. There's nothing else like it."

I didn't tell him that I had seen the bumpy landing and overheard Andrew berating him. He was certainly a confident young man.

Andrew shook his head at Lucas. "No rides. One minor detail: It's not your plane. You do remember that it belongs to the Royal Air Force, don't you?"

I could see that Lucas's spirits were dampened for all of three or four seconds. He grinned again. "That's true. Perhaps Lady Thomasina's first lesson could involve her sitting in the pilot's seat with me. I can show her all the controls. We couldn't cause any damage that way."

"Excellent effort, but no," Andrew said.

"Why did you land here?" I asked. "Isn't it dangerous to land just anywhere?"

"Pilots practice landing on all types of terrain," Andrew said. "Lucas, we need to take off again. This time, try not to make me feel like I'm going to fall out the back. A little less steep on the ascent, please."

Lucas put his hands up in the air like he was surrendering. "You take away all the fun, but if you insist, I'll fly it like I'm driving my grandmother to church. Goodbye, Mina, my ladyshipness." He attempted another elaborate bow and again nearly fell over.

"I hope you won't be meeting the king soon," I said. "It's generally considered bad form to fall over in Buckingham Palace, especially if you knock the king over in the process."

"You can give me lessons." He went to the front of the plane and put a hand on the propeller. "We'll trade. Flying lessons for bowing lessons. We could start with the bowing part. I do intend to meet the king someday."

"I'm sure the king will be delighted to meet you, once you are presentable," I said, trying to sound as serious as possible.

"I thought he would," he said as he spun the propeller. "Must get dull sitting around in a palace all day."

The engine started up. He said something else to me that I couldn't hear and then climbed into his seat. Andrew just rolled his eyes and climbed into his own seat.

I watched them take off. Lucas got the plane up very high very fast. If he drove his grandmother that fast, the poor woman must spend the time holding on for dear life. I watched until the aeroplane was out of sight.

I walked back to the garden pondering what I'd just witnessed. Lucas had acted as if they were just out for a fun flying lesson, but Andrew's words that I'd overheard chilled me. What was Lucas going to have to survive? I had already been suspicious of Andrew's claim that Lucas was an aeroplane designer, and what I'd just witnessed confirmed it. How could Lucas design planes if he needed lessons on how to land them?

With nothing else to do, I spent the rest of the day in the garden weeding and pruning, except for a quick bite of bread and cheese begged from Mrs. Brickles. For the first time ever, the garden didn't hold much interest for me. I kept looking up at the sky, imagining what it would be like to fly with Lucas. I'd never done anything as exciting as flying, but I didn't think I'd be scared. I had a silly fear of bats and I wasn't too fond of snakes, but I'd never had a fear of heights. Though anyone with a bit of sense would be a little nervous flying with Lucas. I could just picture him doing loops to impress a passenger.

I also tried to fit together their flying lessons with the possibility I would be helping Andrew. I couldn't make a connection. Frustrated that I still didn't know what was going on, I didn't pay enough attention to the rose I was pruning until I realized I'd turned it into a plant small enough for a pixie garden. I groaned, wondering what I could say to Mr. Applewhite. I didn't think I could convince him that pixieing roses made them grow better.

I straightened up, noticing the long shadows from the beech

tree nearby. It was later than I had realized, and that meant I needed to figure out what I was going to wear for dinner. I was not going to appear before everyone in one of Margaret's old garden party frocks. I could ask Margaret to loan me something, but I didn't think she would. She'd tell me to wear something of my own because her clothes were too sophisticated for someone my age. That was true, but I still wanted to wear something nice. If my mother had been home, she would have intervened, but since she wasn't, I needed a new plan.

Thinking of my mother gave me an idea. She had some lovely dinner dresses, and I thought they would fit me now. I knew exactly which gown I wanted. I hoped my mother hadn't taken it with her on her trip. When I went into her dressing room, the dress was hanging just where it always had. My mother favored shades of blue, and this one was midnight blue velvet beaded with metallic thread. A silver beaded butterfly ornament decorated one side of the waist. It fit me perfectly.

Pleased with the result, I decided I might as well put my hair up too, even if Margaret would disapprove of that as well. I couldn't wear my hair down forever, and I was old enough to be done with childish plaits. The only problem was that I didn't know how to do my hair. I needed Lettie to help me. My mother had taught Lettie how to do hair, and the girl was very good at it. I went down to the kitchen to see if Mrs. Brickles knew where she was. Lettie had taken on so many tasks, she could have been anywhere.

Mrs. Brickles was rushing about the kitchen, which was unusual for her. "I haven't seen her and I wish I knew where she was. I need her help. She was supposed to be back from the village an hour ago. She said she had an errand to do. It's not like her to dawdle. Is there anything I can do?"

"No, I'll see to it myself."

I went back up to my room and made a hopeless mess of my hair. As I was about to give up and put it back in a plait, I heard a noise in the hall. I listened. A door closed, but the sound came from the wrong direction, the opposite end of the hall, where all the bedrooms were closed off.

I got up and opened the door. Hannah came dancing down the hallway, twirling round and round. When she saw me, she stopped short. "Excuse me, Lady Thomasina, I forgot where I was. I like to dance sometimes, and the hall makes a nice space for it."

I'd never thought of that, but I supposed she was right. "Is there anything wrong?" I asked. "I thought I heard a door closing."

"No, I was just checking to make sure water hadn't come in the window of that yellow bedroom at the end. The frame needs to be fixed, and sometimes when it rains, water seeps in."

"Oh. Thank you. I'll have to ask Miss Tanner to get someone to fix that."

"No need. I've already told her." She looked at my dress. "That's very nice. Would you like me to do your hair to go with it?"

"You know how to do hair? That's wonderful!"

We went back into my room and I sat down at the dressing table. Hannah went to work, chatting the whole time. "I used to do my mother's hair, but there's not much call for it at the moment," she said. "She isn't in the best of health and is pining for warmer weather. Her rheumatism bothers her something terrible. But once she gets out in her garden, it takes her mind off it. You should see it! Not that it compares to anything here, of course, but she has some beautiful roses and grows the prettiest pinks. She has to live very quietly, so she does like to hear about my days here."

She paused for a moment and took a step back to examine my head. I didn't know what she wanted to see, but whatever it was caused her to take down one part and start again. "I told her all about Lord Tretheway and how distinguished he looks," she said, picking up the comb once more. "Like he was made for the part." She straightened up, raised her chin, and put her hand on her stomach in an uncanny imitation of the way my father stood with his thumb hooked in his waistcoat.

I'm not sure the girl even realized she was imitating my father, though, because then she switched to a different stance, her hands behind her back and her chin drawn in. I knew right away she was mimicking Mr. Norris. "But that valet, Mr. Norris, he didn't like me by half, that one," she said. "He's a bit of a stick-in-the-mud. Seemed surprised I asked him some questions about the visitors." She changed back to her normal posture. "Who wouldn't be curious, I told him, with all the fancy motorcars and chauffeurs here?"

The girl was a natural actress. "Mr. Norris is very dignified," I replied, trying to pick my words carefully. I didn't want her to get in trouble with Miss Tanner. "And I'm sure he felt he couldn't say. You understand, don't you? He feels like he shouldn't talk about my father's business. I'm sure he wouldn't tell me if I asked." I hoped this would be enough of a hint to make the girl realize she wouldn't get anywhere with Mr. Norris.

"He'll get used to my ways eventually," Hannah said, not taking the hint. "There." She put down the comb and gave my hair a final pat.

I turned my head from side to side so I could see it in the mirror. "It's perfect. Thank you."

"I miss doing hair." She looked over at the clock and dropped the brush. "Oh, I should go. I'm supposed to be setting the table!"

"I'm sorry I kept you," I said. "If Miss Tanner notices, tell her it's all my fault."

"If I hurry, she might not notice." She dashed off toward the back stairs so fast that I hoped she didn't run into someone on the way down.

When I came down, I saw Lucas and Andrew standing in the entrance hall. I took the steps slowly, hoping I wouldn't trip. Lucas looked up at me and smiled, not the grin I'd already seen, but a slow smile that turned up on one side. I felt my ears turning hot and knew I was blushing. I ducked my head to cover my embarrassment.

"There you are, Mina," Andrew said. "I was hoping we could talk in the library before dinner." He didn't remark upon the dress. I'm not sure he even noticed what I was wearing.

We went into the library. Lucas followed us, closing the door behind him.

"I need your help with something." Andrew went over to my father's desk.

I tensed up. Finally, I'd find out why I'd come home and what I could do to help.

He picked up a roll of paper and took off a paper wrap, then unrolled it on the desk, placing paperweights to hold down the corners. I moved closer to look at it. The paper was blank except for a few irregular lines drawn on it.

"We're working on some maps for our pilots," he said.

"How am I supposed to help you with that?"

He tapped the drawing. "This one is for the area in Germany where your mother's cousin had her house. The government would like as much detail as possible about the village and the surrounding area, down to the individual houses and shops. I know you won't remember everything, but it is a very small village and your father said you knew every inch of it. He said your aunt could never keep you in the house because you wanted to play outside all the time."

I looked down at the paper and then back up at him. "My father had me come home for this? A map of a village?" My mother's first cousin had married a German man, and before the war they lived on a lovely country estate in the Rheinprovinz near the village of Winnefeld. We'd gone there every summer and I had loved all of it, from the tiny fairy-tale villages to the castle ruins to the wooded hills and valleys. The house had been shut up since the beginning of the war, when my cousins went to Switzerland.

"You learn not to ask questions when you are in the military," Andrew said. "You aren't told why and you don't ask. You have to assume someone has a good reason for wanting this information, and your father decided you were the best person to give it."

I supposed that was a reasonable answer, but something about it didn't feel right. "You've been there too," I said. "I don't remember how many summers you visited Crispin there, but it was at least two or three. Why can't you do it?"

Andrew looked down at the map and then took out a cigarette and lit it before sitting down in my father's chair. "I tried, but I've discovered my memory is not as good as I'd thought it was. Too much has happened and too many years have passed. I could remember a few details, like the house where the blacksmith's daughter lived, because Crispin and I thought she was very pretty, but your father wants more detail than that."

It was true that the village had felt like a second home to me. Every family had been there for generations, much as in our own village. They'd made a bit of a pet of me because I was so intent upon learning to speak perfect German. I felt a pang at the memory of how much fun we'd had during our summers there.

I glanced over at Lucas. He had pulled up two chairs, and was sitting down on one while indicating that the other was for me. Andrew held out a pencil. "Draw as much as you remember. This line is the main road through the village." He pointed at a double line. "And here is the bridge over the stream. Does that get you oriented?"

I took the pencil and studied the paper. "Yes, but I've never drawn a map that had houses on it."

"I remember back when you wanted to be a pirate. You drew treasure maps then," Andrew said. "They were good. I'm sure you can do this."

"You wanted to be a pirate?" Lucas sounded amazed.

I felt a little pinprick of annoyance. "Why is that so surprising?" I said. "Doesn't every child? I've always liked adventure stories."

"It's just . . . I mean . . ." He stopped as if he was confused. "I'd have guessed princess rather than pirate. You don't look like a pirate."

"Well, of course not!" What a silly thing for him to say.

"She is also good at imitating pirate talk, as I recall," Andrew said.

Lucas smiled. "I have to hear that."

"Only if we find a treasure map," I said. "Pirate talk is not appropriate at other times."

Andrew tapped the paper. "Let's concentrate on this map," he said. "Just draw in little squares and label them with as much as you can remember. If you know who lived there, even if it's just the first names of children, put that down. If you remember someone's occupation, that will help too."

I didn't understand why a pilot would need that information, but Andrew had already made it clear one wasn't supposed to ask. I began to draw as much as I could remember. Lucas leaned in close to watch. I noticed that he had a nice minty soap smell to him that distracted me. I hadn't known soap could smell so good.

It took me about an hour to finish, because after I had drawn in the buildings, Andrew began to ask about landmarks. Lucas paid close attention, as if he was trying to memorize all the details himself. It became very obvious that Andrew was not telling me the whole truth about why he wanted the map.

Finally, when I couldn't remember any more, I set down the

pencil. Andrew said, "That's excellent, Mina." He lit another cigarette. "I'm sorry I don't remember more myself. I do remember something about a house called *das Hexenhaus*. Do you know which one that was?" Lucas leaned forward.

"Yes, it's this one." I pointed to a house near the bridge. Hearing that phrase made me smile. "Crispin named Frau Weber's house *das Hexenhaus*, the witch house, because she disliked children so much. He used to make up stories about all the dreadful things she would do to me if I wandered into her garden. She did have a lovely garden, every color of flower imaginable." With a garden like that, I didn't believe she could have been as awful as Crispin claimed.

Andrew picked up another pencil and made a small "x" next to the house. "What about any of the other names you or Crispin gave them? If they have odd names, it helps people remember them."

I thought that was a little strange, but I did what he said. There were several we had called by other names. When I was done, Andrew rolled up the map. "Thank you. I'm sure the mapping people will be very pleased."

"Is that all the help you needed from me?" I asked. I couldn't believe I'd come all the way home just to help with a map. Disappointment swept through me. Was I supposed to go back to school now, to the dull routine of lessons and meals and schedules? I didn't think I could stand that.

"This was an enormous help, even if you don't see it now. You may never know how it helps. That's the nature of war. We all have our parts to play." Andrew stood up.

I realized I'd been given the smallest of bit parts, but I forced myself to smile. "I'm glad I was able to help." My teeth were clenched so tightly that my jaw ached. I stood up too. Lucas went to the library door and opened it.

The front bell rang and a moment later I heard Mrs. Underdown's voice. "So nice of you to invite me for dinner, Lady Margaret. I do so want to talk to you about a little project of mine. And I'm looking forward to getting to know your young houseguest. When I met him and Lord Andrew on the road, I was quite intrigued by him."

I'd completely forgotten about Mrs. Underdown. She'd said she was going to stop in during the afternoon. How had she finagled an invitation to dinner?

"Save me from that woman!" Andrew said. "What are we going to do?"

"What do you mean?" I asked.

"She'll try to find out every detail of why we are here."

I didn't point out that I didn't know every detail of why they were here and I also wanted to know. "Don't worry. I can handle Mrs. Underdown," I said. "We'll just change the subject whenever she brings it up. We should go. We can't hide in the library forever." I walked out, and Lucas and Andrew followed.

I pasted on a bright smile, bracing myself to match wits with an opponent who was far more skilled than me. If my only other job was to protect Andrew and Lucas's secrets, I'd do my best.

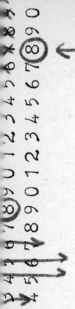

CHAPTER SEVEN

AS SOON AS we sat down in the dining room, I heard the front bell ring. I couldn't imagine who it would be. There had been no sound of a motorcar, and it was late for someone to be arriving on horseback or for anyone but Mrs. Underdown to be driving around in a pony cart. I looked over at Margaret, wondering for a moment if she had invited her mysterious beau to dinner. Just as quickly as that thought came, however, it went. There was no extra place set at the table.

A moment later Miss Tanner came into the room with a

young woman who was wearing a stylish coat and a hat, though the hat was nearly falling off and there was mud on her coat.

"Miss Gwendolyn Slade," the housekeeper said.

Margaret got up, as did Andrew and Lucas. "Gwendolyn! I didn't expect you until tomorrow," Margaret said. I hadn't expected anyone at all; Margaret hadn't told me we would have another guest.

"I took an earlier train and asked a nice young man at the station to give me a ride," the girl said. "I was so eager to come back. I had such a lovely time when we were here before." She smiled at all of us. "Please sit down," she said. "I'm so sorry I arrived at such an awkward time."

I wanted to ask her more about the nice young man, but couldn't figure out a polite way to do it. It had to have been someone on their way to Cranwell, because we didn't have an abundance of young men driving about the county. And I was sure I would have heard a motorcar. It surprised me that any of Margaret's friends would want to come to Lincolnshire. Her kind of friends usually didn't relish country sports and activities. This girl looked made for London. She had a prewar, china-doll gloss about her, all perfect blond hair and perfect alabaster skin. I couldn't imagine her traipsing about Lincolnshire.

"It's not awkward," Margaret said before doing the introductions. When she introduced Andrew, the girl's smile dropped from her face for an instant and then recovered. "How do you do?" she said, offering her hand. It was almost as if she knew him, though Andrew gave no sign of recognition.

"Hannah will set a place for you." Margaret motioned to the girl. "And Miss Tanner will take your things."

"Oh, but I'm not dressed for dinner!" Gwendolyn protested. "I didn't know you were having other guests. I'm so sorry."

"It's fine," Margaret said. "No one minds what you are wearing. Please join us."

Hannah set another place and then she and Miss Tanner left the room. At first it was all very awkward. Lucas didn't appear at all comfortable in his suit. He couldn't sit still, his hand constantly going to his collar as if it was strangling him. Andrew didn't participate in the conversation at all.

Mrs. Underdown dominated the room, focusing her attention on Lucas. I waited, ready to intervene if necessary. When she found out he lived on a cattle ranch with his grandparents, she wanted so much information about cattle herding, it sounded as if she planned to take it up herself. I could just picture her organizing cows into perfect ranks as they marched out to graze.

"I'm quite fascinated that you design aeroplanes while helping to run a cattle ranch," Mrs. Underdown said.

There it was. I'd known she'd bring it up sooner or later.

"That does sound fascinating!" Gwendolyn exclaimed. "Oh, do tell us all about it."

I jumped in. "Don't press him. I've already discovered that Mr. Miller is a very modest and shy young man. He'd be embarrassed to tell you of all his accomplishments. Isn't that right, Mr. Miller?"

He opened his mouth and then closed it. I didn't wait for any other response. I turned to Gwendolyn. "Have you been doing any war work, Miss Slade?"

Miss Slade gave a start of surprise, as if she'd heard a loud noise. She didn't speak for a moment. The silence stretched long enough to be uncomfortable before the girl stammered a reply. I caught something about working in a soup kitchen for returning soldiers and something about also being needed at home.

"Where do your people live?" Mrs. Underdown asked the girl. I swear Mrs. Underdown's eyes actually gleamed at having a new person from whom to extract information.

Miss Slade regained her composure and spoke more clearly. "I'm from Somerset. My father is a doctor there."

"Oh, how nice," Mrs. Underdown replied. That was apparently enough for Mrs. Underdown to slot Miss Slade into her proper place in society.

Mrs. Underdown turned away from her, took a deep breath, and then looked first at Margaret and then at me. "Since you are both home, I have a great favor to ask, a very great favor." She paused. "I'm planning a little entertainment for some of the officers stationed at Cranwell and for our convalescents in the neighborhood."

Warning bells went off in my head. I wished I could change the subject before the next words came out of her mouth and we were trapped. Musical evenings to help the war effort had replaced parties as social events, and even though I liked to sing, it embarrassed me to sing in public. But because every girl who had the slightest talent in either voice or in playing the piano was expected to do their part, too many people had been forced to listen to my mediocre attempts. The worst part of it all was that I couldn't imagine it helped the war effort at all. I'm sure soldiers on leave had many other things they'd rather do, like meet their friends in a pub, than pretend everything was going perfectly with the war.

Before I could think of a reason to refuse a request, however, Margaret said, "We've never been known for our singing or playing, but Mina is far better at singing than I am. I'm sure she will volunteer."

"Oh, it's something much more exciting than singing," Mrs. Underdown said. She spread her hands like she was bestowing a blessing upon us. "We are putting on a musical opera the day after tomorrow, a delightful production by Mr. Gilbert for the officers at Cranwell and some of the convalescents in the county. And my very great favor is that I was hoping we could hold it here."

It took me a moment to understand what she was asking. I hadn't expected that sort of request, and judging by Margaret's lack of response, neither had she.

Mrs. Underdown took advantage of our stunned silence and kept talking. "Yours is the only large house in the neighborhood not housing the wounded or convalescents, and I remember how your hall worked so well for Crispin's theatricals. We've been practicing in the village hall, but it's so drafty and damp there, and difficult to store the props, especially with the way the roof leaks. If you'd allow us to have it here, we could invite many more men."

The mention of my brother made my heart clench. I didn't

know if I'd ever be able to say his name so casually. Even though my father and mother held out hope that Crispin was in a German prison camp somewhere, I didn't believe he'd ever come home. If he had been captured, we would have had word of it long before now. I stared down at the tablecloth, trying to control the tears that were threatening to slip out.

I waited for Margaret to respond. When she didn't, I looked up and tried to catch her eye to signal a no. Even if I didn't know all the reasons Lucas and Andrew had come to Hallington, I was sure the last thing Andrew wanted was a collection of people traipsing around the house.

But Margaret didn't look at me. "If it's just a matter of providing space, I suppose we can do that," she said.

"That's wonderful!" Mrs. Underdown clapped her hands. "I knew you'd be willing to do your part. It is quite a humorous play, and the members of the Cranwell Orchestra have agreed to provide the music. I've always adhered to the admiral's philosophy—if you are going to do something, don't hold back."

Mrs. Underdown never held back. And that meant we couldn't either; into the breach we'd go. I supposed it would give me an excuse not to go back to school, at least. If Andrew didn't need me here anymore, I could claim Margaret needed my help.

"May I ask what play you are performing?" Miss Slade said. "I love theatricals."

"It's a delightful show by the name of *Princess Toto*." Mrs. Underdown gave a surprisingly girlish laugh. "It involves a princess who is extremely forgetful and two rival suitors and many misunderstandings."

"That sounds like a promising setup for a good story," I said, forcing thoughts of past theatricals and Crispin away. I was intrigued by the idea of a forgetful princess.

Mrs. Underdown nodded. "Oh, it is. Princess Toto has been betrothed from birth to Prince Doro, but he disappears and is presumed to have been eaten by wolves. The princess's father arranges for a new husband for his daughter, a Prince Alfie, but right before the wedding Prince Doro returns from having joined a band of brigands. And it goes from there as they both try to win her hand. I know you'll love it."

I glanced over at Lucas, who was leaning back in his chair, an amused expression on his face. "Mina, it sounds like one of your plays," he said.

"It does, rather," I agreed, "though I'd never name a prince Alfie."

I had the feeling that Lucas was watching the rest of us as if we were part of a play too. It had to all seem ridiculous to him. I knew our little part of the world had always been sheltered from the reality that most people lived, especially now with the war on, but this was the first time I had imagined how someone from outside must view us. Did he realize that all of us knew there were cracks in the perfect picture? Did he know we were desperately trying to ignore them because we didn't know what else to do?

"The theatrical sounds so exciting!" Miss Slade exclaimed. "I wonder if I could ask to help. I know it's presumptuous of me, but perhaps you will need help backstage."

"That would be lovely, dear," Mrs. Underdown said. "And we

may have a very special guest." She leaned forward like she was going to tell us a secret. "I've been told Prince Albert is stationed at Cranwell, and I am of course hoping he will attend."

I heard a little gasp from someone and then a cry rang out. Lucas pushed back his chair and jumped up, darting over to Hannah's side. He took hold of a tureen, the large silver one used only on special occasions. Half the soup was on the floor, a pale green puddle soaking into the carpet.

Hannah burst into tears. "I'm so sorry," she wailed. I hadn't even realized the girl had come back into the room.

"This is too heavy for you," Lucas said. "I can't believe you carried it all the way up the stairs yourself." He took it over to the sideboard and set it down.

"Hannah, you should have asked for help," Margaret scolded. "Please go tell Miss Tanner what happened. She'll tell you what to do." She turned to us. "I'm very sorry. It's so difficult without footmen."

"I could serve the soup," Lucas said. "I know how to use a ladle."

"There's no need for that," Margaret said, aghast. "You're a guest. Miss Tanner will be along shortly."

I could tell by the expression on Lucas's face that he thought we were being silly. I jumped up. "I'll do it."

"Mina, do you think you can manage?" Margaret asked, as if I were attempting something extremely difficult.

"Yes," I said, a little irritated by the implication that I couldn't serve soup. Just because I had never done it didn't mean I was incapable.

"I'll help." Andrew got up to join me, motioning for Lucas to sit back down. Margaret began to speak, but Andrew held up his hand. That halted her, though Mrs. Underdown's eyes looked as if they might fall out of her head. I could just imagine the woman telling all her friends about Lord Andrew being forced to serve soup.

We managed without spilling too much on the sideboard. A ladle was harder to handle than I had thought. I also sloshed some soup out of Lucas's bowl as I set it in front of him, but luckily none of it spattered him. Hannah came back with Miss Tanner, who raised her eyebrows slightly at the sight of the soup servers. She dealt with the spill, signaling to Hannah to pour more wine.

As soon as everything had settled down again, Mrs. Underdown went right back to talking about Prince Albert. It actually was exciting news. I'd never met the prince, but I knew Margaret had danced with him at a ball the year before the war. She hadn't said much about him except that he stuttered but it wasn't to be talked about.

"I've heard he insists that everyone treat him as a regular officer, so naturally he'd want to come to an officers' entertainment, wouldn't he?" Mrs. Underdown said.

I wasn't so sure about that. Our little entertainments were nothing compared to what the man would have seen in London and on his travels. Some of the older girls at school kept postcards of both the dashing Prince of Wales and Prince Albert on display, endlessly speculating about who and when they would marry, longing for the excitement of a royal wedding, though everyone knew no wedding would happen during wartime.

"What is Prince Albert doing at Cranwell? He's not a pilot, is he?" Miss Slade asked. "That seems very dangerous."

It *was* dangerous. I'd seen a report on my father's desk listing the average number of months a pilot survived. Not years—months. It was another of those facts of war that we were supposed to accept. I knew Prince Albert and his older brother, Edward, were both in the military because they were often photographed with their father, King George, but I'd just assumed they had jobs that wouldn't put them in too much danger.

"He's there under a different name, and no, he's not a pilot," Mrs. Underdown replied. "He's in charge of the boys being trained as mechanics and such. I imagine they are quite overwhelmed to have the prince with them. Such an opportunity for them. If he attended our little entertainment, it would be quite a treat for our convalescents as well."

"If he's at Cranwell under a different name, I assume he doesn't want people to know he is here." Margaret set down her glass so forcefully that some of her wine sloshed on the table.

"Yes, Margaret is right. Prince Albert would be a very high-value target for Germany," Andrew said. His voice was cold. "I'm sure his people won't want him to come off the base for something like a theatrical. How did you know he was here?"

Mrs. Underdown gave a little titter of laughter. "My dear Lord Andrew, everyone around here knows. Something like that can't be kept secret, but he's in no danger from the people of Lincolnshire. Of course, if he comes to our performance, we'll have to try not to draw attention to him."

I wondered exactly how that would work if Mrs. Underdown wanted the convalescents to meet him.

Mrs. Underdown held up her hand as if she didn't already have our attention. "Now, we should start practicing right away so our actors can get used to their performance space," she said. "Say, tomorrow afternoon at two? The performance is the day after tomorrow, and we'll need the actors to get familiar with the staging area." She paused and looked around the table. "There is just one more favor I must ask. The rector had a role, but his gout is acting up, so unfortunately he has had to bow out. He's most disappointed that he can't take part."

I had a bad feeling about what Mrs. Underdown was going to say next. Surely she wasn't going to ask Andrew to step in for the rector. She didn't. Her eyes locked on mine.

"I hope you can play the part, Lady Thomasina," Mrs. Underdown said. "I still remember how you made us laugh when you played Falstaff in Crispin's last production."

Before I could bring myself to speak, Margaret made a choking sound. "I remember that. You were hysterically funny, Mina!"

If I had been close enough, I would have kicked my sister. That particular performance hadn't taken any great acting skill. People had laughed at Falstaff because Crispin made me wear an oversized costume and I was so nervous that my lines came out squeaky and high-pitched.

Mrs. Underdown pulled a small book out of her bag. "You're such a good actress, you'll have no trouble learning the part. And there's one bit where you sing a short solo, only four lines. Very easy. Here's the script. I've marked all your lines so you can memorize them before tomorrow." She held it out to me and I had no choice but to take it. "It's all going to be splendid," she said, beaming at us.

I doubted if "splendid" was going to be the right description for it, but I'd do my best to contribute to the effort. At least I'd be wearing a costume. It was always easier to play a role in costume.

I saw Margaret put a hand to her head for a few seconds. I suspected her headache had come back. "Should we move to the drawing room since everyone is finished?" she said, cutting off something Mrs. Underdown had begun to say. Margaret rose without waiting for anyone to reply, so we all followed.

Once we were in the drawing room, I hoped we could manage to politely rid ourselves of Mrs. Underdown sooner rather than later. I didn't want her to start questioning Lucas again. Gwendolyn sat down close to Lucas. I felt a flash of jealousy and wished the girl weren't quite so pretty. "So, Mr. Miller, are the Americans behind President Wilson and his push for America to enter the war?" she asked.

"Yes," Lucas said. "Most of them, at least now. The first part of the war, most wanted to stay neutral, seeing as how it was viewed as a European war and no concern of ours."

"I hear by the end of May over one million American troops will be in France," Gwendolyn said. "That should help our boys."

"Yes, we need more men." Andrew got up and poured himself a brandy. "The pilots we have are a grand lot, but we need more. There is a Canadian fellow I've heard about who has absolutely no fear and will push a plane to its limit. I hope we get more like him. I suspect the Americans are going to be something like the Australians—an enormous help, but with a tendency to engage in hijinks that will get them in trouble." He glanced at Lucas, and I could imagine he was thinking of their plane ride. I wished he hadn't brought up flying. It might start Mrs. Underdown off again.

Andrew drained his drink and then poured another. He smiled, but I thought it looked forced. "I heard quite a story from a friend of mine who has a couple of Australian air squadrons in France under his command," he said. "Our soldiers may grumble about the tinned milk, but they make do. The Australians aren't quite satisfied with always making do when it comes to milk. They somehow always manage to find cows in the middle of a war zone, and for the cows' own safety, so they claim, they take charge of them, moving them about in lorries. The wing commander says he can only hope no one raises awkward inquiries as to the cows' provenance."

Everyone laughed except Margaret. It did feel odd to be joking about anything related to the war. I'd witnessed it before, not just with Andrew, but also with the few other soldiers I'd been around. Men seemed to think it best to gloss over anything terrible, as if women were too delicate to be able to bear it.

"We'd call fellows like that cattle rustlers back home," Lucas said.

"They've got a piano they 'found' too," Andrew added. "I suppose they'd be considered piano rustlers as well."

This brought on additional laughter, but Margaret spoiled Andrew's efforts. "I'm surprised their superiors let them get away with such behavior," she said. "Surely the breakdown in discipline has serious consequences on their effectiveness."

"You're wrong," Andrew responded. "The wing commander says he'll put up with anything to keep the Australians in the air. They come up with clever schemes to set traps for enemy pilots, and he says their sense of initiative is something he wishes he could bottle. They do get a bit wild in their flying, though. I've seen their pilots take up people riding on their wings. I wouldn't want to try that."

Lucas laughed. "Now that's an idea." Andrew glared at him and gave a tiny shake of his head.

"I didn't think I'd ever see the day when people would risk life and limb in a flimsy canvas contraption just so they could imitate birds." Gwendolyn shuddered.

"I'm sure after the war aeroplanes will go back to being novelties, something for the few hobbyists to play with," Margaret said. "That is, if the war ever ends. If I have to hear one more bomb, I think I'll go mad."

After that, everyone grew quiet again. Mrs. Underdown announced it was time for her to go and no one protested. After she was gone, Gwendolyn wandered the room, examining all the family photographs as if she was trying to commit them to memory. Andrew smoked cigarette after cigarette. Lucas wouldn't sit still. He roamed the room too, pulling at his collar until I was convinced he would rip it off. Every once in a while he stopped at a window and looked out. I watched him, wondering why he looked different, and then I realized it was in the way he stood. Tension had taken over, removing that loose-limbed ease I'd first noticed about him. When he turned around, his face was different too. Without the grin, he looked older and even a little grim.

I turned my head so he wouldn't see that I'd been staring at him. Gwendolyn picked up a photograph of Margaret and Crispin taken when Crispin was just a baby and Margaret only about three. "You were an adorable child, Margaret," she said. "And your brother was too."

Margaret gave a faint smile. "Crispin had that sweet look until it changed to one of pure mischief. He could never hide that he was always planning something."

Mention of Crispin cast an additional pall over the room. We sat there in silence until I became aware of a noise in the background that didn't belong. I listened and realized it was Jove barking. It was a persistent bark, not one like he was particularly agitated or anything. It was odd.

I stood up. "I'll be right back."

"I can go check on the dog," Lucas offered.

"Let Mina do it," Margaret said. "Why don't you bring him in here, Mina? Poor old thing. I'm afraid he's losing his sight. I think that's why he's been barking at shadows. It's terrible for him that my father isn't here and his world is going dim."

I went to look for the dog, feeling awful that I hadn't noticed the vision problems. That would explain the barking.

I found him sitting outside on the terrace, looking in. I opened the door for him. He bent his head down and picked up something, then trotted inside and dropped it at my feet. It was Lettie's tam-o'-shanter. "Where did you find this?" I asked the dog before realizing it was a very silly question. Jove tilted his head and looked at me, his signal that he wanted to be petted for bringing in a prize.

"Good dog," I said as I reached down to pick it up.

Lucas's voice came from behind me. "Is anything wrong?"

Hearing his voice made me realize how quickly I'd come to like the sound of it, the soft drawl of it. When I heard him speak, it was as if he was pulling me in, shutting out all the bad things around us. Either his voice or just his presence made my skin feel a little tingly.

"Mina?" he said.

I realized that I needed to answer him. "No. Jove just wanted in." Jove was already at Lucas's side, wagging his tail. I set Lettie's hat on a nearby chair. "He's very pleased he found one of the servant's hats. I'll take it to her after dinner." I reached for the door handle to close the door.

Lucas put his hand over mine. "Wait." His touch startled me. I jerked my hand out from under his and then wished I hadn't, berating myself for acting like a scared rabbit. Lucas behaved as if he hadn't noticed. He pulled on his tie and smiled. "It's nice to breathe some real air. It takes a long time to have a meal here. Would it be a terrible breach of etiquette if we went outside for a few minutes?"

It would, but I wasn't going to tell him that. "We can blame Jove," I told him. "Say he ran off with Lettie's hat because he thought we were playing a game." Hearing his name, Jove thumped his tail, unaware that he was going to be the scapegoat.

"Yes, we must rescue the hat," Lucas said. "Jove, you are a rascal, aren't you?" He made a sweeping motion with his hand. "After you, Miss Mina."

The tingly feeling increased. I took a step out the door.

CHAPTER EIGHT

LUCAS FOLLOWED ME out on the terrace and then onto the lawn. Jove, of course, came with us, trailing at Lucas's heels. Lucas had been right. It was nice to breathe fresh air. The grounds were so still, they could have been a landscape painting. Mr. Applewhite had mowed recently and the lawn was lovely in the bright moonlight, a smooth expanse where we had played croquet and hosted our lawn parties. I held on to the thought that someday we'd do those things again.

"Do you play croquet?" I blurted out.

Lucas chuckled. "Why? Do the English have a night version of it? I'd be willing for a game instead of going back inside."

"No," I said, though the thought of night croquet did sound rather fun, especially with Lucas.

As we walked, I began to tell him all about the lawn parties, wanting to prolong the moment. I decided we needed to make an entire circuit of the back lawn. After all, when a guest needed fresh air, I should be a good hostess and provide it.

He pulled again at his tie. "You don't have to dress up for those lawn parties, do you?"

I was about to answer him when a sound caught my attention. It was like a faint moan, the kind of sound I heard in the woods when the wind was blowing. But there was no wind and we weren't in the woods.

The sound came again. I stopped. "Did you hear that?" I asked.

"No," Lucas said.

I put my hand on his sleeve. "Wait."

I looked down at Jove. His ears were pricked up and he was looking toward the old icehouse. It had been designed to fit into the landscape like a grotto, though why a grotto would be at the edge of the lawn was never explained. We didn't use it any longer, and vines had grown up over most of it, though Mr. Applewhite kept them pruned enough that the steep steps leading down to the door were clear. I started toward it. Another moan. I broke into a run, Lucas following. When we reached the steps, I looked down into the cavity, but it was too dark to see the bottom. The moan came again.

My heart skipped a beat. I remembered that Mr. Applewhite

had grumbled about the steps before, complaining that whoever had built the icehouse had never gone down steps made slippery with rain and moss.

Lucas bounded down the steps and knelt before I could tell him to be careful. "It's a girl with dark hair," he called up.

I came down as quickly as I could—it was slippery. When I knelt down next to Lucas, I saw that it was Lettie lying there. She opened her eyes. "I hoped someone would come," she said. "I've been calling and calling."

My heart picked up speed, pounding as I tried to think of what to do. "I'll go get help," I said, and ran back inside. I knew Lucas and I wouldn't be able to get Lettie up those narrow steps ourselves.

The next hour went by in a blur. Andrew and Lucas carried Lettie up to her room. Miss Tanner telephoned for a doctor while Mrs. Brickles saw to Lettie. The pallor of the girl's face frightened me. She was very, very still and no longer conscious.

We all clustered outside the room looking in until Miss Tanner politely shooed us away when the doctor arrived. I recounted to the others how we had found her, as if that would help in some way. It didn't, of course.

As we went back downstairs, I was struck by the emptiness of the servants' quarters. I hadn't been up to them in ages. There were rooms for a dozen housemaids, but with only Hannah and Lettie, that section of the house had the same unsettling quiet as the rest of the place.

We sat down in the drawing room, waiting for some news. I feared how Margaret would react, but she actually held herself together, even convincing Gwendolyn and Lucas to play cards with her. She also decreed that everyone drop all formality and call each other by their given names. Such a small gesture did seem to lessen some of the tension. Both Gwendolyn and Lucas appeared more at ease. I couldn't begin to concentrate, so I sat with a book, not seeing the pages. Andrew went back to smoking what seemed to be endless cigarettes.

I jumped up when Miss Tanner finally came into the room. "How is she?"

"The doctor says Lettie is concussed, but he thinks she will recover," she said. "There is nothing more to be done tonight. Mrs. Brickles is sitting with her until we can get one of Lettie's sisters to come tomorrow."

"I can sit with her too," I said. "Mrs. Brickles shouldn't be up all night." I had to do something to help, even if it was just sitting next to Lettie's bed.

"That won't be necessary, Lady Thomasina," Miss Tanner said. "There is the extra bed in Lettie's room where Mrs. Brickles can rest if she wants. And I'm sure Lettie would be more comfortable with her sister. She wouldn't want to impose upon you."

I knew I needed to stay calm because that was what would be expected of me, but I had been trying to make sense of what happened. "Why did Lettie go to the icehouse?" I blurted out.

Miss Tanner frowned. "I don't know, Lady Thomasina. Now, if there is nothing else, I'll go see to the kitchen."

"There's nothing else," Margaret said, standing up. "I'm going up to bed. We all should." Margaret's voice had taken on the tone of a hostess in command, and everyone obeyed her. We trooped upstairs.

Even though I was exhausted, once I was in my room I couldn't sleep. What did Lucas think of all this? And why was he, an American with loads of charm who didn't appear to know enough about aeroplanes to design them, here to prepare for a secret mission? I felt a little like Mrs. Underdown trying to fit people into their proper places. I couldn't figure out where Lucas fit.

The sound of a motorcar coming down the drive drew me to the window. At first I thought the doctor might have been summoned back, but the vehicle had its lights off. As it came close to the house, the driver switched off the engine so that it glided to a stop. Margaret came out of the house with a coat on. A man in uniform got out and took her in his arms, kissing her. After a moment, the two of them got in and drove off.

So Hannah had been right about my sister having a secret sweetheart. I supposed Margaret thought I was still too young to confide in, though I'd have kept her secret even if I didn't understand why she didn't want anyone to know. She was a widow, after all, and there was nothing wrong with her meeting a man. I suspected he was the real reason Margaret had left London. He was also probably the reason Margaret hadn't been happy to see me come home, nor to have Andrew and Lucas as houseguests. I knew I should respect her privacy, but I was too curious to leave the secret alone. It was crying out to be discovered.

I went back to bed, wishing the room wasn't so chilly. I realized that Jove had not tried to join me, and I missed his warmth.

I suspected I'd lost out to Lucas. I found myself thinking about those ridiculous bows Lucas had done out in the pasture, grinning all the while. It would be nice to sit with him in the cockpit of a plane, though I didn't think they were very big. I'd have to sit on his lap, which would also be nice. Feeling much warmer, I fell asleep.

The next morning, as soon as I was dressed, I bolted down some toast in the breakfast room and then went to check on Lettie. Mrs. Brickles came out just as I was about to knock.

"She's sleeping peacefully, Lady Thomasina. Best come back later." The cook hid a yawn. "Her sister will be here any minute."

"Shall I sit with her until her sister arrives?"

"No need for that, Lady Thomasina. Now if you'll excuse me, I want to see how my kitchen looks after I've left it to others for so many hours."

I went outside and weeded the summer border, but I couldn't stop worrying about Lettie. When I went in to check on her again, her door stood open. I looked in. She still appeared to be sleeping. One of her sisters was there.

"Would you come out into the hall?" I whispered to her. "I don't want to wake Lettie."

She hurried out to me. "I don't think we've met," I said. Lettie had nine sisters, but I'd met only one of them, younger than this girl. "I know you must be Lettie's sister because you look so much alike. What's your name?"

"It's Mary, your ladyship," she mumbled, twisting her hands together.

"How is Lettie this morning?" I could see Lettie's color had improved. The night before, she had been so pale that she'd looked like a different person.

"She was awake a little while ago, but she is very confused. I hope her wits come back."

"I'm sure they will," I said.

"Lady Thomasina." I heard Lettie's voice, weak but clear, from the bed.

I went in. "Lettie! I'm so happy you are awake."

"Please sit, your ladyship." Mary indicated the chair next to the bed. I sat down.

Touching the bandage on her head, Lettie said, "I've got a fearsome headache."

"I'm not surprised. You must have hit your head on one of the stone walls when you fell. Those steps are very narrow."

A confused look appeared on Lettie's face. "Steps?"

"That's what I mean, your ladyship," Mary said. "She doesn't think she fell."

"Yes, you fell," I said. "We found you at the bottom of the steps at the door of the icehouse."

"Icehouse?"

"Yes, do you remember going to the icehouse?"

Lettie tried to shake her head and then moaned in pain. "I didn't go to the icehouse. I went . . . Where did I go?"

She was growing pale again. I couldn't keep asking her questions if it was going to make her worse. I stood up. "Don't worry about it now, Lettie. I'm sure you will remember later. Just rest."

Lettie lifted her hand. "Wait. I didn't go to the icehouse. I remember now. I went to the summerhouse."

"The summerhouse? Why would you have gone there?" The summerhouse, at the back of the garden, was a little shaded seating area from which to enjoy the fragrances of the lilies and the honeysuckle when they were in bloom. The latticework that made up its walls meant it was too chilly to use in the spring, and the servants didn't use it at all. I sometimes took a book there to read on lazy summer afternoons, but it wasn't a spot favored by anyone else in the family.

"I . . . I don't remember," Lettie said, "but I'm sure I was there. I smelled something . . ." Her words drifted off and her eyes closed.

"We'll let her rest," I whispered, and tiptoed out of the room, pondering what I'd just heard.

The mention of the summerhouse had sparked a memory. I went back up to my room and took the wristlet out of the drawer, holding it up to my nose again. I had been wrong. The scent on the wristlet was not cucumber—it was borage. The herb grew far too vigorously all around the summerhouse, and without a staff to keep it under control, it was threatening to invade the rest of the garden. But why did the wristlet smell of it?

Perhaps Lettie actually had been at the summerhouse, though I couldn't think of a reason why she would be. She would never go just to sit in it. The indoor staff didn't walk about any of the ornamental gardens; Miss Tanner would have frowned upon that. They only went into the kitchen garden.

I went to the window. I could just make out the summerhouse

behind the shrubs that bordered the walkway to it. I had to go look, though I doubted I'd find any sign that Lettie had been there. No one was about when I went downstairs and out the terrace door. As I headed toward the back, I found myself noticing once again how shabby and abandoned the garden looked. I passed the entrance to the maze, though it was so overgrown that it looked more like a wall of wild shrubbery, adding to the deserted feel.

As I got closer to the summerhouse, I saw it needed a coat of paint. I could also smell the borage. It had spread far more than I had expected, with new shoots sprouting in a wide area all around the entrance to the summerhouse. I picked a leaf and then pulled the wristlet out of my pocket. They both had the same scent.

I was just about to go in when a rustling came from behind me. Before I could turn around, a thick cloth went over my face and a strong arm went around my waist.

"Be quiet and you won't get hurt," a man hissed.

CHAPTER NINE

THE CLOTH STANK of something rotten and I nearly gagged. It was too tight over my mouth for me to scream. I began to struggle, fear pounding through me.

The man cursed and tightened his hold on me. "Drop the watch and I'll let you go," he said.

I dropped it. The man yanked on the cloth, jerking my head back. I could tell he was tying it in a knot at the back of my head. For some reason that forced me into action, and I rammed my elbows back into him, trying to free myself.

"Mina!" Lucas's voice came from somewhere near the house.

The man cursed again and pushed me hard onto the ground.

"Mina!" Lucas sounded as if he was getting closer.

I felt the man grab one of my arms, and my panic increased. I didn't want him to touch me again, so I rolled over and kicked at him, accidentally connecting with him in a place that made him cry out in pain. He let go of me and I could hear him crashing through the bushes as he ran away.

I ripped the stinking rag from my face, gasping for breath. I looked around, but there was no sign of the attacker.

Lucas reached me before I could get up. "Are you hurt?" he asked as he knelt down.

I tried to get some words out, feeling so shaken I wasn't sure if I could get my voice to work.

"I'm not hurt," I said finally. Lucas put his arms around my waist, helping me up. Once on my feet, I was shivering so much I felt like I might fall over.

Lucas shifted so that one arm was still around me. "Lean on me if you need to," he said.

"Did you see him?" I asked, trying to get control of myself.

"Just his back," Lucas said. "He ran off into the woods. Let's go back to the house. We need to tell Andrew and call the police. Do you know who it was?"

"No, I didn't even see his face."

He tightened his hold on me. "I didn't know this sort of thing happened out here in the country. Have you heard of any other attacks?"

"It wasn't random." I told him about Lettie insisting she'd gone to the summerhouse instead of the icehouse, about the wristlet, and about the man I'd seen running away from the house the first night I arrived. "The man grabbed me and told me to drop the wristlet. He attacked me just to get it."

"Is that it?" He pointed to the spot where I had fallen. The wristlet lay there, now a little dirtier than before.

"I suppose I must have landed on it," I said. "That must be why the man grabbed me again when I fell down. He was trying to get to it. Miss Tanner told me the man I'd seen running away was probably a soldier who had been invalided out of the fighting. But why would he still be here?"

"Can I let go of you for a minute to pick it up?"

"Yes, I'm fine." As soon as he took his arm away, I wished he'd put it back. At least I felt a little steadier on my feet, though my insides still felt shaky, as if I had just been on a fast automobile ride over winding country roads.

Lucas picked up the wristlet. "Did you go into the summer-house?"

"No, I was just looking at the plants around it."

"I have an idea. I want to look inside." I followed him, looking back over my shoulder into the woods as I did. I knew the man would not be there, but I couldn't help myself. I hated that someone had been watching the house, watching me work in the garden.

"I thought we'd find this sort of thing," Lucas said as we viewed the interior. A moth-eaten wool blanket lay in one corner, surrounded by crumpled food packets and a couple of empty tins. "Whoever it was has been living here for a bit. Do you think Lettie was meeting him?"

I couldn't imagine Lettie sneaking out to meet a man. "No, she would never jeopardize her job here. Miss Tanner would sack her if she found out."

"We have to tell Andrew," Lucas said. "He's probably still in the library. He got a telephone call after we got back from Cranwell. Are you able to walk?"

"Yes." I brushed away a tear, telling myself that I was not going to cry. Sometimes I cried long after something had upset me. Lucas noticed the tear, but didn't say anything. He just put his arm around me again and kept it there as we went back to the house.

"Why were you looking for me?" I asked, shivering a little. I didn't want to think about what might have happened if Lucas hadn't come along at the right time.

"I wanted to see if you were all right, after everything that happened last night. Andrew said you'd be upset about Lettie. I saw Margaret inside and she told me you could usually be found in the gardens. I've been looking for you everywhere. There are too many gardens here."

"I'm glad you did look." I felt a little less shaky at the thought that he'd wanted to check on me.

Andrew had just finished his telephone call when we went into the library. I was shocked by his appearance. It was as if he were aging more and more each day. He ran his hand over his face like he was trying to wipe away the tiredness. He was about to say something else when he looked at me and frowned. "Are you all right? You have dirt on your face."

Lucas handed him the wristlet and I launched into an explanation. As I told the story, Andrew's expression grew more and more serious.

"This is German," Andrew said, examining the wristlet.

"I know," I said. "I should have paid more attention to that. Miss Tanner said it was probably a hungry soldier, and she also said we shouldn't give in to spy hysteria. There wasn't really a spy here, was there?"

Andrew didn't answer right away. He studied my face and then gave the slightest of nods, as if he'd come to a decision. "I need you not to repeat anything I'm going to tell you," he said. "Can I count on you?"

"Yes," I said, a little frightened by the intensity in his voice.

He gestured at the telephone. "The call I just took gave me confirmation that some confidential matters your father discussed here at his last meeting are now known by the Germans. The information had to have come from someone in the house. They are interviewing all the drivers, and others who were here. If they can't identify the source from among those people, someone from London will be up to interview the household staff. The person in the summerhouse may have a contact inside who is giving him information."

I took a step backward and groped for the chair I knew was close by. When my hand touched its arm, I sat down. The news confounded me. My father was always so careful with anything related to his work. To hear someone had managed to outwit him shook me. If someone could do that, we weren't as safe as I'd thought.

I realized Lucas had moved next to the chair and put his hand on the back of it so that the tips of his fingers were touching my hair. I wished I could just lean back and close my eyes to forget what I'd heard.

"How much do you know about Lettie?" Andrew asked.

"What?" I asked before realizing where his question was leading. "I can't imagine Lettie having anything to do with a spy," I said. The idea was absurd. "Lettie has lived in the neighborhood since she was born, and her whole life revolves around her job and her family. I don't know how she'd even meet a German!"

"You may know less about Lettie than you think," Andrew said. "Most of the people who pass along information do it for the money. Lettie may have need of funds, or someone in her family might. And a German agent does not have to be German. There are many people in a spy chain, all with different motives."

"But how did Lettie end up at the bottom of the icehouse steps?" Lucas asked.

"I don't know," Andrew said. "We'll have to hope she can tell us more when she recovers."

It couldn't be Lettie. I was sure of it. It seemed more logical to determine the person's identity by figuring out who in the house could have met a German agent. Not Mrs. Brickles. That was as absurd an idea as Lettie being the culprit. A German agent wouldn't just approach her at the butcher's and manage to convince her to spy on my father. And Hannah wouldn't stop talking. Spies were supposed to listen instead of talk.

But a memory tugged at me. I remembered Lettie talking about my father's meeting on our cart ride. She had mentioned that Margaret was there with a friend and they hadn't been invited to the dinner. When Gwendolyn had arrived, she'd said she'd been at Hallington before.

"What about Gwendolyn?" I asked, explaining what I knew. I wasn't going to end this conversation until Andrew understood he couldn't just assume it was Lettie. Since Lettie couldn't defend herself, someone had to do it for her. I related Lettie's conversation to Andrew.

"And remember when Gwendolyn came into the dining room the first time?" I added. "Her coat had mud on it and her hat was crooked. What if she helped the man attack Lettie? We don't know anything about her except what she's told us." I told myself the fact that she was pretty had nothing to do with my suspicions. "She says she lives in London. She could have met all sorts of people there who convinced her to work for them."

Andrew considered that. "I suppose it's possible. I'll have someone look into her background."

"What about the maid, Hannah?" Lucas asked. "From what I understand, she hasn't been here long."

Andrew shook his head. "I've spoken to Miss Tanner about her. She says the girl is flighty and talks too much. I don't think it's her. German agents would be very careful in what they say and do." He stopped and frowned. "Are you sure you are all right, Mina? You keep clenching and unclenching your hands."

I hadn't realized I'd been doing that. I also hadn't realized how cold the library could be on a spring day. "I'm fine," I said. Andrew didn't need to worry about me in addition to everything else.

He nodded. "Good. Now, about the man in the garden, I'll tell the gardener to keep a look out for any strangers, but I don't think the fellow will be back, now that he knows he's been seen."

"We didn't see enough of him to identify him," I said.

"He doesn't know that." Andrew put the wristlet in his pocket. "And someone like that is a coward, deep down. You fought back. He won't try again."

I wasn't so sure about that. "What about Margaret?" I asked. "She'll be hysterical if she hears about this. I think she sees the house as the last safe place left."

Andrew grimaced. "We don't need Margaret upset. As long as you are sure you are all right, perhaps it's best to keep this from her. I'll ask Miss Tanner to be extremely vigilant about locking up, but as I said, I don't think the man will be back. I need to make another telephone call." He looked at both of us. "I'm afraid I'm going to have to ask both of you to leave the room. Lucas, we need to go back to Cranwell as soon as I'm done."

We left, though it felt strange to be asked to vacate a room in my own house. We walked out into the hall and both of us stopped at the same time. "Thank you," I said.

"For what?"

"For . . . For everything." I couldn't say, *Thank you for putting your arm around me and please do it again*, though I very badly wanted to.

"You're welcome," he said. He shifted his weight and looked at his feet. It was what someone would do if they were feeling awkward, but I couldn't imagine Lucas ever feeling awkward.

"I suppose I should get the car if we are going to Cranwell," he said.

"You are just learning how to fly, aren't you?" I blurted out the question. I had to know.

Lucas looked shocked. He didn't answer.

"I'm not stupid," I said. "I saw you land in the pasture. I've seen a few other aeroplanes land before, much more smoothly than that. And I heard Andrew say you didn't have much time. And I saw how interested you were in the map I drew. A map of a German village. You didn't even need to be in the room when Andrew was talking about it if it had nothing to do with you. The two have to go together."

"I can't say, Mina," he said softly. "Please don't ask me. The less you know, the safer you are."

"You can trust me, you know," I said.

"It isn't up to me. Andrew is in charge here. I'm to do what I'm told."

He looked so miserable that I knew I shouldn't push him. "All right. I'll stop asking, though I might be better able to help if I knew more."

"There isn't anything you can do to help. I wish there were."

There was no good response to that. I wasn't going to resort to begging. "I'm going to go change," I said.

"Are you sure you are all right?" he asked.

"Yes." I tried to smile, but now that I had a moment to think, I could almost feel the disgusting rag over my mouth. "Yes," I said again, and hurried up the stairs so he wouldn't see me if I started to cry.

When I came back down, I saw that Lucas was still in the hall, wandering around with his hands in his pockets while he examined the pictures on the wall. He was also whistling softly. I recognized the song. It was the same one he'd whistled when he left the train: *So send me away with a smile, little girl, brush the tears from eyes of brown.*

No, there wouldn't be tears from me.

CHAPTER
TEN

I REACHED THE bottom step just as Margaret came out of the morning room. I wished she hadn't appeared, not right at that moment. She glanced at me and then at Lucas, who seemed totally engrossed in a painting of a pastoral landscape full of cows.

"Mina, we've been neglecting our guest," Margaret said. Lucas whirled around. I could tell he hadn't been aware of either of us. She motioned to me. "Why don't you give Lucas a tour of the house while he's waiting for Andrew?"

"I don't want to be a bother," Lucas said.

I noticed Margaret was looking much better this morning, and she seemed happy too.

"It's no bother," she said. "And Mina doesn't have enough to do."

That wasn't true. There was plenty to do in the garden, but at the moment, I had no interest in going back outside. I wanted to think about anything besides the man in the garden. And I wanted to be with Lucas without anyone else around, even if it was just for a few minutes. "I'd be happy to, if you are interested," I said to him. "You can say no, though. I don't mind. We don't have any rooms where kings slept or anything like that, but there are some rather nice parts and some nice paintings."

"I'd like that."

"Good," Margaret said brightly. "I'll leave you to it."

After she left, Lucas pointed at the picture he'd been examining. "What about this one?"

"I'm already a tour-guide failure. I don't know anything about that one. My mother likes the colors in it. I think that's why she put it there."

"I was looking at the cattle, wondering what breed they are," he said. "Nice colors too, though."

I laughed. "I'm not a cow expert. I'm not much of an expert at anything, not even giving house tours. My mother usually takes visitors around, though my father teases that the stories about the rooms change each time. This way."

We walked through several of the rooms. I had a feeling that Lucas wasn't all that interested in who was in what portrait or how old some of the vases were, though I dutifully told him all I remembered. By the fifth room, I could see his interest flagging, so I decided it was time to reveal the best part of the house. Leading him into the Tapestry Room, I said, "The tapestries are some of the most important items in the house, from the early seventeenth century. The four of them depict different fables of Aesop, but that's not the best part of the room. Can you see something different about it?"

"You're smiling like there is a secret here. Is this a challenge?" His face brightened.

"Yes. Let's see if you can figure out why this isn't an ordinary room."

"I'm always up for a challenge." Lucas walked around the room slowly, examining all the walls, the bookcases, and the fireplace. The tapestries covered two of the walls; the third held the door, flanked by bookcases, and the fourth, the fireplace and more bookcases. I had always loved the room, especially in wintertime, when the combination of the firelight and the fantastical creatures on the tapestries enhanced the feeling that the room was a step removed from the real world.

Lucas examined each tapestry and then moved on to the other walls. After the first time around, he said, "Can I have a hint?"

I shook my head. "No."

"I knew you'd say that." He went back to the fireplace and examined the carvings on it. "In stories, there is always something you push on the fireplace to make a secret door swing open. What happens if I push this carved flower thing on the mantel?"

"Nothing happens." I was enjoying this. "Do you give up?"

He made another circuit around and then shrugged. "Yes, I give up. I'm stumped."

I went over to one of the bookcases. "We do have a secret door. See how the frame around this bookcase doesn't look quite like the rest? And there's a little circle carved into the frame. If you push it . . ." I pushed, and with a faint creak the bookcase swung open to reveal a tiny winding staircase going up to the floor above.

Lucas came over and peered at it. "That's amazing. Why was it built? There must be a good story behind it. Who needed to be smuggled upstairs?"

"It was nothing like that, I'm afraid. The story goes that an ancestor had hordes of children and a shrew of a wife. He had the staircase built to go up to a room he used as a bedroom, so he could come and go without everyone knowing."

"Who has the room at the top? If I lived here, I'd want it."

"My brother, Crispin. It's one of the worst bedrooms, because it's small and dark. He insisted he had to have it, though." I remembered the first time Crispin and Andrew had used the stairs to try to frighten Margaret after luring her into the Tapestry Room with some story of a strange visitor and then popping out to scare her. Margaret's screams could be heard all over the house. "We haven't used the staircase in ages."

"Someone has been using it." Lucas pointed to some scuffs in the dust on the steps.

"What?" I leaned down and peered at the marks. "I suppose one of the servants is using it, though they aren't supposed to.

Miss Tanner wants them to use the back stairs. Some of the floorboards are not in the best condition. I'll talk to Miss Tanner about it. Unless Margaret has been using it." I stopped. Did the staircase play a part in her secret romance? Was someone going up and down it to avoid the notice of the staff? If so, it was very strange that Margaret would go to such lengths.

"These are nice carvings." Lucas ran his hand over one of the elaborate designs on the paneling next to the bookcase. The room had several, like wooden versions of still-life paintings with birds and leaves and vines all intertwined together. "I wish my grandfather could see these. He does a little whittling, but this is astounding."

"The carvings were done by a man named Gibbling Griffin," I said. "He was famous, or at least he is now. He's dead, of course." I was getting tangled up in what I was trying to say. "I mean, I don't know if he was famous when he was alive."

Lucas wasn't even listening to me. He had moved on to a painting my mother had done of a monastery in Germany, St. Augustine's.

"That's *Augustinerkloster* in Erfurt," he said.

"Yes. Have you been there? You used the German word," I said, surprised.

"Yes," he said. "When I was about ten. I . . . I had relatives in Germany."

He'd said "had." With the war on, people treaded carefully around past associations with Germany, and it had become awkward to ask too many questions. "So, do you speak German?" I asked, thinking that was a less intrusive question.

He shook his head. "I understand some, but I don't speak much."

His pronunciation hadn't been all that bad. I was curious about how much he spoke, so I decided to test him. "Did you enjoy your visit?" I asked in German.

Lucas said *ja* but didn't expand on it.

That hadn't been enough of a test. I was still standing by the carvings, so this time I said in German, "The work was done by a man named Gibbling Griffin."

"I don't believe you gave him correct information, Lady Thomasina," Miss Tanner said in German as she came into the room. "The carvings were done by Grinling Gibbons, not Griffin. But how nice you have someone with whom to practice German."

Her voice had made me jump. I couldn't get used to how quietly she moved about the house.

"Yes, it is nice," I said, still speaking German. "My school has dropped its German classes, and I don't want to forget mine. Someday the war will be over and things will be back to normal."

"I see," Miss Tanner said. "Very commendable. If you ever wish for more practice, I'm somewhat proficient in it. It is a beautiful language."

I'd had no idea Miss Tanner spoke German. "Thank you," I said, "but I wouldn't want to keep you from your work." I didn't want to feel like I was back in school.

"I do have some time. Whatever you choose, though," she said as she left the room.

"Thank you," I said again. I turned back to Lucas. "As we have learned, this carving was done by Grinling Gibbons, not Griffin."

"Okay, I didn't understand any of what either of you said in German, except the name. My German isn't that good. I'll be sure and remember it's Gibbons, though." Lucas smiled. "That seems to be an important fact. It would take a lot of effort to learn about all the things in this house. How many rooms are there, anyway?"

We walked back into the hall. "I don't know. I've never counted them." I tried to do a quick count in my head, but with Lucas standing there, my concentration left me. I had that skin-tingling feeling again, and I wanted to think of something else I could show him so we'd have a few more minutes together. Since Lucas seemed to be waiting for an answer, I said, "About thirty, I suppose, not counting the servants' quarters."

"What do you do with all of them?"

"What do you mean?"

"Why do you have so many rooms?"

"I don't know. We just do." I was taken aback by his questions.

"I've always wondered why people want such big houses."

"Well, how many rooms does your grandfather's house have?"

"I've never counted them. I suppose eight or nine. He grew up in a big family. We use them all, except for some of the spare bedrooms. It seems like here there are a lot of rooms just to sit in."

His remarks made me feel defensive. "It's not like my father built this house. Some ancestor did, and they thought they needed all the rooms. What were we to do, tear them down?"

"No, it's just strange to me." He went back to studying the cow painting while he talked. "Hannah told me if there wasn't a war on, there would be at least a dozen servants who would take care of the house, not counting the ones in the kitchen."

"Hannah told you that?"

"She brought up a tea tray early this morning. I told her I don't drink tea, but she said I might grow accustomed to it. The girl gave me a whole lecture on the health benefits of tea."

I couldn't believe what I was hearing. It was surprising that Miss Tanner had even allowed the girl to take up the tea tray. Before the war, young female maids didn't enter male guests' bedrooms when the guests were there. "I'm sorry if she was bothering you. She's new, and the housekeeper says she's very talkative."

"She wasn't bothering me. In fact, she was very funny. She's quite good with imitations too. She does your sister to perfection."

"I can't believe she was imitating my sister!" I wondered how long the visit to Lucas's room had actually lasted.

"Why not? Are only ladies of the manor allowed to have a little fun?" His voice had turned very cold.

I was about to explain that I didn't want Hannah to get in trouble because Miss Tanner might let her go, but before I could, Lucas turned away from me. He muttered, "I'm going to go get the car." As he went out the door I almost called after him to stop, but didn't. He hadn't even tried to understand, so why should I bother giving him a lesson in the intricacies of how Miss Tanner ran the house? If Miss Tanner fired Hannah, Lucas wouldn't even notice, but the rest of the household would be left with more work.

"That's the last house tour I'll give," I said to the empty hall.

CHAPTER ELEVEN

ANDREW OPENED THE library door and came into the hall. He looked around. "Who are you talking to?"

"No one," I said, happy to see Andrew. He would have understood me perfectly. He wouldn't have called me a "lady of the manor."

"Where is Lucas?" he asked. When I had explained about the car, he said, "Good. I don't have any time to waste." His voice was strained. "There has been a change of plans. I have to go to London right away and may not be back until tomorrow. I don't want to leave right now, but it's important. Will you be all right?"

"Of course." I didn't want Andrew to leave, but I couldn't say so. I tried not to shudder, feeling the same chill I'd felt in the library. I told myself that it was only one night, and it wasn't as if we couldn't manage without him. I'd check all the doors and windows myself, and like Andrew had said, the man was not likely to come back. I smiled at him. "Go. Don't worry about anything here."

"Excellent," Andrew said. "Will you tell Miss Tanner I've gone?"

"Yes. Is Lucas going too?" I asked.

"No, he's to stay here and make himself useful. If I left him at Cranwell by himself, I've no doubt he'd spend the day joyriding around in whatever aeroplane he could commandeer. He'll have less of a chance to get into trouble here." He gave the faintest of smiles, though it just emphasized how drawn and tired he looked. I hadn't noticed before how thin he'd become. "Put him in Mrs. Underdown's play," he added. "I suspect he is an excellent actor. In fact, I suspect he will become everyone's favorite and they will all be dancing to his tune. You'll have to be the one to keep him from getting an inflated head. There is no one better than you for that."

"I suppose," I said. "Though his head is rather inflated already."

Andrew took out a cigarette and lit it, his hand shaking. I hated to see the shaking.

"It feels wrong to be devoting so much time to a silly little play with everything else that is going on," I said.

He looked at me for a long time without speaking. Then he surprised me by reaching over and touching my cheek very gently. "Don't think about that," he said. "If a moment of happiness is within your grasp, take it. There is nothing wrong with holding on to the last gasps of a dying way of life while you can. If it gives people some comfort or sense of purpose, we shouldn't judge, no matter how meaningless the act."

I was shocked by the bleakness of his words. "Nothing is dying!" I cried. "When the war is over, everything will go back to normal."

He sighed. "No, Mina. We've come through fire and have the scars to show for it. The whole world has changed. There is no going back. I'm not sure it was even real then. I look at you and think back on those years before the war like they were a lovely dream. At least I have that."

I was speechless. I just stood there as he turned and went out the front door, stumbling a little over the threshold as if he were making an extreme effort to put one foot in front of the other.

I went to the door and watched Andrew speak to Lucas. Lucas got out of the car. Andrew got in and drove away. It felt like a heavy weight had settled upon me. Andrew was right; there was no going back. And I couldn't avoid thinking about everything I'd seen. The map. The aeroplane lessons. An American who understood a little German. It all fit together—at least what Lucas was going to do. I had no idea why he was going to do it.

As I stood there, a long row of motorcars and carts came down the drive, led by Mrs. Underdown. She pulled her pony to a stop at the steps and instructed two elderly men in the cart behind her to unload what looked like a throne. "We're here right on time!" she called to me.

"It's going to be quite a day," I murmured to myself.

I followed the throne carriers and Mrs. Underdown inside. From all the boxes and trunks that came in after them, I realized that Mrs. Underdown had neglected to tell us she was staging an extravaganza. There was a cast of twenty, along with enough props and set pieces to furnish a London stage, and the Cranwell Orchestra, a group of talented airmen who had put together their own musical group. I held my tongue, remembering what Andrew had said and reminding myself that it was part of the war effort.

Poor Miss Tanner blanched at the sight of everything piled in the entrance hall and the people coming and going. It was the first time I had ever seen a crack in the woman's composure. When Mrs. Underdown asked one of the village helpers to haul some boulders into the house to add realism to the brigands' lair, Miss Tanner pulled herself together. "Mrs. Underdown," she said, "perhaps some fabric draped over some chairs and other furniture would suffice. Your audience will be sophisticated enough to understand the illusion."

After that the housekeeper took over and established order, deciding that the yellow sitting room would be the backstage area. The small parlor off it became the dressing room for the women, while the billiards room was opened up to hold the set pieces when they weren't needed and to be the men's dressing room. She also had some of the helpers move anything of value that could be damaged out of all the rooms.

Mrs. Underdown was in her glory, rushing around trying to

do everything at once. "The costumes are quite remarkable for an amateur production," she told me. "Miss Marshall volunteered to be in charge of them and has worked tirelessly. You'll wear a man's suit in the first part, with a sash to indicate you are part of Prince Alfie's court, but then when your lot pretends to be brigands, you all have pirate costumes. The rector had decided to add an eye patch to his costume, and we thought it quite a good touch. We'll adjust it so it will fit you."

An eye patch? I didn't mind wearing a silly costume in front of my friends and family, but I was not overjoyed at the idea of appearing before dozens of strangers in one. I saw Lucas off to the side, watching all the commotion. I waved to him and called, "Lucas, could we speak to you?"

Lucas came over, looking curious. Apparently Andrew hadn't told him he'd volunteered him to be in the play.

"Lord Andrew suggested that since Mr. Miller has time, he could play a part," I said to Mrs. Underdown, not meeting Lucas's eye. "Perhaps he could take mine."

"Oh, I wouldn't want to deprive you of your part," Mrs. Underdown said. "We lost one of our other brigands because of an ankle sprain. Mr. Miller can take his role, and there are only two lines to learn."

"A brigand? Do I get to have a sword?" Lucas asked, grinning. He mimed swishing a sword about.

"Only a papier-mâché one, but they are very realistic in appearance," Mrs. Underdown said. "I'm so glad you agreed to participate, Mr. Miller. Lady Thomasina, will you introduce the young man to the curate? He's in charge of the brigand costumes." She bustled off.

"Did I agree?" Lucas asked. He was still grinning.

"In Mrs. Underdown's world you did. The curate is right over there."

He swished his imaginary sword again. "I've always wanted to be a brigand. Who are you again?"

"A count and then a brigand too," I said.

"Fantastic! We can practice our sword fighting together, unless you already know how. Do young English ladyships learn saber fighting?" He made a stab at the air. "En garde!"

"No. The sharpest object I've ever held is a needle for needlework. I'm terrible at actual embroidery, though I could stab someone with a needle if I had to."

"You shall make an excellent brigand, then." I was happy we were back on good terms, though I couldn't believe how lighthearted Lucas was. It was as if he could ignore whatever it was that he was preparing for. I didn't think I'd be able to do that in his place.

After I introduced Lucas to the curate, I was about to go find my own costume when I noticed a young man in military uniform come through the front door carrying a package. He looked completely bewildered by the sight of a group of women practicing a procession that involved waving bouquets of flowers from side to side.

I walked over to him. "Can I help you?"

He gulped and looked everywhere but at me. "I have a package for Captain Graham, miss. Can you point him out to me?"

Graham was Andrew's last name. "He's not here. He's gone to London. I'll take it." I reached for the package, but he clenched it more tightly. "I'm not sure I should, miss. I was supposed to give it to Captain Graham. Nobody said what to do if he wasn't here."

"Lady Thomasina! We're ready for you," Mrs. Underdown called.

I knew soldiers felt like they had to follow their orders, but we couldn't stand here all day. "I'm Lady Thomasina Tretheway. Lord Andrew—Captain Graham—is a guest here. I'll make sure he gets it."

The young man turned bright red, handed over the package without a word, then backed out the door as fast as he could. The package wasn't marked with Andrew's name, or with anything else. I squeezed it. It was soft, like it had cloth or clothing inside it. I wished I knew what it was, but knew it wouldn't be right to open it.

However, there *was* one tiny rip in the wrapping. I held it up to my eye. Definitely fabric, a gray wool like soldiers' uniforms were made of, except uniforms weren't gray. They were brown. I decided to put the package in my room until Andrew returned. When I gave it to him, I'd tell him the same thing I'd told Lucas: I'd be able to help them better if I knew more. I carried the package upstairs and put it on the shelf in my wardrobe.

Back downstairs, rehearsals were in full swing. I had to admit Lucas looked spectacular as a brigand, the rakish clothing more natural to him than buttoned-up formal wear.

I caught him staring at me, and I could feel my ears turning warm. I thought he was staring because I was wearing trousers, but then I realized he was staring at my eye patch. "Is there something wrong with it?" I asked. "Do I have it on upside down? Is there a right side up with an eye patch?"

"No, it looks fine. It looks fantastic, in fact." A wistful look crossed his face.

I pulled off the eye patch and handed it to him. "Here, you wear it. I'm afraid I'll fall off the stage if I do."

"We wouldn't want that to happen!" He smiled and put it on, then danced around a bit, waving the sword like he was testing it. I heard him whistling happily under his breath.

As we ran through the play, I realized it was every bit as daft as it had sounded. My own plays were silly, but this was far sillier. Princess Toto's memory was so bad, she forgot she had been married within a few hours. She had two princes in love with her for no apparent reason, and she was obsessed with a brigand named Barberini.

There were so few men that women were playing most of the roles. The play called for a King Portico, but Mrs. Underdown had changed it to Queen Portica and was playing the part herself, and with a flourish. At some point in the play, the queen and her court dressed up as citizens of a recently rediscovered Atlantis, and Mrs. Underdown seemed to particularly enjoy the dance that had been choreographed for the islanders, which consisted of them marching in a circle and raising their hands to the heavens while they sang. Her elaborate headdress made of gold fabric draped over a small lampshade kept falling off during this, but Gwendolyn intervened and adapted it with an extra tie around the chin so it would stay on.

Gwendolyn threw herself into helping with great enthusiasm. She was willing to do anything, from moving scenery to repairing costumes. The costumes had a tendency to rip from some of the more energetic motions of the brigands—especially Lucas—when they ran about brandishing their flimsy swords with zeal. Hannah was interested too. She kept coming in and out of the hall to watch for a few minutes.

By the time rehearsal ended, I was as tired as if I had dug up the entire front lawn. There had been squabbles about who stood where, because everyone wanted to be in front. The fourteen-year-old boy who played Prince Doro was too embarrassed to look the married woman playing Princess Toto in the eye while he pleaded with her to marry him. The boy's voice kept crack-ing, which only added to his embarrassment.

Finally, Mrs. Underdown raised her hand and called out, "Your attention, please." Everyone quieted down. "Thank you. You will make us proud tomorrow." She launched into instructions for the following day. When she was done I did my part, saying good-bye to each person as they left, though I was getting so hungry I had a hard time concentrating; I was too busy wondering what was for dinner.

I shut the door after the last person. As I headed upstairs to change, I heard a girl's laughter from the drawing room. At first I thought it was Gwendolyn, but then I realized it sounded more like Hannah. I was surprised that she would be in the drawing room at that time of day. She should have been in the kitchen or setting the table in the dining room. When I went to look in the drawing room, it was empty, but I spotted Hannah out on the terrace. She was sitting on the wall swinging her feet back and forth. She gave another peal of laughter.

The door to the terrace was partway open, which explained

why I could hear her. She laughed again. "Oh, nobody here knows, but I'm only working as a maid temporarily to save some money. When the war is over, my mother and I are heading back to London. We were in a traveling theater company before the war, and we intend to join one again. I'd like to save enough money to get to America and join a theater company there."

I looked out to see Lucas leaning against the wall of the house.

Lucas said something I couldn't make out and then Hannah spoke again. "No, we don't like it here. My mum hates country life as much as me. It's too dull. And now that I'm older, I'll be able to play much better parts. If they'd asked me to be in their theatrical, I'd show them the right way to play Princess Toto, but they would never ask a servant."

Miss Tanner's voice came from the hall. "I'm sorry, Lady Margaret, there might be a delay with dinner. The table still needs to be set. I'll get Hannah to see to it right away."

Pushing the terrace door all the way open, I said, "Hannah, you must get inside. You are supposed to be in the dining room." The words came out more abruptly than I had intended, but I didn't want Miss Tanner to catch the girl. Hannah nearly fell off the wall. Lucas caught her and stood her on her feet.

"I'm sorry, miss!" Hannah cried. "I was just taking a little rest. I've been up since five o'clock."

"If Miss Tanner sees you like this, she won't be happy," I said.

Hannah gave a drawn-out sigh. "You're right, miss. She's a sour one, is Miss Tanner."

"No, that's not what I meant," I said. "I mean, you might think she's sour, but that's not the reason why she'd be unhappy. And it's not a good idea to say she's sour." I was getting confused about how to make my point. "Housekeepers get upset if they think people aren't working when they are supposed to be. You could get in trouble."

She gave a little sniffle, looking like she was going to cry. I felt terrible. "I just don't want you to get sacked," I added.

"Yes, miss. I should get back to work." Before she went inside, she looked over her shoulder and smiled at Lucas. "Thank you, Mr. Lucas." I noticed that there was no trace of potential tears now.

Lucas smiled back at her. When she had gone inside, the smile turned into a frown. "She hadn't been here all that long, and she's been working hard all day," he said.

"It's not that. You don't understand—"

He cut me off. "I understand," he said as he turned away from me and headed off the terrace into the garden.

I wanted to stamp my foot, I was so frustrated, but I ground my teeth instead. Hannah was turning out to be trouble, just like Miss Tanner had feared. And Lucas shouldn't have acted like he did. If Lucas didn't realize I'd been trying to keep Hannah in Miss Tanner's good graces, he was foolish. But it didn't matter. I didn't really care what he thought of me anyway.

Lucas said nothing to me at dinner, and I was glad when it was over. I excused myself and went to bed early, which was a mistake, because I woke a few hours later unable to go back to sleep. The next few hours were spent writing an enormously long letter to Dorothy declaring that I had decided never to marry and intended to take up the study of obscure languages and devote my life to the furtherance of human knowledge.

At some point, I fell asleep in midsentence, and woke to find my head on my desk and a giant blot of ink on the paper. I finished the letter, trying to delay going downstairs until Lucas would be finished with breakfast. I knew I'd have to see him at some point during the day, but I didn't want to see him alone.

Eventually, I decided I couldn't hide in my room any longer. As I opened my door, I heard another door opening. I knew from the particular way the door squeaked that it was Crispin's room. The secret staircase led to his room.

"Who's there?" I called out.

CHAPTER
TWELVE

I HADN'T EXPECTED to see Gwendolyn come through the door. "Hello!" she said brightly. "It's just me. I've been hearing strange noises from this room and I was getting worried. At home, we've had birds come down the chimney, and they make an awful mess if you don't get them out right away. I couldn't find anything, though. I guess it was just old-house noises."

"Yes, it can be quite a creaky old house," I said. I wasn't sure I believed Gwendolyn's story, though I couldn't very well accuse a guest of lying. Why hadn't she just told Miss Tanner?

"I didn't mean to pry, but while I was in there, I got distracted by some of the photographs." She laughed, and her whole face lit up. "There is another adorable one of Crispin when he was a baby. Your brother has such a funny expression on his face, as if he's surprised by the world."

I knew which one she had seen. I had always loved that picture of Crispin. His black hair came to a tuft at the center of his head and his round eyes looked out at the world with amazement. He'd kept that look as he grew older, though more than a bit of mischief crept into all of his later photographs. My parents could hardly keep him contained. He'd wanted to explore everything without a thought for his own safety. Though I hadn't been told what he was doing when he disappeared, I was sure it was something dangerous he'd been the first to volunteer to do.

I realized Gwendolyn was still standing there. I found it odd that she was so interested in our family photographs, but I knew it wouldn't be polite to comment on that either, so I just said, "Yes, it's a nice photograph."

I was glad she didn't seem to want to talk after that, because I didn't want to talk any longer about Crispin. When she mentioned something about checking the costumes, I left her to go downstairs.

At breakfast I discovered that Lucas had volunteered to take the pony cart into the village to pick up more supplies, so I didn't see him at all. I tried to make myself useful, but Miss Tanner and Mrs. Brickles kept saying they didn't need any help, though they clearly did. It was amazing that Lucas had managed to convince them they should let a guest help yet I couldn't, though he'd probably just grinned at them and they'd given in.

By afternoon, preparations were pitched into a frenzy after Mrs. Underdown's troupe arrived. Helpers had been tasked with moving every available chair into the hall, and Mrs. Underdown kept changing her mind as to whether we should serve the refreshments in the dining room or in the drawing room. One actress who played a lady's maid named Jelly had a fit of nerves and burst into tears, claiming she'd never be able to remember her lines.

Gwendolyn became the steady voice we needed. She steered Mrs. Underdown into choosing the drawing room, she calmed the crying actress, and she handled every costume mishap with a smile, as if she enjoyed it all.

Mrs. Underdown had also decided all the actors and the orchestra should have a light dinner there at Hallington to keep them in the "spirit of the company," and Mrs. Brickles provided sandwiches for everyone. I could only imagine what was going on in the kitchen.

While we were eating, scattered about among the dozens of chairs now in the hall, Gwendolyn came over and sat down by me. "I think the play will be a great success," she said. "I participated in a theatrical in Somerset for some men training there, and they enjoyed it immensely. It doesn't matter that it's just an amateur production."

"This is very amateur," I said. "I'll be amazed if we get through it without some major mistakes."

"Don't worry. The play is so farcical, the audience will concentrate on that. They'll be so surprised by Mrs. Underdown in her queen of Atlantis costume that nothing else will matter. In fact, they may be laughing so hard they won't even hear the lines."

"I hope so. Thank you for all your help."

"You don't need to thank me! I'm having a wonderful time. I feel so lucky to be here."

"I'm glad." She had been a major help, and I decided I liked her better than many of Margaret's other friends I'd met.

"You should get ready," she said. "It's almost time."

I went back up to my room to change, wanting a little time away from everyone else.

As I was changing, I glanced over at the wardrobe. The door was ajar, but I was sure I'd shut it when I'd put Andrew's package away. The latch didn't work properly, so I always shut it firmly to make sure it would catch. If I didn't, it banged open and shut with any breezes coming in.

I walked over to it and noticed a bit of brown paper on the floor, the same sort of paper that was covering Andrew's package. Looking in, I thought the package wasn't in exactly the same place as it had been before. I took it out. The bit of paper had to have come from it. As soon as I looked at it, I could tell someone had opened the package and tried to rewrap it. They hadn't done a good job. The rip was much larger, revealing more of the gray fabric and a bit of braid. I realized what I was looking at.

It was a German uniform.

Shuddering, I dropped the package on the bed and stared at it. I hadn't wanted to believe where the clues were leading me, but I knew now. Lucas was going to fly into Germany and, for some reason, go to the village where my cousin had lived. It was incredibly reckless. I didn't understand why Andrew was letting the plan happen. I didn't understand any of it. I could feel anger growing inside me. Did Lucas think this was some sort of lark, one he could charm his way through? How could he be so careless with his life?

I heard footsteps going down the hall and opened my door in time to see Andrew going into his room. He was carrying something. I grabbed the package and ran to the door that he'd closed.

"Andrew, I have to talk to you!" I said, trying not to let my panic get the better of me.

He opened the door and his eyes immediately went to the package. He looked up and down the hall and then motioned for me to come in, shutting the door behind me.

I handed him the package. "Someone took it out of my wardrobe and opened it. It's a German uniform, isn't it? Are you going to tell me what's happening?"

His face turned white. "Are you sure someone opened it?"

"I'm sure." I explained about the rip.

He put the package down and grasped my hands. "I hate involving you in this, but I don't have a choice. We're in trouble."

"You're scaring me, Andrew." My mouth went dry. I'd wanted to know what was happening, but now that he was about to tell me, it became all too real. It was no longer a game.

"Someone in the house is definitely working for the Germans," he said.

I pulled away from him. Even if I had suspected it, hearing it made me feel sick. "Who? It can't be Lettie. It can't be Mrs. Brickles. We know that doesn't leave too many possibilities. It's either

Hannah or Gwendolyn or, or . . . Miss Tanner." Why hadn't I thought of her before? It would explain so much, and she spoke German.

"That isn't everyone," he said quietly.

"Yes it is," I said. "Except for the village girls Mrs. Brickles brings in when she needs them."

Andrew didn't say anything. He just stood there like he was waiting for me to figure it out.

I ran through everyone in the house once again, as if I could have forgotten someone. "Who? It can't be Mr. Applewhite. Not only is the very idea ridiculous, he never goes into any part of the house except the kitchen area. He lives over the stables. There is no one else in the house except . . . except Margaret. No. You can't be thinking it's Margaret."

His expression didn't change. I stared at him, waited for him to laugh and say of course it wasn't Margaret. He didn't.

"No!" I shook my head. "It's not Margaret! That's absurd!"

He grabbed my hands again. "I don't think it is Margaret, but we can't eliminate any possibilities based just on our feelings. Right now I need you to do something for me. It will take all your acting talents. I don't have time to find out who it is. Lucas and I need to leave tonight, but no one can know. Tomorrow, I want you to act like we are still here. Act as if we've gone to Cranwell very early. Act as if you saw us leave."

Letting go of my hands, he went over to the desk and pulled out a piece of paper, then scribbled something on it. "Tomorrow afternoon, go and do some gardening at the entrance of the park. When you come back, you'll pretend someone from

Cranwell delivered this. It says we've been called to London unexpectedly."

I took the note. "You have to tell me more than that. It's something in the village where my cousins lived, isn't it? Lucas said he used to have family in Germany. That's part of the reason, isn't it? He's going to Germany and it has something to do with his family and something to do with the village."

Once again, Andrew didn't answer. I wanted to shake some words out of him. I tried to remember if Lucas had said anything else about his background. I couldn't think of anything. I decided to use a different tactic. "You have to realize he'll never make it. His German isn't good enough to get by even as a tourist in normal times. How can you let him go?"

For the first time, I noticed what Andrew had brought into the room. Two rucksacks lay on the bed. I tried to tell myself it didn't mean what I thought it did. It didn't work, and there was no escaping it. Two rucksacks, two people. I took a step back and grabbed hold of the desk chair to steady myself. "You're going too, aren't you?"

He went over to the window and looked out. "Don't press me, please, Mina. The less you know, the safer you are. You need to get down to the play. Everything has to seem normal."

I couldn't just walk out of there and ignore what I'd seen. "Is the German uniform for you?" He didn't answer. "I'm not leaving until you tell me," I said. "I have to know."

He sighed. "I suppose it doesn't matter if you know now. Yes, it's for me. I'll wear it because I won't stand out so much. Any man my age would be in uniform. And it's an officer's uniform,

131

so I can use that authority to deflect questions if I have to. My German is good enough for that. Please go now, Mina, and after the play, do what you can to keep attention away from us when we leave. Lucas doesn't know about the change in plans yet. I'll pull him aside as soon as I can. I'm going to have to time our departure so no one notices."

I made myself walk to the door. I didn't know how I'd bear it if Andrew didn't come back. He'd always been part of our lives. Our family couldn't stand one more part being ripped away. But I wouldn't fail him. I'd felt helpless ever since Crispin disappeared. This was my chance to actually do something rather than just watching everyone else take on the burdens of the war.

Numb, I went downstairs, hoping that by some miracle the war would end tomorrow and there would be no need for them to throw themselves into danger.

Every step through the house reminded me of our lives before the war. As I passed through the entrance hall and saw all the furniture had been moved, a picture flashed in my head of the first time Andrew and Crispin had let me take part in their games. It had been so blustery and cold that we were all stuck inside. The two of them had the brilliant idea to reenact the Battle of Crécy. They had spent ages rearranging all the furniture to make hiding places and base camps. I was recruited to play a dead French soldier lying on the floor so Crispin could leap over me to advance on the English forces. Since I was willing to do anything to get to play with them, I took my role very seriously, holding as still as possible. I had loved every minute of it.

A stray tear sneaked out of my eye, and I wiped it away as I went into the yellow sitting room, our makeshift backstage area. I put a smile on my face, determined to help where I could. Mrs. Underdown, out overseeing the arrival of the guests, kept coming to the door and calling for quiet. People took turns peeking out to watch the crowd grow.

"It's going to be a full house," Hannah announced as she came in. Gwendolyn had recruited Hannah to help keep track of costumes, and the two of them began helping people with last-minute adjustments to their headdresses.

The show started. I forced myself to concentrate, though all I could think of was the sight of the two rucksacks on the bed. I was waiting for my cue when Andrew came into the room; I hadn't expected to see him again. He motioned me over.

"Have you seen Miss Tanner?" he asked in a whisper. "No one seems to know where she is."

"No, I haven't seen her for a while. I just assumed she would be overseeing the setting up of the refreshments."

"She was, but she's not there now. If you see her, tell her I need to speak to her."

He left and I went back to trying to listen to the play.

"Is everything all right?" Gwendolyn's voice came from behind me. I had forgotten that Gwendolyn and Hannah were in the room. I turned around. "We saw Lord Andrew come in. He looked worried."

"Everything is fine," I choked out.

Mrs. Underdown rushed in, nearly plowing into Hannah, who was now by the door. She held up her hands for silence. "I want you to know that we have the very great honor to have His

Majesty, Prince Albert Frederick Arthur George, in the audience. I myself greeted him." The gasps were so loud that they could probably be heard in the hall. Mrs. Underdown continued, "Now, I've been told he doesn't want any special notice, but please try not to turn your back on him as you move around the stage."

That would make for some rather awkward scenes, but I decided not to argue. When I was finally onstage and just standing in place, I took the opportunity to locate the prince. He was easy enough to spot. I couldn't tell if he was enjoying the performance or not.

All in all, only minor mishaps occurred. One of the swords broke, a few people forgot their lines, and the actress playing the maid had a bit of a cry when her costume ripped. I went backstage to change and found the girl dashing about the dressing room looking for a needle and thread. Gwendolyn and Hannah had gone, so I helped her tie an extra sash around the tiny rip, assuring her that no one would notice.

Luckily, Prince Doro's voice stayed even, and he managed to at least look in Princess Toto's general direction as he declared his love for her. The audience laughed in the right places, and laughed in some extra places as well. Mrs. Underdown beamed throughout the play, even during the parts where her character was supposed to be serious.

When the show ended, we went out to bow, and then Margaret came up onstage and invited everyone to the drawing room for refreshments. I had wanted to stay on the stage for only a few moments, but so many people came up to speak to me that I couldn't get away. The prince hadn't stayed, no doubt fearing he'd have to deal with Mrs. Underdown fawning over him.

As we stood there, I realized that I didn't see Lucas anywhere. I wished I'd been able to say goodbye to him. Better that I hadn't, I told myself; I wouldn't have wanted him to see me cry. If they were strong enough to face going off into such danger, I was strong enough to let them.

As soon as I could, I went down to the kitchen to thank Mrs. Brickles and the rest of the staff. I knew my mother would have done that, and I wasn't sure Margaret would think of it. The kitchen was still bustling. Even Mr. Applewhite had been recruited to put away the heavy pots and pans. Mrs. Brickles looked exhausted. No Miss Tanner, though.

A girl came in, one I recognized as someone from the village who helped out whenever we had large parties.

"Why aren't more of the trays back down?" Mrs. Brickles asked her. "I don't want to wait all night to put things away."

"We're trying, Mrs. Brickles, but Hannah said she had to leave, so it's just me and the other girl from the village," she said.

Mrs. Brickles put down a plate. "Where did Hannah go?"

"She had to go check on her mother, who's been ill and taken a turn for the worse."

Mr. Applewhite snorted. "If that woman is ill, I'm ready to meet my maker. She was in the village earlier today, lording it up in the apothecary's, boasting how she's bound for London soon, having come into a nice windfall. She made a rude remark about the mud on my boots too, saying she'd be glad to get back to London so she'd never have to see mud again. How John Davies saw fit to marry her, I don't know. I know he left home trying to make more of himself, but he took a wrong turn with that woman."

"What are you talking about? She wasn't married to John Davies," Mrs. Brickles said, putting away some of her knives. "John and my sister Betsy were planning to marry when he died. My da went to collect his things from his room in Lincoln after his accident to bring them home to his mother. He lived by himself in a rented room. There wasn't a wife."

"What?" Mr. Applewhite exclaimed. "That woman told the apothecary she'd come back here because her dear husband John had spoken so fondly of the place. She even cried a few tears about how he was taken so early in the accident at the docks."

"That's strange," I said. "Hannah told me her mother loved it here, and loved her garden, but couldn't work in it much due to her rheumatism."

Mr. Applewhite snorted again. "That woman has never been in a garden, I wager. And if she's got rheumatism, she certainly doesn't act like it."

I remembered overhearing Hannah tell Lucas that she and her mother had been in a theater company. She had mentioned then how much her mother hated the country, which certainly didn't fit with her mother's supposed love of gardening. It almost sounded as if Hannah's mother was two different people.

Or that Hannah was.

"Excuse me," I said. "I have to get upstairs."

CHAPTER
THIRTEEN

THE FASTEST WAY upstairs from the kitchen was by the back stairs. I ran up two flights, but neither Andrew nor Lucas was in his room. I looked out the window. There were still people leaving, but I couldn't tell if any of the remaining cars belonged to Andrew.

Thinking they might be out in the old stable where Andrew kept his car, I went back down the main stairs in time to see Lucas come through the front door. Andrew came out of the drawing room.

"I've been looking for you everywhere," Andrew said to Lucas. Neither of them saw me.

"I've been helping sort out the carts and motorcars trying to leave," Lucas said. "Some of the horses pulling the carts needed convincing they shouldn't bolt at the sounds of engines."

Andrew held up his hand. "That's not important now. I've got to—"

I came down the rest of the way so fast that I nearly fell. "Wait," I said, interrupting him. "It's Hannah. Hannah is working for the Germans." I told them everything I'd figured out, plus how Lucas had noticed that someone had been using the secret staircase in the Tapestry Room. "I don't know where she is now. No one does. And no one can find Miss Tanner." I stopped to breathe, hoping I'd made them understand.

"Listen," Lucas said. I heard muffled sounds of laughter. It was a man's laugh.

When it came again, I pointed to the Tapestry Room door. "There's someone in there."

We walked over to it, all of us moving as quietly as possible. Andrew motioned for us to stand back. He pulled open the door.

Over his shoulder, I saw Margaret on the sofa, sitting on the lap of a tall man in a uniform. She was kissing him.

My sister was kissing a stranger in the Tapestry Room.

I was as embarrassed as if it had been me on the stranger's lap.

"Margaret!" I said.

My sister started at the sound of my voice and leaped up. The man stood up as well.

Andrew let out a strangled sound and then bowed. "Your

Highness, I'm so sorry. We didn't mean to intrude. We just thought—"

Your Highness? I gaped at Margaret and the man. It was Prince Albert.

My sister had been kissing Prince Albert.

My sister had been sitting on Prince Albert's lap and kissing him.

"I s-say, a b-bit awkward, isn't it?" the prince stuttered. "Lord Andrew, isn't it?"

"Yes, sir," Andrew said. "I do apologize."

"We just wanted a bit of privacy," Margaret said. "Usually people don't barge in here late at night." She glared at me. "Do you mind leaving now?"

Andrew took a step forward. "Sir, Margaret, we would leave, but Mina has brought some news that is rather disturbing. We think there is a possibility the new housemaid is a spy, and for some reason, she can't be found."

"Hannah?" Margaret laughed. "Don't be absurd. She's just a simple country girl, and not a very intelligent one at that. She can't be a spy."

A faint creaking behind me caught my attention. I turned to see the bookcase in front of the secret stairway move slightly. The barrel of a revolver appeared in the crack as the bookcase opened.

"Watch out!" I yelled, pointing at the revolver.

Andrew reacted first. He sprang toward the secret door. A sharp report sounded and everyone was moving—everyone except Andrew, who was on the floor.

I could see the blood expanding on Andrew's shirtfront, the red shocking against the white. I froze, unable to look away.

Lucas ran over and flung the bookcase door all the way open. He started up the stairs after the shooter, and that brought me to my senses. I knew he would have a hard time catching her. She'd go up one flight and then go down the upstairs hallway to the back stairs, which ran through all the floors in the house. From there, she could go down two flights and out the kitchen door. And if he got too close while he was chasing her, Hannah would just turn around and shoot Lucas too. I had to help him, but it wouldn't help just to chase after him. All sorts of ideas flashed through my mind as I ran out of the Tapestry Room and into the main hall.

A man in uniform burst through the front door. "Where is the prince?" he yelled. "I heard a shot!"

"He's all right!" I said. "He's in there. But call for a doctor! Someone else has been shot. The telephone is in the library." I pointed at the library door and then dashed for the servants' stairs on the main level, behind the main staircase. I could cut her off in the stairwell if I could reach it before she got down to the lower level.

I opened the door and went onto the tiny landing. Light spilled in from the hall, so I closed it, afraid that if she saw the light, she'd know I was waiting for her. At first there was no sound from above, but then I heard footsteps rushing toward me. It was very dark. A thought flashed through my mind—Why did we keep the servants' stairs so dimly lit? It was dangerous for them to go down in the dark. I could barely see anything.

As the footsteps came closer, I suddenly realized I didn't have a plan. I didn't have a plan, and Hannah had a gun. I put a hand on the doorknob. My hand was shaking so badly I could hardly hold on to it. I needed to get back out into the hall. The footsteps grew louder. I could hear her breathing heavily. I could also hear a second set of footsteps. Lucas was coming after her.

I took my hand away from the knob and flattened myself against the wall. I had intended to try to grab whatever arm held the gun and then hold on to her until Lucas caught up, but when she got close, I stuck my foot out instead and she fell. I heard the gun clattering down the lower stairs. Hannah swore and started to get to her feet. I didn't know what to do next, but then Lucas was there. He grabbed her from behind.

"Where's the gun?" he shouted.

"It's down there," I said. Hannah struggled to get away. I was afraid he couldn't hold on to her, so I opened the door out into the hall. "Help!" I yelled. The man who had come looking for the prince came into the hall. "Help him carry her downstairs," I said to him. We'll lock her in the butler's pantry and then call the constable."

She was trying to bite Lucas, but the man picked up her feet and Lucas got a better hold on her arms. "I've already telephoned them," the man said.

"Good." I couldn't wait to be rid of her. "This way." I went first, wanting to be able to explain to Mrs. Brickles what was happening. This went far beyond the typical kitchen upset.

When I burst into the kitchen, Mrs. Brickles gave a little shriek and took one step back. "Lady Thomasina!" She didn't have time to say more before Lucas and the man carried Hannah in.

"We need to put her in the butler's pantry. Can you get the key?" I said.

She gave one giant shudder and then raised her chin. "I can do that," she said, and marched over to the wall where the keys hung.

As soon as they got Hannah inside and locked the door, she began to scream and pound on it.

"I have to get back upstairs," the man said. I saw by his uniform that he was a major. I supposed he was an aide to the prince. He nodded to Lucas as if they'd just finished a game of tennis or something equally casual. I felt like I was in one of my own plays.

To add to the unreality of what was happening, I saw Mrs. Brickles pick up her rolling pin and shake it at the pantry door. "She won't get out, Lady Thomasina!"

"Thank you," I managed to choke out.

"I'll stay here with Mrs. Brickles until the police arrive," Lucas said. His voice dropped. "You should go see Andrew."

Andrew and the red on his shirtfront. I went back upstairs, concentrating on watching myself take one step after another while the scene in the Tapestry Room played over and over in my head. I shouldn't have shouted. I could have picked up a chair and thrown it at the gun instead. I could have done all sorts of things that would have saved Andrew from a gunshot. And now I'd never be able to forget it.

When I got back to the Tapestry Room, Gwendolyn was kneeling by Andrew, who was propped up with a cushion. Miss

Tanner held a cloth against Andrew's chest. A terrible whistling sound came from it. The room spun in front of my eyes. I dropped down into a chair and put my head on my knees for a few moments.

I was still sitting like that when I heard the doctor arrive, and I made myself sit up. He came in and immediately knelt down to examine Andrew, paying no attention to the prince, who stood next to Margaret. "We need to get this man moved upstairs," the doctor said. He looked up, and from the way his head jerked back when he saw the prince, I knew he had recognized him.

"We'll carry him," the prince said, motioning to the major.

I followed them upstairs, but when they laid him on the bed, the doctor made everyone leave except Gwendolyn, who told him that she had helped her father many times in his surgery. I wanted to get back to the kitchen, but Margaret was so upset that I thought I shouldn't leave her. The prince wanted to stay with her, but the major insisted they get back to Cranwell, where it was safer.

After they left, we went into the drawing room. Margaret poured herself some brandy and sat down. She stared at her glass.

"Does Father know about the prince?" I asked.

"Of course not," she said. A tear ran down her face. "It can't come to anything, so there was no sense in telling anyone. We just wanted to forget about everything for a little while." She got up and moved over to a chair by the window, turning away from me.

We sat there in silence for a long time until Miss Tanner came in. "The constable has taken Hannah away," she said.

I jumped up. "How is Andrew?"

"I don't know. The doctor is still with him."

I noticed Miss Tanner's hair was coming down and her spectacles were bent. I'd never seen her like that.

"Are you all right?" I asked.

She brushed her hair away from her face and took a deep breath. "Yes. I must apologize. I'm so very sorry. I should have been more suspicious of the girl."

"How could you have known? She was a very good actress," I said.

"I should have listened to Lettie. When she complained about Hannah, I told her she should realize she was lucky to have the extra help."

There were still some things I didn't understand. "What happened to you tonight? Andrew and Mrs. Brickles couldn't find you earlier."

"Hannah locked me in a room in the male servants' wing," she said. "I had found an unsigned note in my office saying that something was wrong there, so I went to check. It was foolish of me to be taken in like that. I had ordered her to stay in the kitchen and help Mrs. Brickles. I expect she didn't want me noticing she wasn't there."

"So I suppose Hannah was working with the man I saw running away the first night I was home?"

"The constable believes so. I reported what you told me, but asked him not to upset the household by asking questions. I realize now that I should have let him do just that. I had no idea about Lady Margaret's . . . friend."

Margaret, who hadn't said a word, got up and poured herself another drink. She didn't even look in our direction.

"I would have approached the whole situation very differently if I had known," Miss Tanner said. "The man you saw that night was probably passing information from Hannah to someone in Lincoln, who then passed it on to Germany. The constable doesn't know if the man arrested in Lincoln was part of it, but the police will find out." She brushed back her hair again. "Now, can I get you anything? Would you like some tea?"

"No, we are fine. Do you know where Mr. Miller is?" I didn't understand why Lucas hadn't come to find me.

"I haven't seen him. If I do, would you like me to ask him to join you?"

"Yes, thank you."

After Miss Tanner left, we went back to our silence. When the door opened again, Gwendolyn came in. "He's stable," she said. "The bullet went through him, and the doctor says you might as well all go to bed. You can't do anything more for him tonight. A nurse will be in early tomorrow to stay."

"Can I see him?" I asked.

"Better wait until morning," she said. She looked over at Margaret. "Margaret, why don't you let me help you upstairs? I've got some sleeping powder. I think you could use it."

I was relieved when Margaret nodded and got up. She and Gwendolyn went up the stairs. I waited until I thought they'd be in Margaret's room and then went up as well. I stopped at Lucas's door and knocked. No one answered. I peeked in. There was no one there.

I went to my own room, wishing I knew where he was. My brain was so fogged with tiredness, I lay down on the bed and pulled a blanket over me.

When I woke the next morning, the room was frigid, and I realized that no one had lit the fire the day before. I was so chilled I decided to put on my school uniform. The heavy skirt would keep me much warmer than the frocks I'd been wearing, and with everything that had happened, it seemed silly to care about whether or not I looked fashionable. After I'd dressed, I went to Andrew's room. The door was open and I could see Andrew. He was laying very still. A woman in a nurse's uniform sat in a chair next to him. "He's doing better," she said when she noticed me.

I crept in. "Has he been awake?"

"Yes. He was complaining about people making a fuss over him and saying he wanted to get up. That's a good sign. The doctor left a few hours ago but is coming back shortly to check on him. As long as infection doesn't set in, he'll mend just fine, though it's best to let him sleep."

"Thank you," I said. I went downstairs. Chairs still littered the hall and the floor was dull with bits of mud and scuff marks. I decided I could do something to help, so I started to put things back into place.

I worked for quite a long time and when I was almost done, I spotted a glint of gold next to a small table by the door. A necklace lay on the floor, a locket with a broken chain. I didn't recognize it. It was far too old-fashioned for Margaret. When I picked it up, the locket popped open. There, staring up at me, was a photograph of Crispin as a baby.

"Oh, you found my locket!" Gwendolyn came hurrying down the steps and over to me, but stopped short when she saw the locket open in my hand.

"Why do you have my brother's baby picture?" I asked. I examined it more carefully. It was not a photograph I'd ever seen. "Where did you get it?"

Gwendolyn clutched her hands. "It's not of your brother," she said.

"Of course it is. You saw the photograph of Crispin in his room. This one is nearly identical except . . . except . . ." I held it up again, taking in all the details. "There's something different. The eyes are different somehow, but it still looks like it could be . . ." I stopped, confused.

Gwendolyn began to cry, silent tears running down her face. She whispered, "I don't want to keep it a secret any longer. I've been keeping it so long, and you have all been so kind to me. I've wanted to tell you so badly."

"I don't understand." I held out the locket to her and she took it, smiling and wiping away the tears.

She touched the picture with her finger. "It's a picture of Crispin's son," she said. "His name is Gordon." Her smile widened. "He's a sweet boy."

I sat down on a nearby chair, unable to believe what I had just heard. "But . . . but . . . why . . . ?" The sheer magnitude of what I was hearing left me unsure of what to ask or what to say.

Crispin had a son. I was an aunt.

"Did Crispin know?"

"No. By the time I knew I was going to have a baby, Crispin was already missing."

I took a deep breath, trying to think clearly. "How did you even meet?" I tried to remember from Crispin's letters where he'd been and when. He'd never mentioned one girl in particular.

Gwendolyn sat down on the chair next to mine. "I met your brother in Somerset while he was training there, and we fell in love, or at least I did. I hoped he loved me too, but he never asked me to marry him before he left. I guess he didn't love me as much as I had hoped."

I was shocked. My parents were going to be appalled. My father was still very much a Victorian gentleman. A baby—his grandchild—born out of wedlock would be a big blow to him.

A little sob escaped her and it took her a moment before she spoke again. "He saw me in a theatrical and waited after the performance so he could meet me. After that, I lived for the moments when I could see him. He saw the whole world in a different way, as if every day could hold something amazing." She took my hand and squeezed it. "I don't have to tell you that, though. You knew him far better than I."

"Does Margaret know?" I drew my hand away. There was too much happening all at once. I didn't need more to think about.

"No. When I met her in London, I was so happy to have a chance to get to know Crispin's family, but I was afraid to tell her the truth. I thought perhaps if I got to know all of you and you liked me, I could tell you then. I did so want you to like me."

"But where is the baby?" Gwendolyn clearly didn't keep him in London. She wouldn't be able to go out with Margaret and her friends if there was a baby at home, unless she had a nursemaid.

"He's with my parents in Dover. We couldn't keep him at our home in Somerset. Everyone would know, so my father took a job at a military hospital near the port, and they've rented a house."

I was still trying to take it all in when I realized there was something odd about her story. "What about Andrew?" I asked. "How could he not know who you were? He was Crispin's best friend, and when he met you, it didn't seem like he'd ever heard of you. Wouldn't Crispin have spoken of you?"

Gwendolyn looked down at the locket. "I knew Andrew's name. When Margaret introduced us, I nearly fainted. Crispin talked of him all the time. But Andrew was in France when Crispin was in Somerset. I think they didn't see each other during the time I knew Crispin. I suppose he never had a chance to tell Andrew about me. I wish he had."

I tried to think of what to do next. I didn't know if Margaret should be told, or if we should just wait until my father was back. Gwendolyn began to cry again and I realized the girl was exhausted. "You should get some sleep," I said. "Andrew is going to need your nursing skills."

She put her hand over mine and smiled. "Thank you," she whispered, though I wasn't sure what she was thanking me for.

After she went upstairs, I sat there considering what should be done, and I realized that I needed to tell Margaret. It was too great a matter for me to decide on my own.

I got up as Lucas came down the stairs dressed in old clothes, like those a farmer would wear to market. He carried both of the rucksacks I'd seen in Andrew's room.

"What are you doing? Where were you last night?"

He didn't stop walking. "I've been over at Cranwell and in the library on the telephone trying to reach people to tell them what happened. I couldn't get through to anyone who knew enough to understand I needed help." He sounded angry. "This idea of a top-secret mission has backfired spectacularly. It's too secret."

I followed him. "Please don't say you are going on this mission by yourself," I said.

He opened the door and went out. "I'm going on this mission by myself," he called over his shoulder. "Today is the day, with or without Andrew."

I ran after him. "If it was something you could do alone, they would have sent you alone. Why can't you just wait until Andrew has recovered?"

He didn't even look at me as he spoke, and he was walking so fast that I had to run to keep pace. "There is a ship convoy going tonight," he said. "The military has been planning some other big mission for months, and it was arranged for Andrew and I to go along. It's a way to get us partway to where we need to go. But it's going to take Andrew months to recover, and what I have to do needs to be done now. We don't have months."

We had reached the part of the stable that had been converted for motorcars. Lucas opened the doors and went in, and I followed. "A ship is good," I said. "You're catching a ride on a ship. That's safer than a plane." I was confused, but I kept talking.

"That's good. But once you are in Germany, how do you think you are going to get around, speaking just minimal German?"

"How do you know I'm going to Germany?" He stopped, shock crossing his face.

"I saw the German uniform and Andrew told me. I had thought it was just you, but he said he was going too, and it makes sense. He speaks more German than you. You can't go by yourself."

"Some people there have to know some English."

"I'm sure some of them do. But not many people speak English in the area around Winnefeld. And if you can't speak German, you might as well be wearing a sign saying you are a spy. They don't get American visitors during wartime."

"I have to go. I'll manage." He threw his bag in the car and got in.

I ran around to the other side and opened the passenger door. "If you are determined to do this, take me with you," I said without thinking. "I'll be a big help. I'm fluent in German and French, and I know the village. I know the whole area around it." I knew it was an outrageous idea. My heart was racing so fast, I felt like I was going to burst with excitement or fear—I couldn't tell which. I could finally do something real. "Just wait one minute for me. I should write Margaret a note. I'll make up something so she won't know what I'm doing, but I don't want her to worry."

Lucas leaned over and pulled the door shut. "Don't get in this car. You are not going to Germany with me. I can't take a girl with me, especially not a girl like you."

"What do you mean, a girl like me?"

"If you don't know, it's one more reason you shouldn't go."

"I don't know. Tell me."

He pushed the starter on the car. "You live in a big house and you change your clothes three or four times a day. You garden in fancy dresses and you spend your time acting in silly plays and having tea that other people make for you. You'd just be a burden, and I'm not taking responsibility for a spoiled little rich girl."

I started to tell him how wrong he was, but he held up his hand and kept talking. "I'm not finished. There would be no one to wait on you during the trip. No maids, no cooks, nobody. So do you understand? I know girls like you are used to getting their own way, but you are not getting your way today. If you feel the need to be useful, go help nurse Andrew."

Stunned by his outburst, I took a step back from the car. Lucas reached over and pulled the door shut, then drove off fast, gravel flying up behind the tires.

Jove came trotting into the stable yard. When he reached me, he pushed his cold nose against my hand and it brought me to my senses. Lucas had to be stopped. I was not so useless as to just let him go off on his own. I was not just a spoiled little rich girl.

He didn't know me at all.

CHAPTER FOURTEEN

I DARTED INTO the house and ran upstairs. The nurse looked up when I ran into Andrew's room.

"I have to talk to him," I said. "It's very important. It's about his war work."

"Only for a moment," the nurse said. "He's suffered a very grievous injury." She stepped back.

"I need to see him alone," I told her. "I wouldn't ask if it wasn't important."

She frowned. "All right, but don't agitate him. Just for a moment. I'll be right out in the hall."

Andrew lay so still and his skin was so gray that I had to watch his chest to make sure he was still breathing. "Andrew," I said softly.

He opened his eyes and gave the faintest of smiles, then closed his eyes again.

I wanted to put my hand on his shoulder to get him to listen to me, but I was afraid I'd hurt him more. I spoke louder. "Please, Andrew, wake up." He opened his eyes, so I kept talking. "Lucas is going off on his own to Germany today. I tried to stop him, but he wouldn't listen. I need someone else to stop him."

Andrew attempted to sit up, an involuntary moan escaping from him. He fell back. "No, he can't go by himself," he wheezed, sounding as if every word was a struggle. "He won't get a mile before he's captured."

I tried to speak slowly enough that I wouldn't babble. "Lucas took the motorcar. He said he's going on a convoy tonight." I could feel my throat tightening up and the panic rising. "I don't understand. I thought he was flying into Germany."

"No." He grimaced with pain. "He's going to Cranwell. It was arranged for us to be flown to Dover and then to go on from there." He took a few more breaths before he spoke again. "Help me down to the library so I can make a telephone call."

"Andrew, no! You shouldn't move."

"Get the nurse," he said. "Now."

I got her. When he told her what he wanted, she said, "Absolutely not. Only the doctor could authorize that, and I know for a fact he won't. Let the young lady make the telephone call for you. And don't think you are going to help him get up, miss."

She shook a finger at me. "He'll collapse before he gets to the door."

"I can make the call, Andrew!" I turned to the nurse. "Would you mind waiting in the hall again?"

"Only a few more minutes," she warned. "He's going to have a setback if he doesn't rest." She stomped out. "The doctor will be here any moment, and then you'll have to leave."

"Call the Foreign Office," Andrew said to me. "Major Siddons. He's our contact. He can arrange for someone to go with Lucas."

I supposed I should feel some relief at the notion of someone taking Andrew's place, but that meant Lucas was still going. "All right, I'll call right away," I said.

"Wait." He struggled to sit up again.

"Andrew, don't." I leaned in close. "You don't have to sit up for me to hear you. Just talk."

His words came out slowly. "One of our contacts in Germany has been captured. We had to change codes. I didn't have time to teach it to Lucas. There's a book cipher. Lucas has to have the book." He waved at the wardrobe. "There. The pocket."

I opened the wardrobe. An old coat hung there. I searched the pockets until I found the right one and pulled out a small, slim book bound in dark green leather.

The sight of the book seemed to give Andrew some strength. His next words came out clearly. "Call Cranwell and ask for Captain Marks," he said. "He needs to come here so I can teach him the cipher. He can take the book to Dover, to the *Alexandria*, and teach Lucas before the ship leaves."

A shudder shook him. I could see sweat forming on his forehead. He opened his mouth, but no words came out.

I took hold of his hand. "Andrew, you're so weak. I can teach the cipher to Captain Marks. I know several book ciphers. Can you tell me which one it is?"

He made a writing motion with his hand. I grabbed a piece of paper and a pen from the desk and then held a book for him to use as a writing surface. He scratched out a few words. I could barely make out the shaky handwriting.

Arnold variation. Last number–first letter.

"I know that one! But are you sure they can't get a copy of the book in London and get it to Dover from there? London is so much closer. There has to be someone who could take the book and teach him the cipher."

He shook his head and wiped some of the sweat off his forehead. I held out the paper, hoping he would write *yes* to my idea. Instead he whispered, "Too obscure. Too long to find." He began to cough.

"All right, don't talk anymore. I'll make the calls."

I ran downstairs. Once I got through to Major Siddons, it took three tries to explain before he finally understood. Once he did, he was brief. "We'll take care of it," he said, and hung up the phone.

But when I called Cranwell and asked for Captain Marks, the man who answered said, "I'm sorry. Pilots are not allowed to take personal phone calls on this line."

"You don't understand. I must speak to him. Right now. This is Lady Thomasina Tretheway. It's urgent."

"I'm sorry." He hung up. I stomped my foot, wanting to yell at the telephone. I heard the sound of a motorcar. It had to be the doctor.

I ran back upstairs. Andrew looked at me, a hopeful expression on his face. "Everything will be all right. Just rest," I said, picking up the book. I heard footsteps in the hall.

"Tell Marks to look inside it," he whispered. He clutched his side, his face twisted with pain. When he coughed, it turned into a terrible groan.

The doctor rushed in with the nurse. "You need to leave now!" the man said to me, red-faced and furious. He turned on the nurse. "How could you let her disturb him like this?"

I went back downstairs. If they wouldn't let me speak to Captain Marks, I'd just have to go to Cranwell and find the man. I opened the front door, hoping I could manage to hitch Sunny to the pony cart without too much trouble, but stopped at the sight of the doctor's motorcar. Cranwell was only a couple of miles away, and it was urgent. Lucas's life might depend on what I did next.

That decided it. I ran out and jumped in the car, pushing the start button. My father had given me a few driving lessons—I could do this. Captain Marks didn't need to come here. I could teach him the cipher at Cranwell. I'd be back before the doctor even noticed.

The car lurched down the drive, stalling a few times while I got back into practice. I waited to hear someone yelling at me to stop, but no one did. By the time I got to Cranwell, my hands were cramped from clutching the steering wheel so tightly. I came to a jerky stop at the gate. A guard hurried out of the gate-house, his eyes opening wide at the sight of me.

"I need to see Captain Marks," I said. "It's urgent."

"Do you have a pass?" he asked. "Only people with passes are allowed on the base."

I hadn't thought about that. "Can you contact Captain Marks and tell him someone has come from Lord Andrew Graham and needs to speak to him right away? Please."

"I suppose I could try," he said. "Wait here."

The man came back out of the gatehouse a moment later. "Captain Marks isn't here, miss. He's got a short leave. Some family emergency. He'll be back in a few hours. You can come back then."

We didn't have a few hours. Someone had to get to Lucas before he left. I gripped the wheel. I had a car. I could drive there, though I didn't know how long it would take or how to get there. Or I could find someone to drive me. But who? And would I get there in time?

I didn't know what to do. I glanced down at the book, which I had set on the passenger seat. A piece of paper was sticking out of it. Andrew had said Marks should look in the book. I opened it, then took out the paper and unfolded it. There were only a few words on it: *Operation Prometheus. Highest Priority. By order of the Secretary of State for War, the Earl of Derby.* It was signed and stamped.

A motorcar pulled up behind us and I heard a cheerful familiar voice. "Hallo there! Do you mind pulling over and letting me pass?"

I looked back. It was Captain Rigall from the train. I jumped out of the car and ran back to him.

"Lady Thomasina?" he said. "You are the last person I expected to see here. Is something wrong?"

I pushed the note at him, hoping it was as important as it looked. "I've got to get to Dover. Read this. I'm part of Operation Prometheus. Can you arrange for someone to fly me there?"

He was so stunned that I had to repeat myself a few times. He kept looking down at the paper and then at me. "Climb in," he finally said. "I don't know what this is all about, but I'll do what I can." He called to the guard. "Move that motor, will you? She's riding with me."

"She doesn't have a pass," the man said.

"Show him the paper," Captain Rigall said. When I did, the man's eyes widened. He handed the paper back to me and nodded.

Captain Rigall hopped out of his car and came around to open the door for me. "Come with me. I've got to notify my squadron commander. I can't take off without his permission. You understand we don't see orders like this. This is very unusual. I don't suppose you'd like to tell me more?"

I shook my head as I got in. "I can't, but it really is urgent. I do have to get to Dover as quickly as possible."

He got back in the driver's seat and looked over at me as we headed into the base. "On second thought, why don't you give me the note?" he said. "I'll show it to the commander and explain that the passenger is outside, but it's probably better that he doesn't see you. He doesn't think much of women in planes. In fact, he doesn't think much of women in general. I'll just happen to forget to mention that my passenger is female. We'll get out of here much faster that way."

I wanted to hug him. "Thank you!"

He grinned. "No need to thank me. This will be much more entertaining than my usual missions."

We drove up to a small building. "Are you going to get into trouble if he finds out?" I asked. The captain seemed to have almost as carefree an attitude as Lucas.

"Not much." He chuckled. "They need us to keep flying. I'll be back in a tick."

I hoped the commander would not think to check into Operation Prometheus. One telephone call to the right person and he'd find out I wasn't part of it at all. And if I did get found out? What would they do to me? I shivered. Did they put girls in prison for something like that?

Captain Rigall came back out, a wide smile on his face. "We're set. Ready?"

Seeing his face made me pause. Should I really be the one doing this? I'd wanted to do something important, but this affected more people than just me. I had to make a decision. Teach Captain Rigall the cipher and hope he understood, or go myself?

"Ready," I said.

CHAPTER FIFTEEN

"**EXCELLENT!** The plane is all fueled up and ready to go."

I followed Captain Rigall to a rather battered plane. My face must have showed my dismay because he said, "All our machines lose their shine quickly, but this old bird is far more reliable than most. Have you ever flown before?"

I shook my head, not sure I could speak without sounding terrified. It was one thing to want to fly. It was a completely different thing when one was about to climb into an aeroplane.

"You may find you enjoy it. Many people do, but I warn it will be noisy. If you feel sick, just lean over the side." The captain looked around and then yelled at a pilot who had just landed. "Cobby! Can this young lady borrow your scarf and your jacket? We're going up."

The pilot climbed out of his machine and jogged over, unwrapping the scarf as he came toward us.

"How do you get the good jobs?" the man asked, handing the scarf to me and then unbuttoning his coat. "I am condemned to take up elderly staff officers instead of lovely ladies." He handed the coat to me.

"I have better manners than you," Captain Rigall said. "Now, go away." He turned to me. "You'll need to wrap the scarf over your mouth. The engine lets off a spray of castor oil and you certainly don't want to drink it. It's rather revolting if you do."

"Th-thank you," I managed to stammer to the other pilot. The scarf smelled of hair oil and motor oil. I thought that was revolting enough. When I was properly outfitted, the captain showed me how to climb aboard his aeroplane into the seat behind his. Once he was in the pilot's seat, he reached down behind it to pull out a spare set of goggles, handing them back to me.

The takeoff was smooth, but I immediately felt the cold, and the rush of air on my face was like being in a major windstorm. At first I didn't want to look down, but then I told myself I could at least be brave enough to look over the side. I was surprised to see church spires everywhere. I'd known that Lincolnshire had a tremendous number of churches for such a sparsely populated county, but I'd never realized exactly how many. One of the villages we flew over reminded me a little of Winnefeld. If I hadn't been so worried about getting to Dover in time, I would have enjoyed the view.

By the time we landed, I was very cold and my stomach was very unsettled. As we taxied to a stop, I could see a motorcar waiting at the side of the runway.

I looked around. We had landed in the middle of nowhere. I didn't see a city at all.

"Where are we?" I asked the captain. "I need to go to Dover."

He smiled. "You can't just land on the streets of Dover. We're at the nearest airfield, Swingate. The squadron commander back at Cranwell organized a driver for you." He pointed at the motorcar.

"Oh." I hadn't thought about that. It made me a little worried about what else I might not have thought through.

A boy got out and came over to us. He didn't look old enough to drive until he got closer and I could see that he was about my age, with a wispy mustache and uniform trousers that were far too short, as if he'd suddenly grown a few inches. "I believe your passenger is to come with me," he said to the pilot. "Let me help you down, miss. I'm Sergeant Smyth."

"Lady Thomasina, you did fine," Captain Rigall said. "Some people find their first flight so unsettling, they lose their breakfast. If you ever want to go up again, I'd be delighted to take you."

"Thank you, Captain Rigall. We'll see." I couldn't think past the next few hours.

As we drove into the city, I was shocked to see the bomb damage. I'd known that the shipyard at Dover and Dover Castle were major targets, but I'd had no idea how many bombs had gone astray into cottages and gardens and shops. We passed a group of men in the road repairing a bomb crater.

The size of the shipyard and the number of men working there overwhelmed me. I'd been to Dover before the war, but the place was unrecognizable now. The sheer number of men in uniform was the most startling. The motorcar careened around several corners, passing by warehouses and workshops. I felt as if I went around each corner a little faster than my stomach did, thinking about how I'd never have expected to find myself wishing to be back up in a nice, smooth aeroplane.

"Here we are!" the sergeant announced as we screeched to a stop on the pier at the foot of a ship. I didn't know much about types of ships, but this one towered over us, and it was covered in big guns.

I got out of the car. "Thank you," I said. "I don't think I could have gotten here any faster."

Sergeant Smyth grinned and tipped his cap at me, then sped off.

I took a deep breath and walked up the gangplank. Right before I stepped onto the ship, a man in an officer's uniform caught sight of me. "Who do you think you are?" he said, crossing his arms and barring my way.

"Could I speak to the captain? I have to come aboard. I need to give Lucas Miller some information." I handed the man my note.

He read it, looked me up and down, and then shouted to a younger officer, "Get that Miller boy up here right away." He handed me back the note. "I am the captain. I don't have time for this. You have five minutes to talk to the boy. We're leaving momentarily."

Five minutes? I needed more time than that. I hoped "momentarily" meant a lot longer.

The captain motioned to a spot on the deck. "Stand there and wait." I did what he said. "Don't move," he added and then walked away, glancing back to give me a final glare.

While I waited, I looked around at all the activity. Everyone moved quickly and quietly. There was none of the joking that Captain Rigall did. Whatever was happening here was deadly serious. I had been rushing so much that I hadn't stopped to think about the convoy and where it was going. I knew it was a risk for anyone to be at sea now, with the enemy U-boats patrolling. The German submarines had sunk hundreds of ships since the war began.

Another motorcar pulled up and a young man in civilian clothes got out. He saluted the officer and called out, "Lieutenant Warnford reporting to Lucas Miller. Permission to come aboard?" Even though the lieutenant was wearing a workman's clothes, his bearing and his voice just screamed *English officer*. Dorothy would have deemed him dashing. I hadn't been able to envision Andrew passing as a German, and this man certainly wouldn't pass as one either.

I hadn't realized the captain had returned until I heard his voice. "Permission granted."

I saw Lucas before he saw me. For some reason, he had a green ribbon tied in a bow through one of the buttonholes of a very shabby coat. "I don't know how you got here or why you came, but you have to go away," he snapped at me.

I jumped right into my explanation, "I have to explain the new cipher. There wasn't time to teach it to someone else who could get to you before you left." I was bending the truth a little, but I thought he didn't need to know that.

The captain came back over to us. "Your five minutes are up. We're leaving now."

I saw sailors below removing the ropes that moored the ship to the dock. I looked out at the ocean and then back at the captain.

"I need to go with you," I said to the man.

He gave one harsh bark that might have been his version of a laugh. "Are you daft, little girl? You aren't going on this ship."

I shoved the paper at the man again. "You have to take me. They need the information I have." The captain read it and then looked up at me as if he'd like to throw me overboard.

"You won't even know I'm here," I said. "And once we are back in Dover, I'll get off the ship and you won't have to bother with me anymore." I looked over at Lucas. He was stone-faced. I had no idea what he was thinking.

The captain straightened up and said in a very formal voice. "I must state that I cannot believe I'm expected to take a young girl on a military mission, and I shall make it clear in both my log and my report that I do not agree with this order," he said. "We have our own vital mission to carry out, one we've spent months planning. You can come along because I have no choice, but you are not to interfere in our mission in any way."

His voice changed to a more conversational tone. "I have to warn you, none of us are expecting to come back from this. Once we are underway, you can't change your mind. If the ship goes down, you go down too." He looked at me, waiting for my reaction. I gulped. Surely the mission couldn't be that dangerous. He was just trying to scare me so I wouldn't go.

"I understand," I said. My voice came out a little more wobbly than I had intended, but that couldn't be helped.

"Suit yourself," he said, shaking his head. "But stay out of the way," he continued. "Some of the men are still superstitious enough to think it's bad luck to have a woman on board, so I'd prefer it if you'd go below to the officers' mess. They know you are here, but there's no sense in your being a constant reminder. We have hours to go, in any case. We won't reach the coast until midnight."

He gave one last shake of his head and then stomped off, barking a rebuke at some poor sailor who had the misfortune to be in his way. I stood there waiting for Lucas to say something. A horn sounded.

Lucas just glowered at me.

Lieutenant Warnford cleared his throat. "I say, I was briefed on our mission and shown a map and such, but not told about the one involving these ships." He swept his arm toward the sea at the assortment of ships, including two old ferryboats whose peeling paint identified them as the *Daffodil* and the *Iris*. "This is quite a rum collection of ancient vessels. I can't believe some of them are even seaworthy."

"All these ships are going to Zeebrugge and Ostend on the

Belgian coast" Lucas said. "Once we are there, some of the ships will be blown up to block the harbors so the German U-boats can't get out into the open sea. See those old ships? Those are the blocking ships. They are filled with concrete and explosives. When they get into place, the crew is going to scuttle them, blowing them up so they'll sink right at the mouth of the harbor. All the other ships are along to provide protection and to shell the coast to keep the Germans busy while the ships get into place. It's going to be very dangerous for all of them." He looked over at me. His face was tense.

The lieutenant gave an admiring whistle. "I'd like to meet the chap who thought the plan up."

I thought the person behind this idea was daft. "So how does this get you into Belgium?" I asked Lucas.

"When all the commotion starts, we're taking a small boat to shore. It's our way in. The idea is that the Germans will be too busy firing at the large ships to even notice our boat."

This seemed like the worst plan I had ever heard.

A soldier hurried by, staring at us. "We should get below," Lucas said. "You heard the captain. Mina, you're going to have to stay out of sight."

CHAPTER SIXTEEN

LUCAS, THE LIEUTENANT, and I took over a corner of the tiny mess room. We settled ourselves at a cramped table next to the galley, where two cooks were busy at work chopping vegetables and frying onions. In other circumstances, I would have loved to explore the ship, but now was not the time. As the ship moved farther out into the ocean, I began to feel the roll. It added to my already unsettled stomach.

A gray cat wandered in and jumped up on a nearby ledge, pretending to ignore us as it proceeded to give its face a thorough cleaning. It was the final touch on the unreality of the past day. I knew if I tried to write of all these events to Dorothy, my friend would never believe it. Between Hannah, Prince Albert at the house, the aeroplane ride, the ship, Lucas, the dashing officer, and a cat of all things, it was just too much to have happen in twenty-four hours.

The ship took a sudden dip and my stomach told me I needed to get up on deck. My stomach didn't care about superstitious sailors. I didn't bother to explain. I just bolted up the stairs. Outside, I leaned over the railing and took in big gulps of the cool air. I stayed there for several minutes, ignoring the stares, until I felt steadier.

When I went back down, the lieutenant seemed a little shaken. The man pulled out a pipe and put it in his mouth, then forgot to light it. "That's a fine kettle of fish, if I do say so," he said to Lucas, but he didn't elaborate. He took a puff and then took the pipe out of his mouth and tapped it, then put it back in his mouth, still not lighting. "I suppose we'll just have to trust to luck."

"What do you have to trust to luck?"

"He can't tell you," Lucas said. The tone of his voice was remote, as if we didn't know each other at all. I understood that he was focusing on the mission, but it made for an awkward tension between us.

The cat jumped down from the ledge onto the bench where Lucas sat. He sniffed at Lucas's sleeve for a moment and then climbed onto his lap, holding up his chin to be scratched. Lucas obliged.

The lieutenant nodded at the cat. "Perhaps you have a bit of it. The superstitious types think a ship's mascot will single out only the lucky ones. Let's hope it's more than a superstition."

One of the galley workers came out carrying a bin of silverware. "Right you are, sir. That's one lucky cat. Unsinkable Sam has survived two sinkings with no more than a fit of temper at getting a dunking. Both times he was picked up swimming to shore steady as you please. Quite a good ratter too."

The cat ignored the praise. He jumped down from Lucas's lap and trotted off.

"I don't know how much time we have," I said. "I need to show you what you need to know. Can I explain it here?" I glanced over at the kitchen and the men working there.

"Yes," Lucas said. "These men were all carefully selected for their own mission, and at this point, anything they overhear won't be something anyone else could put together to use against us."

I went over the information Andrew had given me and showed them the book, which was called *Himmel Lieder*. I opened it up and saw that it was a book of poetry in German.

Lucas picked it up. "I recognize '*lieder*,'" he said. "'Songs.' I don't know the other word."

"It means 'sky,'" the lieutenant explained. "Very smart to use this book. It would be the sort of book someone might carry about with him."

I hadn't thought about that. It made sense, if they were captured. My stomach turned over again. I swallowed and pushed the thought away. "You're to use the Arnold Cipher," I said, trying to keep my voice from shaking. "Here, I'll show you an example." I wrote out some numbers for them to practice with, and when they seemed comfortable with the cipher, I gave the book to Lucas.

After that, the hours passed slowly. Lucas and the lieutenant were both quiet, lost in their own thoughts. I went back up on deck, feeling better in the open air. While daylight remained, I tried to count all the vessels in the convoy. I couldn't see them all, but of the ones I could see, I ended up with two dozen, though the line of ships extended far back into the distance. It was the strangest collection of ships I'd ever seen. We traveled in three columns, our ship in the column closest to the British coast. One ship in particular had been altered so much I wasn't sure what it resembled. Guns and ramps sprouted all over the upper deck, and mattresses hung around the control tower, leaving only a small space to see out.

Rain began to fall, spitting down from heavy gray clouds almost the same color as the sea. The sailors moved about as if they didn't even notice. I went below and sat, trying to think of anything but the motion of the ship. As night fell, I could sense a change in the mood of the officers who came in and out of the mess. Lucas and the lieutenant came down to get something to eat and then went back up, both carrying their rucksacks. I followed, unable to stand one more minute below. I joined Lucas and the lieutenant at the railing.

"Almost time, men," the captain called out. "Before we get started, there's a cup of soup for everyone and a tot of rum for those who choose." The thought of food made my stomach nearly turn itself inside out, but the sailors all hurried to the area where they were serving the soup and the rum.

Some carried their mugs past me and the scent drifted over. I could tell it was chicken soup. My stomach settled a little at the thought of soup and I realized I should try to take a few sips. I waited until all the sailors had been served and then asked for a mug of my own. It wasn't as good as Mrs. Brickles's soup, of course, but I felt better after I drank it.

Sometime around midnight, I could feel the excitement building aboard the ship. When small motorboats began to zip back and forth to the east of us, I knew it was time. The boats bounced above the waves like flying fish, with the men aboard throwing out canisters that began emitting thick smoke until I could no longer see the shore. Searchlights on the coast switched on, their long beams of light arcing back and forth, cutting through the smoke. Some of the larger ships began bombarding the shore. And with that, the night sky lit up. Shells exploded high above, some looking like stars, and some like giant, glowing green beads. They hung in the air long enough to light the whole area.

"Why are they shooting up in the sky? Are there aeroplanes up there?" I yelled over the din.

The lieutenant yelled back, "Those are tracers, so they can see where to aim their guns."

We watched as ships approached the seawall in front of the harbor. As soon as the one with the ramps and the mattresses reached it, I understood why the ship had been altered in such a peculiar way. Men lowered the ramps on the upper deck to make a bridge so they could cross to the seawall. Machine-gun fire from somewhere on the wall felled all the men who first attempted to cross over, but more kept coming. I couldn't believe the bravery of the ones who ran forward, after seeing the men in front of them cut down. It was the most horrific thing I had ever witnessed.

A sailor came up to Lucas. "We've got to lower the skiff and get you on your way so we can move in closer to do our job. Good luck." He went over to the small craft and began to undo the lashings.

More shells burst from the battery onshore, the booms startling me so much I had to grab hold of the rail to keep from falling. One shell came screaming toward us and I could feel my own scream welling up inside me. Lucas pulled me down onto the deck. Everyone around us acted as if they didn't hear or see a thing. In those few seconds, I realized that Lucas's actions wouldn't have changed our fate. If the shell had hit its mark, we'd be dead. I put my hand over my mouth to try to keep my horror from spilling out in a babble of words.

The shell hit the water only a few feet away and exploded, sparks spraying out, some of them landing on the deck.

"Mate, if you want in this skiff, you should go now," the sailor said. Lucas looked at me. I nodded. I knew he had to go, though I couldn't bear to think of what he would face. He started to say something to me and then stopped, just took my hand and squeezed it gently. As he climbed down the ladder, he yelled up, "Look for me in three or four days!"

The wind switched and the smoke blew past us out to sea, leaving all the ships exposed to the German battery onshore. It seemed as if that was enough to spur all the enemy weapons into action. A hail of noise exploded over the sea and then a bombardment of shells rained down upon us. Ships all around us were hit, bursting into flames.

Our own was rolling so badly, I feared it would swamp the skiff. I could see water sloshing over the side of it as Lucas tried to keep his hold on the bottom of the ladder so the lieutenant could climb down. Our ship began to fire back at the shore, gusts of black smoke exploding out with the shells. The whole ship shuddered each time a shell was fired, and I could hardly keep my balance. I had never imagined a sea battle would be like this. Choking smoke was everywhere, and I wondered if I'd be able to hear once the noise stopped. The lieutenant gave me a little wave and began to climb down the ladder.

I was leaning over watching his progress when a shell hit the deck. I felt myself launched into the air, the breath jolted out of me. I hit the water hard as pieces of the ship, some ablaze, rained down around me. Stunned, I sank down, but the cold water shocked me into struggling to get back to the surface.

Desperate, I gave a kick and came up. When my head broke through the water, I took a breath, but breathed in so much smoke that I began to cough and nearly went under again. Debris surrounded me, some of it on fire, but the water was freezing. It was an effort to even stay afloat. My wet coat and skirt weighed me down, and as I tried to swim, my skirt tangled in my legs, making it even harder. It was as if someone had attached weights to me. I tried to take off the coat, but all my efforts just pushed me under the water. At the surface, with the waves so high, I couldn't even see if there were any other ships nearby.

I fanned my arms furiously to stay afloat, but knew I wouldn't be able to reach the shore, not in my heavy clothes. The waves tossed me about so much that it was all I could do to keep my head above water. I couldn't think of a way to take off my skirt to get rid of some of the weight without using my hands, but I'd sink if I didn't keep them moving.

"Mina!" I thought I heard Lucas calling my name, but couldn't see anything over the waves. "Mina!" As I bobbed about, the skiff came over a wave, nearly hitting me. "Mina!" Lucas, alone in the boat, was fighting with the oars to get the boat beside me. I reached out and he leaned over, putting one of the oars within reach. I grabbed it, but couldn't keep ahold of it. The next wave brought the skiff closer and, giving one strong kick, I pushed myself to it, reaching up with one hand. Lucas took it and pulled me close enough that I could take hold of the edge. Nearly sobbing, I tried to pull myself up, but I didn't have the strength.

"Mina, hold on!" Lucas tried to pull me in, but the boat tipped dangerously.

"I can't do it!" I gasped.

"Yes you can! Get one leg up, and then I'm going to move to the other side of the boat. That will tip it enough to bring you partway out of the water and I can help you then."

It took three tries, but finally I was in the bottom of the boat, coughing and sobbing at the same time.

A few small motorboats were darting back and forth, and I saw them stop to pull other people out of the water. Lucas yelled to try to get their attention, but it was too dark and there was so much noise that no one heard. He tried rowing toward them, but without a motor, our boat was quickly left behind. The remaining ships were moving in closer to the seawall, concentrating their fire on it.

Debris bumped against the boat and Lucas maneuvered it around a jagged piece of metal. The boat bobbed up and down so much, I feared I'd be sick. I wanted to help row, but all I could do was hang on, trying to get enough breath into me. As the searchlights swung back and forth, a gleam in the water a few feet away caught my eye. I tried to make out what it was. It moved toward us, bobbing up and down.

"Stop rowing!" I yelled.

"Why? We have to keep going."

"No, I see something!"

CHAPTER SEVENTEEN

ANOTHER PASS OF the light and I realized what it was. "It's the cat!" I yelled. The creature was paddling for us, his front legs moving furiously. I leaned over the side and reached out a hand, grabbing him by the scruff of his neck. I put him in the bottom of the boat. He gave out a furious yowl, and then, spotting Lucas, scuttled under his seat to huddle by his feet.

The smoke boats went back to work, racing back and forth to create a screen for the British ships. Soon, we were in a black fog, unable to see more than a few feet away even when the searchlights swept near us. Lucas kept yelling to try to catch the attention of the smoke bombers, but the guns that were still firing were so loud that I couldn't imagine anyone would hear him.

"Lucas, the bottom of the boat is full of water!" I shouted, not knowing if he could hear me. I was sitting in at least three or four inches of it.

"There's too much coming over the sides!" Lucas shouted back. "We need to get to shore before we sink." I watched as he strained to get the boat to shore, fighting the waves. As we drew close, he shouted, "When we beach, you're going to have to get out and help me pull it in." A wave pushed the boat in and Lucas jumped out. I got out too, falling partway into the water and then picking myself up. I tried to drag the boat up, but my hands were so numb and my legs felt so weak, I didn't know if I helped at all.

We pulled the boat far enough in so the bow was on sand. A vast expanse of empty beach faced us. Crossing it to the dunes beyond without being seen appeared impossible.

"Watch the searchlights," Lucas said. "When I say run, run, and don't stop for anything." He reached into the boat and grabbed the rucksack, put it over his shoulders, and then reached back to scoop up the cat.

"Heh, buddy, you're good luck, right?" He put the animal inside his jacket, holding him close to his body with one hand. "We could use some of that luck right now, so how about going for a little ride?"

The searchlights passed right over us and I tensed, waiting to see soldiers pouring out of some of the concrete bunkers or the sound of shots being fired at us. A boom sounded down the beach and an enormous tower of fire spouted from the seawall, reaching hundreds of feet into the sky. I was nearly deafened by the sound, but I could see Lucas mouthing the word *"Now!"* as he grabbed my hand and pulled me along.

We half ran, half stumbled across the open beach. As soon as we reached the dunes, I fell to my knees. "I need to stop for a moment," I gasped. My teeth started to chatter. I could feel the wind biting into me. It felt like the cold was seeping inside me. I sat and wrapped my arms around my knees, putting my head down to keep as much of myself away from the wind as I could. It didn't help.

"If you like," Lucas said. "I could put my arms around you to warm you up. That is, if you want me to." I felt a light touch on my shoulder.

"Yes, please." I scooted over close to him and he took me in his arms, in a manner of speaking. The cat was still in his jacket, his head sticking out, looking back and forth between the two of us, but making no move to give up his spot. I supposed he must have been very cold from his swim in the ocean. Even though Lucas was wet too, I could feel the warmth of him. We sat there for a few moments.

"Did you see what happened to the lieutenant?" I asked when my teeth had stopped chattering.

Lucas didn't answer for a moment, and then tightened his arms around me slightly. "Something hit him, like a piece of the ship. He's dead."

"How do you know?"

"He couldn't have survived what happened to him." I felt a shudder pass through him.

We just sat there as the enormity of what had happened sank in. What a fool I'd been to wish for adventure. I closed my eyes. Now Lucas was stuck with me, the girl he'd thought was too spoiled to help. I'd have to show him I wasn't going to be a burden.

All I wanted to do was stay where we were, but I knew we couldn't. "What do we do now?" I asked.

"We need to move a little farther along the beach. We are supposed to come even with the spire of a church and then wait there until the contact comes. Do you think you can try? We don't have to go fast."

"Yes, as long as we can go slowly."

We got up. I was amazed the cat still made no move to try to get out of Lucas's coat. We crept forward through the dunes, the booms and flashing lights in the distance disorienting me. Men were still trying to get onto the seawall, but dozens and dozens fell into the sea, their arms waving like they were doing some weird acrobatic air dance. Small boats darted around trying to rescue the men in the sea, but there weren't enough of them. Shells shrieked all around.

"There! I see it," I said, pointing to a spire black against the sky.

Lucas found a spot shielded from the battle and we sat down. "Now we just wait," he said. "You're still shivering." This time he didn't ask before putting an arm around me. I leaned back against him, ignoring the squawking of the cat, who was forced to move over a little.

"Are you getting a little warmer?"

"Yes," I murmured, though I was actually still very cold.

We watched the force of the battle slow and I could see some of the British ships moving away. As they disappeared into the darkness, I realized we were actually on our own. It hadn't sunk in before.

"What do we do if no one comes?" I asked, sitting up straight, panicked at the thought of being here without knowing whom to trust. "Can we go on by ourselves?"

"I don't know. Andrew knew some of the plan, but he said it was better if I didn't, in case we were captured. If we were, I was supposed to claim ignorance and play on the fact that I was American and say I'd been duped into the scheme by the British. And I suppose the lieutenant was told that too. We'll have to assume people will show up when they are supposed to."

"Don't you think it's about time you told me what you do know, where we are supposed to end up, and what we're supposed to do once we get there?"

He looked at me. "It's complicated," he said.

"What does that mean?"

Before he could answer, a small figure popped up from behind one of the hillocks and I nearly screamed until I realized it was a girl. She was about eleven or twelve years old, wearing an oversized coat and a cap far too big for her that nearly covered her eyes.

"Hello. No one said anything about a lady on this job," the girl said in French to Lucas. She leaned in closer to examine the cat, who was still peering out from the top of Lucas's jacket. "Or a cat," the girl added. "But what can you expect from the English?" she said, as if she was talking to herself.

I translated for Lucas and then took a closer look at the girl. Even in the dark I could see that her ragged clothes hung on an almost skeletal frame. Her face was smudged with dirt and her eyes were enormous in her pinched face.

"Are we supposed to have some code word or something?" I asked Lucas. "I can't believe they'd send a little girl for us."

"There aren't any code words for this place, at least none Andrew told me about."

"You shouldn't be speaking in English," the girl said in French. "Anyone overhears you and you'll be arrested right away."

I switched to French. "He doesn't know French," I said, nodding toward Lucas, "so you'll have to talk to me. What's your name?"

"People don't use their real names," she said, disgust dripping from every word. "You can call me Danielle. That's a good name."

"All right, Danielle, if you are here to take us somewhere, let's go."

She motioned to my coat. "First you need to do something to your coat. You can't wear a British soldier's jacket in Belgium." She muttered "English" again and rolled her eyes.

I'd forgotten the coat was the one the aviator had given me at Cranwell.

"We have to get rid of the braids and the patches," I said to Lucas. "I hope there is a knife in your bag."

"There is." Lucas got a knife out of his rucksack and worked on the coat, cutting off the braids, which resulted in holes through the fabric in some places. When he was done, the coat looked just as shabby as his.

The girl inspected us and then nodded. "Follow me and don't say a word. I know every inch of this beach," she boasted. "Once we get off the beach, if we get stopped, just show them your papers and tell them you're on your way to visit your sick grandmother."

I translated again for Lucas and then said to the girl, "I don't have any papers."

The girl stopped in her tracks. "They sent you here without any identification? The Germans ask to see it all the time, even if you just look at them sideways. If you don't have papers, you'll be arrested."

I explained to Lucas what Danielle had said. "I've got papers for me, and Andrew's are in my rucksack too," he told me. "I was going to use them if mine got damaged. But if you are asked and you show them Andrew's, they'll certainly notice you aren't a man." He took the cat out of his coat and set it down, causing the animal to meow in protest. "Sorry, fellow, I need two hands." Lucas pulled a folded piece of oilskin out of his rucksack, unfolded it, and took out two pieces of paper.

The girl took one of the papers from Lucas and held it up close, rubbing her fingers over it. "This will work for him," she said to me. "It looks and feels real. If a soldier stops us, pretend you don't understand German. No Belgian will willingly speak that language now, and the Germans will be suspicious if you do." She looked over the other paper. "If they don't look closely, this one will work for you. If they notice it has a man's name on it, that will be a problem. Maybe you'd better use a pretty smile and speak German and just hope the soldiers like you. They'll look the other way if a girl is friendly enough."

I didn't translate that part for Lucas, and I didn't want to ask the girl exactly what she meant by "friendly."

She handed the papers back. "Keep them on you instead of in the bag. It's safer that way. Let's go." We set off and I noticed that the cat followed us, sticking close to Lucas's heels.

As soon as we reached the edge of town, Danielle stopped us. "There's a curfew, so the idea is not to be seen. From here on, don't talk unless it's life or death."

"We're not supposed to talk," I told Lucas.

Danielle led us on a winding path around buildings and through narrow alleyways until I was unable to tell which way we were going. The town seemed deserted, lit by only a few streetlights, and those were so dim that they gave off just enough light to avoid running into buildings, almost all of which were completely dark. I wondered if there were people huddled inside them or if the town was empty of all but soldiers.

At one point, Danielle took us through a bombed-out warehouse, directing us around and over piles of rubble, showing us where to put our feet. Both she and the cat hopped nimbly about, acting as if it was no more trouble than walking through a field, and Lucas didn't have much trouble either, but I found it hard to keep my balance.

The cat dashed ahead, as if he knew how to get out. As we drew close to the other side of the building, I saw his gray shape stop and then, as my eyes focused on him, he raised his hackles and arched his back. Danielle held up her hand to halt us. I froze in place.

At first I didn't hear anything, but then came a soft sound of footsteps outside, slow, as if someone was creeping along, trying not to be heard. A door creaked open, letting in a faint sliver of light. Someone slipped inside—a man, judging by the height. By his furtive motions, I could tell he didn't want anyone to see him. Whoever it was had a bundle. He walked in a few feet and knelt down.

I tottered a little and Lucas put up a hand to steady me. I hoped the cat wouldn't move and attract the man's attention. If he looked our way, he wouldn't miss seeing our silhouettes. But the man was too intent upon his job to even glance around. He shifted aside a section of roof that had fallen to the floor. I couldn't see what he was doing, but I heard a sound like something metal being stacked up. A few minutes later, the man stood up, replaced the piece of roof and then went back outside. We waited until his footsteps moved away and then I took a deep breath, glad to get enough air again.

Danielle darted over to where the man had been, hurrying to uncover whatever it was that the man had hidden. When we got to her, she already had a tin in her hand. "My lucky day!" she said, pulling back the lid and sniffing the contents. "It's tinned beef!" She stuck her fingers in it, scooping up some of it and jamming it in her mouth. The cat ran over and wound around her legs, meowing. "You want one too?" the girl asked the animal between bites. "There's plenty!" She opened another one and set it on the floor. "Go ahead and help yourself," the girl said, stooping down to get another. I saw stacks of food tins, dozens of them.

"What is this?" Lucas asked.

Danielle didn't answer until she had finished the second tin and had started filling her pockets with the rest. "Someone is using this place to store what they are selling illegally. Perfect timing for us. Take some, if you want. I'm coming back to get all the rest. Look at all this! I haven't seen this much food ever."

"She says it's food someone has taken to sell illegally," I told Lucas. "What if you get caught?" I asked the girl.

"I won't. I don't think he'll be back tonight, so if I clear it out before morning, it will be safe enough. Whoever it is would move what's left as soon as he realized some of it is missing." The cat finished his tin and then sat down to wash his face, purring with contentment. "Do you want some?" the girl asked. I could tell she wanted us to say no.

"You take them," I said. "Shouldn't we get going?"

"Don't worry, we are almost there."

"Um, do you mind telling us where 'there' is?" I asked. "We weren't given much information."

"And you came anyway?" She smirked, but before she could comment on the English again, I stopped her.

"I know, I know," I said. "The English are incredibly incompetent. Just tell me."

"You are better than most." She gestured at Lucas. "Though I'm sorry you didn't get a better traveling companion. If that one speaks no French, he must not be very intelligent." She shook her head sadly.

"What is she saying?" Lucas asked. "She looks like she's just declared me a lost cause."

"Don't ask," I said. "It will take too long to explain." I turned to the girl. "Tell me where we are going."

"You are going on the canal to Brussels, on a coal barge. The barge leaves at six in the morning and the crew reports a half hour before then, so you must be on board and in place before that. The captain will be there a few minutes early to show you where to hide."

A barge doesn't sound so bad, I thought, as I explained it all to Lucas.

"Whatever it is, I just want to get there before daylight," he said.

We followed the girl to the canal, the cat trailing after us. When we reached the docks, they were far more deserted than I had expected.

"I don't like the look of this. Ask her why there aren't any guards," Lucas said. "There should be some."

"Where is everyone?" I asked the girl.

"There are a few sentries at the main gate, but the important dock is inland at Brugge," the girl said. "That's where they dock all the submarines. They know this one is too easily bombed to keep more than barges here. There is a guard at night, but he doesn't patrol much. He likes his naps."

I repeated it all to Lucas. Then the girl pointed to a long, low vessel moored at the end of a long row of similar boats. "That's the barge. This is as far as I go. Climb aboard and go below to wait for the captain."

I told Lucas the last bit as the girl bent down and petted the cat. "What about your cat? Are you taking him with you?" she asked.

"He's not our cat," I said. "I'm afraid he'll have to stay here and fend for himself."

"Do you mind if I take him? We'd be a good team. He could keep the rats away from where I sleep." The girl picked up the cat and rubbed his face. "I'll give you some more tinned beef too," she said to him. "You'd like that, wouldn't you?"

"Yes, please take him. We certainly can't."

"Does he have a name?"

So much had happened that I had to think for a moment. "His name is Unsinkable Sam. And as of tonight, he's just survived his third sinking."

"That is a very stupid name for a cat," the girl pronounced, putting him down. "I think I'll name him Prince. He's got the look of royalty about him. Come along, Prince, we've got things to do." The girl started to walk away.

"Thank you for helping us," I called after her.

She turned around. "Don't need to thank me. I'll get my pay for this. The White Lady will see to it."

"The white lady? Who is that?" I asked.

She didn't answer. "Let's go get some supplies," she said to the cat. Without a backward glance, she disappeared into the shadows, the cat following.

"You've been usurped," I said to Lucas. "I thought all animals found you irresistible."

"You sound jealous. That cat is smart enough to know which one of us is the better bet." He examined the dock in front of us. "We've got quite an open stretch to cover to reach the barge. Are you ready?"

CHAPTER EIGHTEEN

THE LONG DOCK stood exposed to anyone who might be nearby. I just hoped Danielle had been right about the guard. Lucas and I went slowly, trying not to make too much noise, though it felt like the dock was creaking with each step. Lucas pointed to the water and then back along the dock, and I took it to mean we were to go over the side if anyone came along. I nodded, but prayed we wouldn't have to get wet again, especially not in that water. A sheen of engine oil glistened on the surface even in the dim light, and a few floating dead fish gave off a sickening smell.

We boarded the barge cautiously but found there had been no need. It was empty. The main cabin had been fitted with benches in front and some built-in beds in the back. It was far from luxurious, but it was clean, at least. I went back to one of the beds and pulled off a blanket, wrapping it around my shoulders. Elation at making it this far made me feel less tired, and being inside the barge, away from prying eyes, made me relax a little.

However, Lucas was not at ease. He paced back and forth, stopping to look through the curtains that hung over the windows.

"What's wrong?" I asked.

"I was so stupid for thinking it didn't matter that I didn't speak the languages!" He sat down and grabbed hold of the edge of the table. I could see his knuckles turning white. "That girl could have told me she was taking us right to the Germans to turn us in and I wouldn't have known." He let go of the table and pounded a fist on it. "Stupid, stupid, stupid!"

"But she didn't take us to the Germans, and we have made it this far, and you have me to translate, so I'd say we aren't doing so badly." I smiled at him, but he didn't smile back.

He jerked his head toward one of the bunks. "If you want to rest a little, I'll keep watch. We have a few hours."

I was grateful there was a bed. Even the short time in the water had exhausted me, and nothing seemed better than being able to put my head down.

"You should lie down too," I said, "even if you are going to keep watch." I realized I wanted him next to me. "I'm cold," I said. "Do you mind keeping me warm?" I felt my face flushing, embarrassed by what I was asking, but I'd come too far to stop. "It helped when we were on the beach."

He nodded, but didn't speak. I thought he'd make a joke or grin or something, but all he did was wait for me to lie down. He lowered himself carefully onto the bed next to me and put his arm around me very slowly, as if he was afraid I might break. I put my head on his shoulder. I could feel how tense he was by the way he held himself so still. I wanted the other Lucas back, the one who didn't worry about anything.

"There are some things you should know," he said, "before we go any farther."

"What?" I sat up. He sounded so serious that it worried me.

He looked up at the ceiling and spoke at it instead of at me. "There are a lot of things I didn't tell you." He paused and took a deep breath. "My real name, for one. It's Lucas Mueller, not Miller. My father is German." The words came out in a dull monotone, almost like he was reciting them.

I tried to move away from him, but there was nowhere to go. If Lucas's father was German, he was German too. I didn't understand. "Does . . . Does Andrew know?"

"Of course." He turned to look at me. He reached out to touch my face, but I jerked back, bumping my head on the wall. "Mina! You don't have to be afraid of me! I'm helping out the British, helping them because I'm *American*. I can explain!"

I crossed my arms in front of me, wishing I was anywhere but there. I had to stay calm. "Yes, please explain," I said.

"Like I said, it's a complicated story." He sat up too. "My father is one of Germany's lead explosives scientists. There are rumors he's close to a breakthrough on a new type of bomb. Something like that would change the whole course of the war. I'm supposed to convince him to leave Germany and work for the Allies." He paused. I think he was waiting for me to say something, but I didn't know what to say. I was still trying to take in his words.

"I don't know who came up with the original idea," he added. "I don't know if it was the American or the British government, but they worked together on this plan to find me and bring me here." His voice faltered. I could see the strain in his face. "You understand, don't you?"

"Why couldn't you just write to him? I'm sure someone can smuggle letters into Germany." I wanted to believe him, but I was still reeling from his words.

"I asked that too, but they weren't sure it would work since I've had so little contact with him. I haven't seen him for years. He went back to Germany when I was two. I visited him about six years ago, but beyond exchanging a few letters, we haven't communicated. That's why I don't know much German. I can understand some simple sentences sometimes. He got me a tutor, but I wasn't there long enough to learn much. Someone decided he was more likely to agree if he saw me in person. I'm supposed to convince him." He looked away from me. "I'm not sure I'll be able to do that."

"Of course he'll want to come with you!" I said. "He wouldn't want to be on the opposite side of a war from his son." I reached out and touched his hand. "I'm sorry I acted that way. You just surprised me. You did more than that—you shocked me. I understand now, though."

"You do?" He turned to me.

"I do." A yawn overtook me, and then another. It felt like the tiredness had settled inside me and was weighing me down.

Lucas touched my face. I didn't pull back. "Sleep a little. I'll keep you warm."

We lay back down and I put my head back on his shoulder. I thought I'd fall asleep instantly, but I didn't. There was a stranger next to me. Lucas had seemed so uncomplicated, just a happy-go-lucky American out to find some excitement. The whole time he'd been keeping secrets. I'd thought he was one person, and now he was turning out to be someone completely different.

The next thing I knew, Lucas was shaking my shoulder. "There's someone coming," he whispered. I could hear heavy footsteps coming down the dock and someone whistling.

I got up and we stood there, not knowing what else to do. If the person was coming aboard the ship, we could only hope it was the captain. There was no place to hide.

"How will we know if he's the right person?" I murmured.

"Just listen," Lucas said. He opened the rucksack and took out a revolver. I hadn't realized that Lucas had it, and I felt sick at the thought of it.

The man began to sing in French in a deep baritone.

The lady is fair as the rose of dreams,
Her lips so red, her skin so white

"He said '*blanc*,' didn't he? 'White'?" Lucas grasped my arm. "Andrew taught me that word. Did he say 'lady'? I didn't catch it."

194

"He did."

The tension fell off Lucas. "He's the right man."

"Time to start the day," the man announced as I heard him jump on. The boat rocked from his weight. Lucas put away the gun as the man tromped down the stairs. He came into view, a big, beefy man with a walrus mustache. His only reaction to my presence was to raise his eyebrows. He said, "You need to get into place."

"Where?" I asked, looking around the cabin. I had assumed we'd just stay below.

"This way." He led us through a door into a storage area about the size of a cupboard. It was dark and cramped, but I thought I'd be able to stand it for a few hours.

"Can we move some things to make a better place to sit?" I asked. Lucas stood behind me. I knew he couldn't understand the captain, but up to this point the man's actions had been easy to interpret, so I hadn't bothered to repeat anything in English.

"You aren't staying here." Picking up a bucket, the captain pointed to the floor. I saw a handle attached to a floorboard. The captain reached down and pulled, revealing that a section of the floor had been fashioned into a trapdoor. "There's a space down there that was sectioned off from the coal bunker. Climb in and lie down and keep quiet. Not every crew member can be trusted."

"Will we both fit?" I asked, staring at the dark space.

"You'll fit. I've heard they put five in there once, or at least five were caught."

"The Germans know about this?"

The man snorted. "Yes, the previous captain is now in prison for smuggling people out. We don't use it anymore."

"Wait, so why are you using it for us?" I thought hiding in a place where the Germans had caught others was like playing hide-and-seek and picking the same place to hide in each time, only now there was the risk of being shot if we were caught.

"What's he saying?" Lucas asked. "You look scared."

The man laughed. "The Germans will never expect someone to be crazy enough to go *into* Brussels on a barge. They used to catch the ones trying to get out of the country, not in. They won't check unless they have reason to be suspicious."

"I'll explain in a minute," I told Lucas. "How will we know when to come out?" I asked the captain, already dreading spending hours in that small space.

"We'll dock. You'll be able to tell when we have by all the noise. When we are docked, I'm inviting the men to a café for a beer. I'll say it's my birthday. When you hear me whistling as we leave, wait a few more minutes and get off the boat."

"What do we do then?" I asked.

The man pulled an envelope out of his pocket and handed it to me. "This will tell you. Now, if you are going with the boat, you need to get below. The crew will be here soon." The captain left and I heard him a few moments later, stomping around overhead.

"Captain!" a voice shouted from outside.

I started, knocking over a broom. I knew there wasn't time to open the envelope.

"We have to get inside," Lucas said.

"You go first." I wanted to be closest to the door. Knowing I could get out quickly might make the time bearable.

Lucas lowered himself in and then moved so that I couldn't see him. "Is there really enough room?" I whispered, hearing more footsteps outside.

"Yes, hurry."

Taking a deep breath, I lowered myself in, finding a space about three feet tall and small enough that I couldn't imagine five people crammed inside it. Lucas lay on his side, propping himself up on an elbow. "You'll have to close the door," he said. "I can't reach it, unless you want to switch places."

"No! I'll do it." I reached up and grasped the edge, letting it down slowly. At least there wasn't a latch. No one above us could shut us in. When I let go so it fell into place, darkness enveloped us.

"Are you all right?" Lucas asked. "I can hear you breathing very fast."

"I'm fine," I said, trying to take normal breaths. I thought of Lucas's harsh words about me before he left Hallington. I couldn't let myself complain. If I did, it would just convince him that he had been right. The hiding place wasn't as small as I had feared and I lay down, only to realize that there was a musty blanket beneath me that stank of fish.

After much noise and a combination of raised voices and the clanging of equipment, the barge began to move, with the thrumming of the engine drowning out much of the other noise.

I heard Lucas yawn. "I think we should try to sleep a bit more," he said. "I can't even think clearly. We'll figure out something when we are not so tired." He mumbled something else. I thought he had said, "I'm glad you're here," but when I told him I hadn't understood, he was already asleep.

I couldn't stop shivering from the cold. I envied Lucas, thinking the hours would pass more quickly if I could sleep too. I lay there in the dark wishing I knew how Andrew was. I told myself that Andrew was young and strong and getting good care. He'd be just fine.

I didn't realize I'd fallen asleep until I woke, finding myself huddled in Lucas's arms. Embarrassed, I eased over a foot, and immediately missed the warmth. Lucas didn't stir. I could tell he was dreaming because now and then he would mumble a few words and move his arms around like he was trying to climb something.

A little daylight came through the cracks and I tried to go back to sleep. I didn't succeed. As the day wore on, the space heated up and my clothes and coat dried to mere dampness, stiff with the salt from the ocean. I could feel the salt in my hair as well. Some of the sand on my clothes had fallen off, leaving me feeling the grit every time I shifted.

There was no coal in our space, but it seemed as if coal dust had embedded itself in all the boards. Every time someone walked across the deck above, a fine powder fell on us.

My mouth grew dry and I wished we had asked for some water. I couldn't tell how much time had passed but I suspected we still had hours to go before we got to Brussels, because the barge was moving so slowly. It seemed like less air was getting in. Raising my head up to the deck boards above me, I could feel a tiny bit of cooler air seeping between the gaps in the boards, but it wasn't enough. I wanted to take big gulps of it. It was as if we were shut in a coffin. My heart began to pound and I broke out in a sweat. There wasn't even enough room to move my legs.

Lucas woke up. "Mina, what's wrong?"

"I can't take it. I can't breathe! I have to get out!"

He grabbed hold of my hand. "Shhhhhh . . . It's all right. Look at me," he said, moving closer and placing his other hand on my cheek. "Just at me. There's plenty of air in here, trust me. See? Just breathe normally and you'll feel better."

I tried to slow my breathing, but it still felt like there wasn't enough air in my lungs.

"No, I have to get out!" I didn't care if anyone saw me. I had to get some air. I sat up partway and pushed on the trapdoor.

Lucas pulled me back down to him, putting both arms around me and holding me tight. The sensation of being close to him again distracted me. He smelled of salt from the sea, a clean smell after the mustiness of the blanket.

"Talk to me," he said, brushing the hair from my face. My plait had come nearly undone and my hair was everywhere. "Don't look at anything but me. All right? You're fine. I've got you." He smiled. "Andrew told me that before the war your family traveled all over. Tell me about one of your trips. I've never been anywhere outside the U.S., well, except for Germany and the short stops along the way to get there, and then this trip. Describe it all like you are there."

I didn't think I could, but I tried to concentrate on something besides the misery I felt. My stomach felt sick again, and I wished we had taken some of the tins from the warehouse. Why hadn't either of us thought about when we would need food? I never forgot about eating. My mouth was so parched I couldn't swallow. I couldn't breathe, and I couldn't swallow. I tried to sit up again, but Lucas wouldn't let me.

"Where have you been?" he prompted.

"What?"

"Tell me where you've been. I really want to know."

I breathed in the scent of him again and felt a pleasant lightheadedness. "We have been to Russia several times." Maybe I would just faint and be out of my misery.

"Russia! I want to hear about that."

I didn't say anything for a moment, waiting to faint, but when that didn't happen, I began to talk. I told him about staying at a dacha that was more like a palace than a cottage, and of winter sleigh rides and of ice-skating parties where servants stood at the ready to bring mugs of hot drinks or already warmed fur lap robes. When I was in the middle of telling how shy I'd felt meeting the czar's four daughters, I stopped, knowing it would just add to his impression of me as a spoiled rich girl.

"Go on," he said. "It sounds like something out of a book. It's so different from my life. I'd like to see someone ask my grandfather's housekeeper to bring them a warmed blanket. She'd slap them on the side of the head as an answer."

"So tell me about the ranch," I said. "My mother grew up traveling around the western territories, but I've never been. She says it's very beautiful, but so unlike England, it's hard to even imagine without being there."

Lucas talked and I listened, concentrating on trying to picture his life. It was so very different from my own. It sounded as if he worked long hours, but the way he described the ranch hands and the land and the animals, I could tell he loved it.

When the barge finally stopped, I found I had forgotten to think about the small space, immersed as I had been in listening to Lucas and thinking that I didn't want him to take his arms away.

After the captain whistled and the boat fell silent, I climbed up out of the compartment as quickly as I could, taking deep breaths of fresh air. I wished we could just stay on the boat, sailing up and down the canal.

It was dusk and the dock was deserted. We jumped off onto the jetty, Lucas motioning to some barrels stacked nearby. There was just enough space behind for the two of us to sit.

"I wish we had some water," I said.

"I should have thought of that. I'll get back on the barge and find us some."

"No, it's too dangerous. We don't know when someone is going to come along. Let's figure out what we do next."

Lucas opened the envelope and took out a very creased piece of paper. A photograph fell out of it. "It's a letter in either a code or some language I can't read." He handed it to me and then bent down to pick up the photograph.

The paper had a faint scent of roses, and it was written in a tiny hand, so small I had to hold it close to see. It was addressed to someone named Gunther:

Gunther drug serdechnyi,

Keamc uroyx aywf tom hetv etertsl athtc nsurw htgira wnode tob hetr orbrahi, heta uerz esdq rsehcuobw, ah etertss ndi- heba hetp irottabav. Dsneirfj ofl hetn teihwz dyaly itawaa ouyn ati erbmunk enethgiec. Owhse emhtb hetu phargotohpd soz eyhtl lliwi ownkv ouyw.

Maria Eton Duoversa

"Can you read it?" Lucas asked.

"Only a few words. The names 'Maria' and 'Gunther' and the two words after 'Gunther.' They're Russian, meaning 'my heart's friend,' which is the Russian equivalent of 'my love,' but it's not a phrase people use much in real life. It's more like something you would read in a book. But the rest of the message isn't in Russian." I scanned it again just to make sure. "One of the words in the signature could be two Latin words together. 'Duo' means 'two,' and 'versa' means 'reverse,' but nothing else is in Latin. The rest of it doesn't look like any language I know." I paused. "Actually, I don't think it is an actual language. This is a code."

"It's not the code you came aboard to teach us how to decipher?"

"No. It's different."

He sighed. "We've got a problem. When you were up on deck, the lieutenant said he'd been taught a simple code after he'd agreed to come on the mission. You came back down then, and it didn't occur to me to ask him to teach it to me. I thought he'd be with me." He tapped the photograph. "Whatever it says, since it came with the picture, maybe it means we're supposed to meet this girl."

I took the photograph from him. It was of a young, pretty woman who wore something like the elaborate traditional dresses I had seen peasant girls wear in Russia on festival days. The headdress that topped the girl's head was nothing like anything I had ever seen, though. The intricate white pleated construction resembled a giant fan. If she was going to meet us, she wouldn't be wearing what she had on in the picture. No one dressed like that on an average day.

I handed it back to him and studied the letter again. Thinking it might be a variation of my father's code in the telegram, I tried every one I could think of. Nothing worked.

"Do you really think it's a code? Wouldn't the Germans have code experts to figure it out if we were caught?" Lucas asked.

"Yes, but it may be that it's not a common code, so it would take them some time to decipher it. Or it's not a difficult code and the people using it know it will eventually be deciphered, but they don't care, especially if it's for a meeting that is about to happen, because they count on the fact that it takes some time to break a code. They hope by the time someone figures it out, it no longer matters, because their meeting has already occurred."

I studied it again, trying to find common words. The lieutenant had said it was a simple code. It felt like English, as if I could almost read it. The frequency of the letter combination "het" had to be a clue, because it looked like "the" scrambled, with an extra letter added. That was the problem with a lot of simple codes: Words frequently used in English were difficult to disguise.

Gunther drug serdechnyi,

Keamc uroyx aywf tom hetv etertsl athtc nsurw htgira wnode tob hetr orbrahi, heta uerz esdq rsehcuobw, ah etertss ndiheba hetp irottabav. Dsneirfj ofl hetn teihwz dyaly itawaa ouyn ati erbmunk enethgiec. Owhse emhtb hetu phargotohpd soz eyhtl lliwi ownkv ouyw.

Maria Eton Duoversa

The third time through, I nearly laughed out loud. "I know this."

"What does it say?"

"It's one of the codes Crispin thought up when he was at Eton. Crispin and Andrew used it to write messages to each other. They did it at home too, thinking they could fool me, and they were so angry when I figured it out. That's why it says 'Eton Duoversa.' Crispin had so many codes, he named them to keep track of them. The 'duoversa' is the key. You take the last two letters of a word and move them to the front of the word, then you write the rest of the word in reverse. For the final step, you add a random letter to the end of each word so it doesn't just look like scrambled English. This first word, 'keamc,' is 'make.'"

I deciphered it word by word, reading it to Lucas because we didn't have a pencil.

"Make your way to the street that runs right down to the harbor, the rue des Bouchers, a street behind the abattoir. Friends of the White Lady await you at number eighteen. Show them the photograph so they will know you."

"Andrew must have explained it to someone in the Foreign

Office," I said, "though I don't know why they used this instead of some other code."

Lucas didn't respond. He was already peering around the side of one of the barrels. "Let's go," he said. "I guess we look for the abattoir. I suppose it will be obvious. Slaughterhouses always are."

It was obvious. A huge building dominated the area right by the docks. I shuddered at the thought of it. The area around it was empty of people. I thought that with the food shortages, the building would be empty too, until I heard the lowing of a single cow inside. I kept my gaze away from it and walked as fast as I could.

As we moved up the street, the area looked more like a shopping district. I looked around, trying not to let shock show on my face. The Belgium I knew from before the war had been nothing like this. Then, the streets had been spotless and every shop front looked as if it had been freshly painted. Now everything was faded, overlaid with grime and neglect. Everyone walked with their eyes on the ground, their shoulders hunched. Their clothing was so threadbare that my own stood out as far too fine, even stiff with salt water and coated with coal dust from the boat. We passed a bootblack putting away his brushes, and his stare made me feel as if I might as well be wearing a sign that read *English*.

Number eighteen was a big, rambling old house, slightly less shabby than the houses around it, with a tiny front garden. Someone had set out flowerpots that looked as if they were waiting to be planted, and the front walk had recently been swept. I knocked, and when the front door opened, I held out the photograph. A man motioned us inside.

"Our guests are here," he called out. "Come into the kitchen," he said to us. Leading us down a cold, dark hallway past several closed doors, he took us to the back of the house and into the kitchen. The kitchen held far more warmth and it was crowded with furniture, as if they had moved their entire parlor in as well. An old woman with fluffy white hair sat in a rocking chair, mending a shirt, while a younger woman stirred a pot of soup on the stove. The younger one frowned when we came in, but the older one put down her sewing and examined us curiously. The man went to one end of the table and sat down, pulling out a newspaper that had been folded into a small square. He unfolded it and began to read as if we weren't even there.

"Sit down," the younger woman said. "I expect you are hungry. We have some onion soup. That's all I can offer you." She banged two spoons down on the table.

I translated, a little shaken by the woman's obvious belligerence.

Lucas felt it too, even if he didn't understand the words. "Please tell her, 'Thank you, ma'am,'" he said. "But tell her we don't want to put them out."

The older woman raised her head at Lucas's words. "Are you American, boy?" she asked in heavily accented English.

"Yes, ma'am," he said.

"You won't be putting us out. The only reason we haven't starved is because of the food the Americans have sent. There wouldn't be anything left of the Belgian people otherwise. You'd do well to remember that," she said to the woman at the stove, switching languages. The younger woman ducked her head at the rebuke, but didn't reply.

The old woman set her rocking chair in motion, still watching us. "When you get back to America, you will have to tell everyone we appreciate the food." She chortled and pointed at an armchair by the stove. "We use everything they send us."

I saw a cushion on the chair and went over to pick it up. It was made from an old flour sack. The words on it read *Belgian Flour Relief, The Moody and Thomas Milling Co., Peninsula, Ohio*. It had been embellished with elaborate embroidery in red and yellow and black. The embroidery was exquisite. Red, yellow, and black. "These are the colors of the Belgian flag, aren't they?" I asked.

"That they are," the woman replied, rocking faster. "We are not allowed to fly the flag or wear ribbons of that color. That's why we wear green instead." She nodded at the ribbon in Lucas's buttonhole. "They can't stop us from using what we have to clothe ourselves. They've taken all our cloth for themselves. But we are smarter than they think."

She stopped rocking long enough to reach down into a leather bag that sat beside the chair. She pulled out another ribbon and a scarf with the same beautiful colored embroidery enhancing the letters. "Little girls wear them as dresses and women use them as scarves. Every day we remind the Germans that we have friends in other places. So we welcome friends to our home. Sit down and eat," she said, handing me the ribbon and resuming her rocking. "Put this through your buttonhole. You'll fit in better."

The younger woman set two bowls of soup down on the table.

"It's not much, but we eat what we have, when we have it." Her voice had softened.

"That's fine," I assured the woman. "It smells good." It tasted good too. The warmth spread through me and I felt some of the tension drain away. It would be nice to stay for a while in a safe place. I took a drink from the mug she offered and nearly gagged.

"It's coffee made from strawberry leaves," the older woman said. "We've gotten used to it. It is terrible, isn't it?" She smiled.

"At least it's hot," Lucas said, drinking all of his down. I couldn't manage another sip.

Lucas finished his soup and then pushed his bowl away. "Thank you. That was very good."

"Yes, thank you," I said, hoping they wouldn't mind that I hadn't finished the drink. I took the last spoonful of soup, wishing I could stretch out the moment. Having a meal, even if it was just soup, felt normal and reminded me of being at home.

"We weren't told the details of the next step of the journey," Lucas said. "The White Lady is supposed to tell us how we can get into Germany."

The woman stopped rocking. "You're going by train. We planned it because it has worked before, but I don't know how you, young lady, will make it," she said, meeting my eyes. "The boy, he looks strong, but you—it will go hard on you."

"Why do I have to be strong to ride on a train?"

The woman shook her head. "You're not riding inside like a passenger. You're riding outside on a ladder. You're to take a freight train full of coal. They stop for water at an unmanned tower and it's there that you are to climb up the ladders between the cars. It's about a three-hour ride, which is a long time for a young girl to hold on to a ladder. Especially a young girl like you. You don't look like you've seen much hard work."

I ducked my head, feeling ashamed that yet another person saw me as useless.

"Grandpapa!" A young girl ran into the kitchen, her blond braids tied with green ribbons flying behind her. "I saw Monsieur Janssens outside watching the house when the strangers came. He left and I followed him and he went straight to the secret police. You were right. He is a stool pigeon! They'll be coming!"

I bolted out of the chair, fear running through me. I'd thought the house was safe.

Lucas stood up too. "What did she say? What's happened?"

"The secret police have been told about us," I said to Lucas. "We have to leave."

The older man patted the girl on the head. "Good girl. Now you go off to visit your aunt. We'll fetch you later." The girl gave one quick look at us, ran over and hugged the younger woman, then dashed back out the door.

The old woman stood up, picking up a leather bag. "At least we have confirmation now about Janssens. There's no more time, my young friends. Come out the back door with me."

Someone pounded on the front door and shouted for us to open it.

"They are quick tonight," the old woman said. "We hurry now."

CHAPTER NINETEEN

LUCAS GRABBED HIS rucksack and we followed the old woman out into a walled garden and then through a door at the back of it and out into an alley. The woman led us through several backstreets until I could tell we were heading out into the country.

"Won't the police want to know about the strangers the man reported?" I asked. I didn't want the family to be put in danger.

"Yes, they'll ask. My husband will make up a story. He is good at it," she said. "They haven't caught us yet." The pride came through clearly. "Now, we are going to have to go down a street that is more populated. Walk behind me, as if you don't know me."

She hurried off and we went after her, trying to keep several paces back. When the woman turned a corner, we quickened our pace to make sure we didn't lose her. Right before we turned the corner, a gruff voice rang out just around it. "What are you doing out this time of night? Your papers, please," a man ordered in German.

I saw that Lucas had the same thought I did. Both of us dived for a nearby doorway that was set back enough into the building to provide some shadows.

"I don't understand," the old woman grumbled in French.

"Papers!" the man shouted, first in German and then in French.

"Papers. Ah. Why didn't you say so? Yes, yes, here they are." The old woman sounded annoyed. "Please hurry, young man. I'm a midwife and there is a woman whose time has come. They waited too long to send for me, and I'm afraid this one is going to have a difficult time. So unless you have some skill in birthing babies, I suggest you let me go on my way."

The soldier didn't respond to that. There was silence and then the faint sound of paper being unfolded.

"All right. Go along," the man barked. "I'll be checking up on you at headquarters." He walked back toward us.

Lucas took my hand and squeezed it. He leaned in and pulled me close to him. I heard the man's footsteps coming closer, his boots clicking on the cobblestones. Lucas was so close to me I could feel his breath. My own breath stopped.

I wished I could look out to see where the soldier was, but I was afraid he'd spot me. The footsteps came closer. I felt Lucas's arms tighten around me. I could tell the soldier was only a few feet away.

The footsteps clicked on by us. We stayed still until they faded away. I took a big breath of air and looked up into Lucas's eyes.

He kissed me. I felt warmth spread all over my body as I kissed him back. I tightened my arms around his neck, wishing I never had to let go. All I could think of was how I wanted him closer to me. I leaned back against the door, pulling him with me.

Lucas stopped kissing me and with a shock I remembered where we were. "We should go find our guide," he said, his breath coming in ragged gasps.

"Yes, right." I tried to act as if I regularly kissed people and that my knees weren't wobbling.

The old woman was waiting for us. The fear I'd felt came back to me. "Did you understand what the soldier said?" I asked the woman. "He claimed he was going to check your name."

"I understood him just fine. He understood me too. We all pretend we don't speak each other's language, and the Germans have been told not to trust any Belgians who are too cooperative. He won't check on me. My papers say I have a right to be out after the curfew because of my profession. Not even the Germans can make women have their babies on schedule."

We walked at least another mile until we were on the very outskirts of town, by some railway tracks. "This is where you go on alone," the woman said. "Follow the tracks until you come to a water tower. It's a good number of miles from here, so keep walking until you see it. Once you are there, wait until a freight train stops for water. With luck it will be tonight. Don't get on one that stops after 2:00 A.M. That would get you into Aachen too close to daylight. If a train doesn't come at the right time tonight, you'll have to find yourselves a place to wait until tomorrow night."

"Aachen is in Germany, isn't it?" Lucas asked.

"It's right across the border."

"There isn't a timetable?" I asked, thinking of how hard it would be to find a place to hide for an extra day.

"Not for freight trains in wartime. The Germans run the trains when they need them." She opened her bag and took out a bundle of something wrapped in a piece of cloth and tied with a string. "Take this. If anyone stops you and asks what you are doing, tell them you're trying to sell your grandmother's lace. There is lace in here, if anyone looks. It is beautiful lace. My sister made it before the war." I took the bundle, wishing I could pay the woman for it. It was no small gift.

The woman continued, "When the train stops, climb up near the end of the train, but not between the last two cars, because there might be a guard on the rear car. Once you pull into Aachen, get off on the left side as you face toward the front of the train."

"What then?" I didn't like the idea of getting off at a train station full of German soldiers.

"There is an old man who sells something at the station.

I wasn't told what. You'll need to figure it out. Buy whatever he is selling, and pay him too much. He'll know what to do then. Now I have to get back." She pointed at the ribbon in my buttonhole. "Don't forget to take those off when you get to Germany. It's only for Belgium. I wish you Godspeed."

An old man who sells something? That was too vague. I realized my head was aching and all the muscles in my jaw were so tight that I must have been clenching my teeth. I didn't want to let the woman leave. Once she left, we'd be on our own again. "Wait. Before you go, can I ask a question?"

"You can, but I may not answer. We live in an age when questions can be dangerous."

"Are you the White Lady we keep hearing about?"

"No, dear, I'm not the White Lady, though I'm delighted you think an old crone like me would be someone so special. The White Lady is an old legend, a specter who appears to members of the Hohenzollern family to herald the end of the dynasty."

"I don't understand," I said. "People talk as if she's a real person."

"We've taken her name to inspire us. She's not a real person, but she lives inside us." The woman made a fist and put it on her chest. "We who are trying to get our country back want to be like the White Lady. We may be ghostly in our appearances, but we will cause the downfall of the occupiers. No matter what it takes." Her voice had turned fierce.

"I think you will," I said. "Thank you for your help."

"No need to thank me. We do what we must." She turned to go.

"Your family back at the house—they'll be all right, won't they? Our being there won't get them in trouble, will it?"

The woman looked at me for a long moment. "We will carry on," she said, and then walked away briskly, as if just out on an errand.

"What do you think she meant?" I asked Lucas. "They'll be all right because the officials didn't find us there, right?"

"We should go on," Lucas said. "Here, let me put the lace in the rucksack so you don't have to carry it."

He took the revolver out and stuck it in his belt before he put the lace in. I felt a chill at the sight of the gun. I knew if he actually had to use it, our situation would be desperate at that point.

I forced myself to move. It was hard to take the first step, knowing that each step would take us farther into enemy territory. I tried not to think of anything but where I was putting my feet. It was very dark, but we could just see the train rails.

"They're brave people," Lucas said. "I feel like they've put their lives in danger for us when we are doomed to failure."

I stopped, shocked by his words. I had never expected him to sound so discouraged. "How can you say that? We aren't going to fail. We've come so far already."

"The more I think about it, the more I don't believe my father can be convinced to leave Germany. He signed the Manifesto of the Ninety-Three." He sighed. "The British should have realized it's a clear signal he has no intention of leaving Germany."

"I don't understand. What manifesto?"

"All these important scientists and scholars signed a document saying they supported Germany in all her military actions, military actions they say Germany had to take because of the aggression of other countries."

"Wait, that doesn't make sense. Germany is the aggressor."

"*We* know that, but ordinary Germans don't seem to know it. And even supposedly brilliant scientists don't seem to know it. Andrew told me there was so much propaganda put out to the German people that they actually thought Britain would side with them against Serbia when the war started."

I tried to comprehend how two groups of people could see things so differently. "Maybe he was forced to sign it."

"Maybe. But he is an important man in Germany. He likes that. People call him Herr Doctor Professor Mueller and ask his opinions on everything. When I was visiting, I saw his reaction to someone who didn't treat him with what he thought was the proper respect. He was furious. If he hasn't cared enough to come see me all these years, why would I have any influence over him? He loves his country more than . . ." Lucas's voice trailed off. "I shouldn't have agreed to come."

"But you did. You must have hoped it would work. Otherwise why did you come this far?"

When he spoke again, his voice was harsh. "Because it's my duty, and once I've done my duty, I want to be done with him. He's listed as my father on my birth certificate, but that doesn't mean much. If Andrew hadn't come to see me, I'd have been perfectly content never to think of him again. And how could I say no? Andrew told me it was a vital mission. With America in the war, I have to do my part."

A sharp crack of a stick sounded off to the side. We stopped. I felt my muscles tense.

"Halt!" someone shouted in German.

Lucas pulled me behind a tree. A weak light played over the place where we had just been standing and then we heard the sound of someone moving slowly toward us.

"I know you are there," the voice called out. "I will shoot if you don't come out."

"Stay here," Lucas whispered. Before I could protest, he dropped the rucksack, stood up and said "wait" in German, then moved out into the open.

I didn't know what to do. I inched forward enough that I could see. A soldier had a rifle with a bayonet pointed at Lucas and was motioning for Lucas to put his hands above his head. "Show me your papers!" the man shouted.

Lucas obviously understood this because he took out the forged identification. I held my breath, hoping the man wouldn't find anything suspicious about it. I felt a little better knowing that Lucas had the revolver with him, but I also feared a shot would draw too much attention to us. The last thing we needed were more soldiers here.

"What are you doing here so late at night?" the soldier demanded.

Lucas didn't answer. I feared there had been something in the sentence he hadn't understood. I had to do something. Thinking about how the old woman had dealt with the soldier earlier gave me an idea. I grabbed the rucksack and put it up under my skirt.

With one hand on it so it wouldn't fall out, I called out in

French, "Don't shoot me!" and then emerged from behind the tree.

"Who are you?" The soldier swung the bayonet in my direction, looking as scared as I felt. He was extremely young and reminded me of the driver in Dover, Sergeant Smyth, right down to the wispy mustache. His uniform was far too big for him, and I could see his hands were shaking as he held the bayonet.

Knowing I needed to make sure he understood, I decided to speak in German. Making my voice sound close to hysterical, I said, "Please, let us go! My brother doesn't have all his wits about him and I'm about to have a baby! He is taking me to a midwife. The baby is coming soon, I can feel it! Can you help me? I'm afraid I'll have it right here!" I moaned to give authenticity to my story. Lucas just stood there, so dumbfounded that I hoped the soldier would believe he really was simple.

The soldier seemed almost as dumbfounded. A sharp scent of sweat emanated off him, and his forehead was beaded with it. I wondered if he'd ever stumbled upon anyone on patrol before. He stared at me, like he couldn't believe I was real. "Where do you come from?" he asked.

I didn't know what to say. I knew no names of towns anywhere nearby. "A farm near here," I said. "Please, let us go." I gave out what I hoped sounded like the cry of pain of a woman in labor. The soldier looked horror-stricken. All his attention was focused on me. I saw Lucas nod in my direction, but I didn't know what he wanted me to do, so I moaned again, this time louder, and acted like I was going to collapse. The soldier took a step forward.

Instantly, Lucas had the revolver out, swinging the grip at the soldier's head before the man could react. The butt of the gun hit the man in the temple with a dull thud, and both Lucas and the soldier crashed to the ground, the rifle and its bayonet between them. I ran forward, unable to see if Lucas was hurt, but he was on his feet before I reached them.

"Come on," he said, reaching down and picking up the rifle. He tossed it away. "We have to get out of here. He'll only be out for a few seconds."

A man called out in German from nearby, "Reiner, where are you?"

We plunged right back into the woods, though it was nearly impossible to see. I could hear branches breaking behind us and then the same man's voice. "He's here. Someone has knocked him out." I pulled Lucas to a stop. "They won't know which way we went," I whispered in his ear. "We should be quiet so they don't figure it out."

He nodded. We clung to each other while we listened. I heard more voices. "Can you understand what they are saying?" Lucas whispered.

"No, they aren't talking loudly enough. I think we should move, but as quietly as we can."

I realized I had no idea where the railway tracks were. I had been too busy trying to dodge trees and stay on my feet to pay attention. "You lead," I said.

"I think it's this way."

It took us several minutes. There was a bad moment when we had to stop at the noise of something moving through the trees near us. "It doesn't sound like a person," I whispered. "It's probably an animal." Whatever it was moved away and we continued on our way. When we came out into the open and saw the tracks again, I grabbed hold of Lucas and ran, pulling him after me as if someone or something would reach out from the trees and drag us back in.

"Are you all right?" he asked.

"Yes, I'm just glad to be out of the forest." I looked back over my shoulder, afraid I'd see something or someone coming out of the woods. "Let's keep moving."

"That was a close one," Lucas said as we walked along. "How did you come up with the idea to pretend to be having a baby?"

"The midwife gave me the idea. I didn't know what else to do."

"It was perfect. He was terrified when he thought you might have a baby right there. I might have believed you if I hadn't known better. You're a good actress." He raised his head. "I think I see the water tower."

It was up ahead of us, a blacker silhouette against the already dark sky. We walked up to it and looked around. There was nothing to see but more tracks and more woods. "We can't just stand here for hours," I said.

"You're right. We need to move back, because it's the engine that will stop here. If we need to climb onto a car at the rear, it will be back the way we came."

We walked back to where we estimated might be a good place to wait. "We don't really have any idea how long the train will be," I said. "This might not be the right spot. I have no idea how many cars a German coal train has."

"There should be enough time for us to get to where we need to go. I hope we don't have long to wait." Almost immediately, I caught the distant rumble of a train. We moved farther away from the track, going just into the fringes of the forest so we couldn't be seen.

"Remember, it might not be the right kind of train," Lucas warned. "We don't want to run out and find ourselves trying to climb on a troop train." I shuddered. After our one encounter with the young German soldier, I didn't want to run into any others.

The sound of the train grew louder and we could feel the ground shaking beneath us. I could feel Lucas close by, restless in his movements. The train slowed, its wheels screeching. The engine went past and we could see the engineer and the fireman, then the tender, then the first car. It was a coal train, car after car of it. As it slowed to a stop, I realized we were still too far forward. Lucas did too, and the two of us ran toward the back of the train. There was no caboose, which meant no guards. That was a piece of luck.

"Here," Lucas said, pointing at the third car from the end. "You climb up. I'll be right behind you." He pointed at the ladder. I scrambled up on the coupling, then stepped onto the first rung of the ladder. I wanted to say I was scared, because I was terrified, but I didn't want Lucas to know.

"Okay?" he asked.

I tried to keep my voice even. "Yes," I said as I climbed up higher to make room for him. He came up behind me so that his head was just below mine and his arms were on either side of me as he got ahold on a rung.

Even with Lucas so close to me, the next three hours were some of the worst of my life. I could never have imagined that riding on a train ladder would be so terrible. Within a few minutes, my hands were already tired of grasping the rungs. The metal felt slick and greasy under my fingers. I tried to adjust my hold, wrapping my arms all the way around the ladder to take some of the strain off my hands. My feet soon developed muscle cramps from perching on the narrow rung.

I lost all sense of time, but knowing I had a long time to go made it worse. I had never realized how hard it was to just stand still, holding on. There was a steady stream of fine coal dust blowing off the open cars, and I could taste it with every breath, my eyes watering constantly from the tiny bits that blew into them.

Eventually, I began to fantasize about just jumping off every time the train slowed, thinking I could give myself a few minutes to run along beside it and then climb back up before it sped up too much. I knew Lucas wouldn't let me do it even if I begged, however, so I didn't try. After that I tried counting the sounds the wheels made as they went around each time, but stopped when I reached two thousand. We passed through many small villages, but the train didn't slow, and the dark cottages came and went like parts of a fast-moving dream.

Just when I thought I couldn't stand it any longer, the train crossed a bridge and I could see the river far below. I felt a surge of hope that it was the one running through Aachen. The train passed over it and then slowed slightly. Soon enough, buildings began to appear on either side of the tracks and the train whistle sounded. I wiggled my toes as much as I could within the confines of my shoes, hoping my feet would work so I could climb down the ladder. The train came to a stop.

I tried to climb down, but my muscles were so stiff, I fell. Lucas was there to catch me. "Mina!" He put his arms around me and swung me away from the train, pulling me close. He hugged me, his lips brushing my hair. "Are you all right?"

"I think so. My feet are so stiff."

He picked me up and carried me away from the train, back behind one of the train sheds, and set me down.

"I wish I didn't have to ever stand up again," I said, wiggling my toes and stretching my legs. I unlaced my shoes and pulled them off. "I used to like trains. I'm not sure I do now." I wiggled my toes some more.

"It would be nice to go on a real train ride again with you," Lucas said. "You could keep me entertained by yelling out the window whenever you felt like it."

I felt my ears getting warm, but I also felt a little bubble of happiness inside. "And how would you entertain me? It would only be fair if you did something too."

"Oh, I know exactly what I'd do," he said, moving closer to me. His expression was one I couldn't read. It was so focused on me that it made me shiver, but not from cold. "First, I'd close the curtains," he said, his voice growing softer as my heart beat faster, "to shut out the rest of the world." He put his hands on either side of my face and whispered, "And then I'd do this." He kissed me, and every bit of me went weak.

This time it was some voices on the other side of the building that brought us to our senses. I pulled away from him, feeling disoriented, like I was waking up from a heavy sleep. Lucas looked as if he felt the same way.

What were we doing? We shouldn't be kissing. There were people all around us who wouldn't hesitate to arrest us if they found out who we were. I couldn't let myself forget that, as much as I wanted to. And then I looked at Lucas and remembered Andrew's words: *If a moment of happiness is within your grasp, take it.*

I'd had my moment of happiness, and if I wanted more moments, we needed to move.

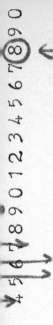

CHAPTER TWENTY

IT WAS TIME to hunt for the old man. I reached for one of my shoes, giving my toes one last stretch. "The longer we stay in one spot, the more likely it is that someone will see us and get suspicious. And the sooner we find the old man, figure out where we are going, and get there, the sooner I can take off my shoes again."

"I don't think we should go together," Lucas said. "You stay here and I'll go look for him."

I stood up. "Don't be ridiculous. Remember your one problem? You don't speak German. I'll go and you stay here."

"I speak enough to point at something and hold up fingers to show how many I want. I can say thank you."

"I'll go," I said. "That way if a soldier stops me, I'll be able to talk to him."

After only a little more arguing, Lucas gave in. "All right. I don't like it, but it makes the most sense." He opened the rucksack. "There's money in here."

I took some German coins, half marks and different denominations of pfennigs. "Whatever an old man can have to sell at a train station, it can't be worth much."

"Be careful," Lucas said. His voice was strained.

"I will."

"Wait," he said, pointing at my coat. "Don't forget to take off the ribbon."

I had completely forgotten about it. I untied it and put it in my pocket and then checked around the edge of the building. There was no one nearby, though there were workers loading bags onto a train parked on one of the tracks.

No one paid attention to me as I walked around in the train station. There was a mix of both civilians and military personnel. They all looked like the people we'd seen on the street in Belgium, worn down by the war.

I saw a woman trying to sell dried plums who wasn't getting much business. The fruit looked so old and cracked that it had probably been dried years earlier.

A few soldiers who looked like guards stopped talking when I walked by them. I dropped my head and tried not to hurry. I was afraid it would look suspicious if I acted like their presence made me nervous. As I walked around, I saw plenty of old men, but no one selling anything. I began to fear that Lucas would come looking for me if I didn't get back to him soon.

An elderly man shuffled by me carrying a bag. I watched him take up a spot by a pillar and lean against it. He opened the bag and took out a much smaller bag made of burlap and tied at the top with a string.

He held it up and called out, *"Walnüsse!"*

Walnuts. The man was selling walnuts.

I walked over to him, my hand in my pocket. "How much?" I asked in German, jingling the coins so he could hear them.

He stared at me. He mumbled something that it took me a moment to understand. *Fifty pfennig for four nuts.*

I realized that I didn't know how much extra I was supposed to pay him. I got out three fifty-pfennig coins and handed them to him. He examined them like he'd never seen a coin before. I waited. If he handed two back to me, he was the wrong man.

"You'll like these," he said to me in German. "But let me get you a better bag." He reached in and pulled out another bag of similar size, but it was tied with twine instead of string. He handed it to me.

"Thank you," I said. I walked away, worrying that I'd see Lucas wandering around the station looking for me.

When I got back to our resting spot, he was still there, though he was pacing around. "Mina! I was just about to come looking for you! Did you find him?"

I held up the bag. "I did, but I haven't opened this up to see what's inside." We sat down and I pulled it open so fast, the nuts tumbled out, as did a tiny slip of paper. I picked it up. The lettering on it was so small I had to hold it close to my eyes. "This is the book cipher," I said. "See, the first number refers to the page, the second to the line, and the third to the word, though in this case we just use the first letter of the word. We need the book."

As Lucas opened the rucksack, my breath caught. The bag had been soaked in the skiff. It was stiff with the dried salt water. The book might be ruined. We might be unable to go any farther.

He pulled out an oilskin bundle and unwrapped it.

"Thank goodness," I said. "I hadn't thought about protecting the book from the elements."

"I did. I wrapped it up on the ship when you were up on deck."

Even though the cipher wasn't long, it took more time than I wanted to decipher it, but I was relieved at the result. It pointed us to the abbey in the hills above the village and to a nun named Sister Ann. We were to wait behind a henhouse until a nun came to find us. I knew the abbey. I'd seen it many times on my rambles with my cousins.

When I told Lucas about it, he said, "I remember that from one of the maps. It's only a few hours' walk from here."

My stomach rumbled. "Before the war the nuns kept bees and sold the honey to people in the surrounding villages. I hope they still have some."

He took my hand. "Let's go see. I could use about a gallon of honey right now."

As we walked, all the awfulness of the train ride dropped away and I didn't feel quite so exhausted. With Lucas next to me, I could almost pretend that we were just going on an outing. We shared the nuts between us, which did a little toward calming the growling of my stomach. We came to a small stream and Lucas jumped across. I tried, but nearly fell back into the water when the far edge of the bank crumbled beneath my feet. Lucas pulled me up.

"So even if I don't speak German well, I guess I'm good for something," he said.

"I almost made it," I said. "I can't help it if I'm not as tall as you, but yes, you are good for something." I smiled. "More than one something." Like kissing, but I didn't add that. "So I've been wondering, what would you have done if you had arrived here and there was no contact to meet you?"

He grinned and shrugged. "It doesn't matter now, does it? We're here and we know where to go. No sense in worrying about something that didn't happen."

I couldn't help but grin back at his unruffled attitude. "Right. We go this way."

As we walked, I wondered how much the village had changed. I knew it wasn't realistic to think it would be the same, but I wanted to keep my memory of the way it had been before, during all those splendid summers I spent there. My cousins and I had been out from dawn to dusk, exploring the countryside and the village. I clung to the hope that the village was so isolated that it hadn't been forced to change much.

It didn't take us as long as I thought it would to get to the abbey. We came over the crest of the last hill to see the abbey below us, halfway down the slope. Shadows still darkened the valley, but the rays of the sun illuminated the church that dominated the cluster of buildings, making the stones glow as if lit from within.

The abbey was a beautiful place, but it had always felt to me like it was protected from time, the nuns moving about their activities as they had for hundreds of years. Even now it had a peaceful air about it, the old gray stone of the buildings barely showing through the ivy that grew up it. The gardens were mostly bare now, but in the summer they exploded with color and the faint droning of bees carried through the air.

"Look, I see some wooden outbuildings," I said. "The henhouse is probably somewhere around there."

We ventured down through a meadow full of flowers just starting to show their yellow blooms. Our passage startled a covey of quail, which burst up and overhead, breaking the silence. As we drew closer, I felt a growing sense of unease. The only signs of life came from a fawn-colored goat staked in an area just beyond a vegetable garden. The goat bleated at us, eyeing us curiously. We crossed a small grove of apple trees and a cluster of cone-shaped beehives. The first few bees of the day had crawled out of the hives and up the sides and were resting on the coiled ropes as the sun warmed their wings.

"The whole place looks almost empty," Lucas said.

At that moment a keening cry came from a nearby building, a man's voice calling out, "Help me!"

We both stopped.

"Maybe the abbey is being used as a hospital," I said. "Nuns in England are doing quite a bit of nursing, so the same is probably happening here. Should we go see?"

"Someone is coming," Lucas hissed.

I took his hand and we ran until we came to a small building. We darted around behind it, startling three chickens pecking in the grass. The birds squawked and flapped their wings, running a little way away before they stopped and resumed their pecking.

I flattened myself against the wall, Lucas next to me. I heard someone humming as they came closer. "Humming means they probably aren't dangerous, right?" I whispered.

"I don't know," he whispered back.

Something was poking me in the back, and I looked behind me to see a flowering branch that had been fastened to the building. I realized that the entire structure had flowers fastened to it, scattered randomly over the sides, a combination of wildflowers and some early garden flowers. Someone had made crude metal brackets out of wire that held canning jars filled with water as makeshift vases. There were also feathers nailed to the walls, and little brackets that held unusual rocks.

I heard a woman's voice. "Anything to share this morning?" she asked. At first I thought the woman had seen us, but then I realized that she was talking to the hens. I peeked around the corner. It was a nun. I hoped it was the right one.

She went into the chicken coop and came out just a moment later. "Mrs. Feathers, I confess I am a little disappointed," she scolded. "Only one egg today from Mrs. Cluck, and none from you. Perhaps tomorrow will be better." She walked a few feet away and smiled, raising her voice slightly. "We've got some freshly baked bread in the kitchen," she said, "and a bit of honey."

Did she think the chickens were going to follow her to the kitchen for bread and honey? I didn't know much about chickens, but I didn't think they ate honey. When she spoke again, I realized she knew we were there. "All friends of the White Lady are welcome to it. Walk with me."

Lucas must have understood some of it, because when I looked at him, he nodded and then went around the corner of the hen-house. I followed him, still nervous to be in the open.

The woman couldn't hide her surprise at seeing me, but when she spoke, she made it sound as if it was not unexpected and that we had just arrived for a nice visit. "Hello. I'm Sister Ann. You are right on time. We'll send word that you've arrived safely and then we'll find you some food. I expect you are hungry." She began to walk away.

I hung back. "Won't the soldiers see us?"

The woman stopped, turning back to beckon us forward. "No. We feed many hungry people who come our way, and besides, the soldiers who are brought here no longer have the capacity to care about the world outside." She took hold of the cross she wore around her neck and murmured something. Speaking louder, she said, "Most have little time left on this earth. And the healthy ones who bring them here only want to leave as quickly as possible. None of them are here now. Very few want to linger among the dying. You have nothing to worry about. This way."

She led us down the hill to a young man digging in a garden, a basket of seeds next to him. The boy looked up at us, and I recognized him. Even for a German, he was very fair. His hair was silvery blond, almost white, and his eyes were a very light gray.

They were wide-set and large, which had always made him look younger than his age.

"Are you . . . ?" I struggled to remember his name. "You're Oscar, aren't you?" It had been years since I had seen him, back when I had visited my cousins every year, but I'd have known him anywhere, though he'd grown tall. He'd always been on the fringes of the group of village children who played together, never saying much. He'd been a year or two younger than me. That would put him at about fifteen now.

He nodded but didn't speak.

"You know our Oscar?" the nun asked.

"Yes," I said. "I used to visit the area years ago. I remember he lived in the village."

"I see." The woman smiled at Oscar. "Now, we need the bird for Düsseldorf for our friends here," she said to him. He nodded and headed for a gate in a stone wall.

The nun motioned for us to follow him into an herb garden that looked as if it could have come right from the Middle Ages, down to the sundial in the middle of it. I would have liked to linger, to take in the scent of newly sprouted plants, to forget we were tired and cold and far from home, but Oscar made straight for a small garden shed at the opposite wall. It was decorated in the same fashion as the henhouse, with swirling designs of stone and metal all over the outside. I could hear the faint cooing of birds inside.

We followed Oscar in and watched as he opened a cage full of pigeons and pulled one out. The sister took a jar full of grain off a shelf. She opened the lid and reached inside, pulling out a stub of a pencil and a small glass bottle that held thin strips of paper. Taking one out, she wrote on it quickly, then handed the paper to the young man, who carefully attached it to the pigeon's leg with a gray metal band. He cooed at the bird and stroked its feathers as he carried it outside, cradling it in his arms. "Come back and visit us," he whispered to it. The pigeon struggled to get away, clearly eager to be free. Raising it up in the air, Oscar held it for a moment and then let go. Immediately the pigeon rose, flapping its wings. It circled once and then flew off to the north.

"Aren't they amazing creatures?" the sister said.

"Amazing." I watched until it was out of sight, wondering who the friends in Düsseldorf waiting for news of our arrival were.

I turned back to see the nun smiling at us. She handed me one of the tiny pieces of paper rolled up, like the one the bird carried.

"This came yesterday. I haven't read it. Don't read it until you leave. If something happens before then, get rid of it." I held it carefully. It was so small. It would be easy to lose. I was very tempted to read it then, but I put it in my pocket instead.

"Come along to the kitchen now," the woman said. We followed her. Oscar came too, trailing a few feet behind us. I was confused as to why he was there. His mother was a washerwoman, and her house in the village had had clotheslines strung in front and in back, always full of clean laundry waving in the breeze. When I'd last been here, Oscar helped her with the laundry, hauling water from the village well one pail at a time. I didn't remember a father.

When we went into the kitchen, I was nearly overwhelmed

by the scents of baking bread and dried apples and beeswax candles. I could almost imagine countless candles burning over the hundreds of years the abbey had been there, their fragrance permeating the stone walls.

The sister set down her egg basket. "Now, I'm sure you'd like something to eat, then a wash, and then a place to sleep until you leave tonight. I've made some prune soup, and we do have bread and honey, even if it's just black bread. The honey helps with the taste. Please sit."

She brought out the food and arranged it, then bowed her head, saying a prayer. Lucas, who had been reaching for a piece of bread, stopped, abashed.

When the sister had finished, she smiled at Lucas. "Please, go ahead. I know you must be hungry. Young men your age always are." She looked at me. "Young ladies too."

I had never tasted honey so good. I tried not to bolt it down, but I was so hungry, it was difficult to be polite. "The honey is delicious," I said, trying to slow down.

"We've found the best honey comes from rapsflower. Do you know it?"

I shook my head.

"It's what's growing in the meadow above the abbey. When it blooms, the whole meadow looks as if the sun itself has loaned us some of its color and light. The bees like our other flowers as well. Oscar does such a good job of coaxing them to grow."

Oscar came over and sat with us, across from me. He didn't eat, but he watched us, smiling the whole time.

"I like gardens too," I said to Oscar. "I can't wait to get home to mine." He nodded and then suddenly pushed back his chair and jumped up, hurrying into the other room.

"Does he live here now? I remember his mother from the village," I said.

"He has lived here for several years, ever since his mother passed away." The sister offered us more food, but when we declined, she began to put it away. "He grows quieter each year, though. I worry about him. He'll soon be old enough to fight, but I don't know how he will survive. He's such a gentle soul. It's the young soldiers who pay the price for war."

Oscar came back into the room, carrying a cut piece of paper painted gold. He laid it down gently on the table, smoothed it out, and then handed it to me. It was a paper crown. Smiling broadly, he took it back and put it on his head.

"Oh, I think I see," said the nun. "You are the English girl who was so kind to him and let him be part of your games. We heard all about it, how you had him act in your play. He has always cherished this," she said, indicating the crown.

The memory came flooding back to me. I had written a play, one of dozens over the years, about a treasure hoarded by trolls and a group of children who went on an adventure to get it. There had been too many parts for just the children of the household, so my cousins and I had recruited village children to act in it. One of my cousins had made the crown, and I'd given it to Oscar to be the troll king.

"It was nice of you to include him," Sister Ann said.

I hadn't included him to be kind. We'd needed someone to play the troll king because the others wanted more lines. We'd made him sit on an old stump that was the troll's throne and ordered him to roar at us at certain parts in the play. I remembered how angry I had been when he grinned with delight after he roared, ruining the scary part of the performance. I even yelled at him for it.

"It's nice he remembers," I managed to say, feeling guilty that I'd been so bossy then.

Lucas yawned so loudly his jaw popped.

"Young man, you can use Oscar's room for the day," the sister said to Lucas. "He'll be working outside and won't need it until nightfall. It's right over here off the kitchen, and it's always nice and warm because it's so close to the ovens. There's clean water in the basin for you."

"Thank you, Sister," Lucas stood up and then stumbled a little as he walked into the room the sister had indicated. He looked almost asleep on his feet. I realized I'd concentrated so much on the misery I'd been feeling at different points that I hadn't given enough thought to him.

"I'll show you to your room too, if you'd like to rest," she said to me. "Oscar, we will need another grave dug by tomorrow or the next day at the latest. The weather is clear now, so perhaps you should dig it today." She said it as if she was asking him to dig a vegetable patch. I thought of the man we'd heard moaning in pain.

Still smiling, the boy got up and pulled a coat off a peg on the wall, then went out the door as if he had been sent to fetch water.

The sister led me down a narrow hallway lined with doors, each one opening into a small room like a cell. The wing had to be part of the original building, because it was all stone and the doorways looked as if they had been made for much shorter people. The chill from the stones seeped into the air, and I wished I could have stayed in the kitchen. The sister stopped at one door and indicated that I should go in.

Ducking my head, I went in. The room held a narrow iron bed covered with a thin frayed blanket, and a small chest of drawers with a basin on top. A cross hung over the bed, but otherwise the room was empty of decoration.

"I apologize for the blanket. All our better ones are used by the patients, but at least it's not too chilly in here today."

"I hope I'm not putting someone out," I said.

"You aren't. So many of our sisters have gone to stay at other hospitals, we have only about a third of the number we had before the war. There is plenty of room."

I couldn't get over the fact that we were in a German abbey being treated like we were guests. "Sister, I don't understand why you are helping us, and also helping the German soldiers."

The woman took hold of the cross she wore around her neck. "Life is so full of choices. Germany is my country, but my first responsibility is to God. I do not care who wins this war as long as it ends quickly. It is a waste and a tragedy. I prayed long hours about it and decided I must do what small bit I can to make it stop. But I will also give help to the dying." She let go of the cross. "Get some rest and I'll wake you after vespers."

After she left, I took off my shoes and lay down, pulling the thin coverlet over me. It smelled of lavender. I thought about Mr. Applewhite and our old housekeeper before Miss Tanner arguing over lavender, Mr. Applewhite saying it wasn't suited for Lincolnshire and the housekeeper stomping around saying he should grow it anyway because she needed it to keep the sheets smelling nice. The last thing I remembered thinking before I went to sleep was how much the bees must like the lavender.

When I woke, I could tell it was late afternoon. I washed and rebraided my hair, wishing I had both a brush and a mirror. When I went out into the hallway, there was absolute silence. Tracing my way back to the kitchen, I found it empty as well. Getting nervous, I went over to the door to the room where Lucas had slept and listened, but didn't hear anything. Pushing open the door, I peeked in and was relieved to see Lucas there, asleep, sprawled on his back, his hair tousled and his expression untroubled.

He didn't stir, so I decided to let him sleep and went outside instead. It had turned out to be a beautiful day. The sun streamed across the garden under a clear sky. The silence made me feel as if the entire abbey was slumbering, keeping quiet while waiting for peacetime to return.

I walked around looking at the gardens. As I drew closer to the church, I could hear distant sounds of singing coming from the chapel. Oscar was working among the apple trees, pruning them. He saw me approach and I raised my hand to wave to him.

"Hello," I said. He beckoned to me, smiling and pointing to an area beyond the beehives and then walking toward them, urging me to come along. I followed him past the cemetery to an area that looked to have been a garden in the past, now mostly given over to nature. There were bird cherries in bloom, their white flowers letting off a fragrance that scented the entire area.

Oscar smiled again and pointed downward. There, at the base of the tree, was a garden in miniature, with tiny paths of pebbles and bits of moss growing as if it were lawn. A little house made of bark stood in the center. There was even an area made into a pond, where a chipped glass bowl had been dug in to hold water.

"It's wonderful! Like a fairy garden!" I said, kneeling down to examine it more closely. It was like I was Alice in the looking glass, grown huge and seeing the world made small. I knew I had to try to make one of these gardens at home. We sat for several minutes in companionable silence until Oscar touched me on the shoulder, motioning to me to go back to the abbey.

Lucas and Sister Ann were just coming out of the kitchen when I came around the corner.

Lucas ran to me. "Mina! Where were you? I was worried."

"I took a walk and found Oscar. I didn't think I was gone that long."

"All is well," the sister said, giving a small package to me. "I've made up a package of food for you to take. Best you go along before it's completely dark."

Oscar came around the corner and looked at the bundle and then at me. He frowned.

"Our friends need to leave," Sister Ann told him.

"You are a wonderful gardener," I told him. "Thank you for showing me what you've done."

Oscar took a small, smooth gray stone out of his pocket. He held it out.

I took it.

"I like stones," he said. "This one is nice and smooth, isn't it?"

"Thank you," I said, not knowing what else to say. I put the stone in my pocket, trying to think of something I could give him. I had no jewelry on, and there was nothing in the coat pockets except the green ribbon. I pulled it out and handed it to Oscar.

When Oscar took it, a huge smile crossed his face. "Thank you."

"That is a lovely present," Sister Ann said.

"We should be on our way," Lucas said. "Thank you for your help, Sister."

"You're welcome. I will pray for your safety."

I heard automobiles coming up the road. Two black cars with German flags on them turned into the long drive up to the abbey.

"Go now!" the sister said. "And stay out of sight!" She made a shooing motion with her hands. The fear in her voice frightened me. Lucas took my hand and we ran. When we reached a small stand of apple trees, I stopped. "We need to read the message before we go any farther. And I want to see what's happening at the abbey," I said. "Sister Anne sounded so scared."

"They were official German cars," Lucas said.

"But she's German and she takes care of German soldiers." I looked out from behind a tree. The cars were still there. The drivers stood next to them, smoking cigarettes. "Maybe they are visiting a patient." But I didn't really believe that even as I said it.

"Nothing is happening. What does the message say?"

I took it out of my pocket and unrolled it. There were only two words on it.

"It says 'mouse barn.' That's the one that belongs to an old lady who hates cats. Frau Ulrich's barn."

"I remember that from the map," Lucas said.

"How could you? You only saw it once."

He shook his head. "No, I studied it several times. Andrew did too."

Of course. I'd known the map wasn't for pilots, but it hadn't occurred to me to wonder what they'd done with it.

"We should go," Lucas said. I looked back at the abbey. There were people going down the drive toward the cars. At first I thought it was just the men in uniform returning, but then I caught sight of Sister Anne. She was in the middle of the group, surrounded on all sides. One man motioned her into the backseat of the first car. The rest of the men got in.

I grabbed Lucas's hand. "They're taking her away!"

He took my other hand. His fingers were cold. "Maybe it's not what we think. And if it is, they may just question her and let her go. We can't know, and we need to move." He took a step backward, tugging on my hands. "Please, Mina," he pleaded. "We've come this far, and right now there is nothing we can do for her."

I felt sick to my stomach and my head was pounding again, but I made myself turn away from the abbey.

We waited until Lucas said they were gone. We went down the hill and into the woods. The last time I had been in the woods below the abbey, my cousins and I had been pretending to be lost princesses escaping from an evil witch. We had spent the afternoon terrifying ourselves, seeing witches behind every dark fir tree. The forest lent itself to fright, with deep shadows and closely set trees giving it a foreboding atmosphere. But that had been a long time ago, and in more than just years.

As Lucas and I walked, the evening mist came up, adding to the strange atmosphere. There were no sounds, as if the animals had all deserted the forest. A few times, I thought I saw someone through the mist, but I told myself I was letting my imagination run wild from thinking about the witch game. Still, I couldn't shake the feeling that there was a presence there, though I felt a little like Lettie for thinking such a thing. Lucas didn't speak. His silence and my unease made the walk seem long, longer than I'd remembered it to be. I tried to think about how he might be feeling now that we were so close to seeing his father again, but it was hard to put myself in his place. My father had always been a major presence in my life. I couldn't imagine how I'd feel if he hadn't been there.

My cousins' house was down in a valley, just outside Winnefeld. The house itself was an old stone manor that had been added to many times, and it was surrounded by outbuildings and stables. When we came upon it, I could tell no one had lived there for years. It wasn't neglected exactly, but it didn't look as perfectly kept as it had before the war. All the windows were shuttered and the gardens looked as if someone was trying to keep up with them, but couldn't manage. Some of the roses had been cut back, but the blackthorn hedge hadn't been pruned for a long time, and its thorny branches made the house seem a little like a fortress.

I wondered if the house still smelled of cocoa. My aunt had

loved the drink, so of course my cousins had loved it too. They had had it every day in place of tea—another reason I had always been happy to come visit them and stayed for as long as I could. I didn't know why the scent lingered so in the house, but you could smell it as soon as you opened the door. I didn't know if it would ever smell that way again.

"We need to keep going," Lucas urged. I realized I'd been standing there staring at the house. The lights of a motorcar appeared in the distance. The vehicle went past the house and on into the village, traveling very slowly. "That had some sort of official seal on it," Lucas whispered.

I didn't want to think what that might mean. "Frau Ulrich's barn is this way," I said. We dodged and crept through shrubs and around outbuildings until we came to the mouse barn. It was practically falling apart. There were no lights on in the woman's cottage.

I remembered that there was a door on one side that would be better to use than the main one. That one would surely be rusted and creaky.

We went in. Not only could I smell the mice, but I could hear them skittering everywhere. I don't mind mice, but the thought of the hundreds surrounding us made my skin creep. "They're more scared of us than we are of them," I whispered.

"What?" Lucas asked.

"I'm just talking to myself. Ignore me."

There was enough light coming in from between the decaying wood boards of the structure that I could see some old equipment and hay bales. There was even some broken furniture.

"The hay bales will be full of mice," I whispered, shuddering at the thought. "Let's find somewhere else to sit while we wait." I wished I knew how many hours that would be. I hoped it wouldn't be for long.

Lucas made us a bench out of the debris and I sank down onto it gratefully, glad to be off my feet.

I jumped at every sound, convinced I heard someone approaching. As the hours wore on, I relaxed a little. Lucas, after he got tired of pacing, settled down next to me.

"How will we know if something has gone wrong?" I asked finally.

"If no one is here by dawn, then something has gone wrong." He put his arm around me. It felt right, like he had been doing it for years. "You should sleep again if you can. We have hours to go."

I did sleep, though very lightly, thinking I heard mice scrambling about nearby. I wished that we had Sam the unsinkable cat back with us. He would have guarded us while I slept. I was thinking about the Belgian girl and the cat when Lucas said my name very softly.

"Mina, wake up." He took a lock of my hair that had come loose and twirled it around his finger. "It won't be long now." He leaned in close. I thought he was going to kiss me again, but he didn't.

He pulled back. "I hear someone outside."

CHAPTER
TWENTY-ONE

I COULD HEAR someone too. Soft footsteps, barely audible. We got up and went behind a stack of hay bales, crouching down just in time. The door opened and an electric torch played around the barn.

Behind the light, I could make out a man. It had to be our contact. Who else could it be? I was about to call out when I saw the man wore a German uniform.

Lucas saw it too. He got out the gun and lifted it very slowly. The man eased his way in, still playing the light around.

Something about the way the German moved struck a chord of memory in me. As the man drew closer to the bales, Lucas shifted. I could feel him trembling, like he was getting ready to spring. A thin ray of moonlight came through the door and I saw who it was. Before I could speak, Lucas leaped up, the gun raised in his hand.

I yelled, "No!" and threw myself at him, grasping the arm with the gun with both hands. "Don't shoot! It's my brother!" I shouted.

"Mina?" the man said.

Lucas lowered the gun and I let go of him. I ran to Crispin and flung my arms around him, hugging him tightly. He didn't hug me back. I let go and stepped back, trying to see his face. It really was him. I didn't understand why he was just standing there. He didn't seem happy to see me. His face was stony, so expressionless he looked like a different person. Crispin had never been able to hide his emotions. I took another step back. "Crispin, what are you doing here? Why are you in a German uniform?" I asked, unable to comprehend what I was seeing.

"I don't understand," Lucas said. "Your brother is a German soldier?"

"No, of course not," Crispin snapped. "Mina, I can't believe you are here. Are you daft?" He sounded furious. "What on earth is happening? Where is Andrew?"

"If you will stop asking questions, I'll tell you," I said, stung by his anger. He acted as if we were back at Hallington and he had tired of me following him around. "But you have questions to answer yourself, when I'm done explaining." I felt like crying.

He should have been happier to see me. All that time I'd spent thinking about him and missing him, and he was just standing there glaring at me.

I plunged into the explanation, and then stopped in midsentence. It all became clear to me. "Andrew has known all along, hasn't he?" I said. "And he didn't tell me." Anger threatened to overcome me. Andrew had known how torn up I was about Crispin and he hadn't said a word. He had let me suffer, think my brother was either dead or starving as a prisoner of war. I hated him.

I spun around. "Did you know?" I hissed at Lucas.

He shook his head. "I had no idea."

"Andrew knew," Crispin said, "but he was under orders not to tell anyone." He turned to Lucas. "You must be Lucas. Your father is outside. I'll go get him. I'd like to talk more, but we don't have much time. Not everyone in the village can be trusted. I want to be out of here as quickly as possible."

"Wait. You can't just appear out of nowhere without explaining," I said. "Does Father know you are here too?"

Crispin gave a faint smile. "Yes, he knows. He helped arrange it."

"How could he keep it a secret?" I didn't understand.

"No one knew until very recently that I was safely in place. I had a spot of trouble. And there was no sense in telling you I was alive only to find out I was dead."

"'A spot of trouble'? It's been months!"

"More than a spot, I suppose. I was laid up with a badly broken leg in a village north of here. Some kind souls took me in and hid me."

"But how could you agree? It's so dangerous!"

"Someone had to do it. You know my German is good enough to pass as a native. I can do far more getting valuable information out than slogging through the mud with a rifle. Now, I really need to bring in Lucas's father. We can't linger here."

I wanted to keep talking to him to make sure I wasn't in the middle of some exhaustion dream, but he hurried out the door.

Lucas came over and put his arm around my shoulders. "I feel like I'm inside one of your plays," he said. "Long-lost brother reappears. Father and son meet after many years. Though I'd prefer you erase the possibility of soldiers with guns bursting in."

"Me too," I murmured. "I'd erase the mice too."

He squeezed my arm and then took his own away when the door opened again.

The man Crispin brought in looked nothing like Lucas. He was older than I had expected, stooped over and frail. He did fit the image of a university professor perfectly, right down to his thinning hair and wire glasses. I expected him to begin to lecture right then and there.

Herr Mueller stood looking at Lucas, frowning. Lucas's face was expressionless. "I'd like to speak to my son alone," the man said in heavily accented English.

"Mina and I will be right outside," Crispin said. "Hurry, please."

We went out. Neither Crispin nor I spoke. I tried to make out some of the conversation between Lucas and his father, but only muffled voices came through the wall. Crispin shifted and then I heard a cracking sound, as if someone had stepped on a twig nearby.

Crispin pulled me behind a hedge. He held one finger to his lips and then let go of me. I stood still, rigid with fear, hoping Lucas would have the sense to keep his father in the barn. There was no way to warn him.

Crispin peered around the hedge. I moved so I could see too, though he tried to push me back. We both froze when a figure came into view, a man creeping toward the barn door.

The man went to the door and put his ear to it.

Horrified, I watched Crispin pull a knife out of a sheath on his belt and move behind the man, then pick up a stone from the pathway. He threw the stone to one side of the man. The man looked toward where it landed and Crispin sprang at him from behind.

I saw the knife slash the man's throat. The blood spurted out. My stomach turned. I retched and bent down, bracing myself on my knees so I wouldn't fall.

Crispin pushed the man forward onto the ground and then knelt down to wipe his knife on the man's jacket. When Crispin stood up and turned toward me, his eyes were no longer those of the brother I remembered. This hard-faced man calmly putting away a knife did not in the least resemble anyone I knew.

A memory flashed in my head of my brother at home from school on holidays, organizing us all into performing one of the theatricals. I remembered how we'd all collapse into laughter as he acted out parts, showing us how to play an elderly butler or a young girl mooning over a hero. I couldn't imagine this man putting on a bonnet and a shawl and hobbling around playing a demanding old lady, all while barely containing his own laughter. I heard Sister Ann's voice: *It's the young soldiers who pay the price for war.*

"Did you have to kill him?" I whispered.

"I thought we were being followed," Crispin said. "I recognize him. He's rumored to be in the secret police." He knelt down and went through the man's pockets, taking out some money and cigarettes and putting them in his own. He also took the man's revolver, sticking it in his belt. "This fellow has had his eye on me for too long. Let's just hope he didn't tell anyone. He seems to act alone. I think he hoped to bring in a spy all by himself for the accolades it would bring him."

Lucas appeared in the doorway. "It's all right," Crispin said. "Just a potential problem out of the way."

Lucas came outside, staring down for a long moment at the body on the ground. He glanced at me, his face strained. "My father says he won't go."

"Why not?" Crispin asked.

"He says the British will put him in prison. He doesn't believe that they want him to work for them."

"Try again," Crispin said. "You have five minutes. We're out of time after that."

Lucas sighed. "I'll try."

I moved closer to Lucas and put my hand on his arm. "You can do it. He wouldn't have come all this way to see you if he didn't want to be convinced."

He gave me a hug, leaning his forehead against mine for a brief moment, and then went back in and shut the door.

Crispin got his knife back out.

"What are you doing?" I asked.

He turned to me with those eyes, blank and dark.

"You wouldn't . . . You're not going to kill Lucas's father too?" I grabbed his arm. He shook it off. This couldn't be happening. I felt dizzy. "No," I said, my voice catching in my throat.

Crispin sighed. "I have to, Mina, if he won't go to England. He knows who I am now. He may report me to the authorities, but more important than that, we can't have him using his brilliance to benefit the German army any longer. I wanted just to kill him without all this bother of trying to get him to England, but the British authorities overruled me. They really believe he will work for them. They've convinced a few other scientists and engineers to leave." He shifted the knife to his other hand and adjusted his grip. "Get Lucas away, if you don't want him to see," he added. "Get him to go outside, and I'll take care of it."

"No, you aren't going to." I couldn't let him murder another man. Whatever Lucas felt for his father, he wouldn't want him dead. Pushing past Crispin, I ran into the barn. Lucas's father stood by the hay bales, his arms crossed. Lucas was pleading with him.

"Herr Doctor Professor Mueller, you have to come to England," I burst out, frantically trying to think of a way to convince him. "Your talents are being wasted here."

"This is Mina, Father," Lucas said. His voice was calm, but his eyes were wide. He gave a slight motion with his head, like he wanted me to leave.

"Young lady, I've been over this with my son already," Herr Mueller said. "The British will put me in prison."

"No, they'd never do that!" I said. I had to think of some way to convince him. I felt like I could see right through the wall behind the man and to Crispin standing there with his knife.

I remembered what Lucas had said about his father, how he liked to be treated like an important man. "The British will be honored to have you in their country!" I knew my voice was coming out high and strained, and I was afraid he'd detect a false note in it. I had to sound absolutely convincing.

I took a breath and spoke more slowly. "Someone of your brilliance would be wasted in prison."

I hoped I wasn't laying on the praise too heavily. "You'll have your own laboratory to work on whatever you want. My father will see to it. That's one of the reasons I'm here. He sent me to assure you that England needs you. He wouldn't put his own daughter in danger if it wasn't vitally important. Tell him, Lucas. Tell him my father has influence."

"She's right," Lucas said. "Her father, Lord Tretheway, is in the Foreign Office. He is very high up in the government."

Herr Mueller uncrossed his arms. "How do I know he will do this?"

"Because he has always honored scientists," I said. "You will be a valuable contributor to science in England. They will give you all the latest equipment and assistants to help you. Does the German government do that?"

"The government is very short on resources," Herr Mueller said. "They are always pushing, pushing for results." I could tell he was wavering.

"Since the British have allied with the Americans, we don't have such shortages," I said. "The Americans have everything we need. My father is very pleased about that."

The man didn't say anything. "Will you go?" Lucas asked. "We need a decision."

The man hesitated for so long that I feared he would say no. He got out a handkerchief and took off his glasses, polishing them carefully and then putting them back on. He walked around the room and came back to Lucas. "You look well," he said to him. "How are your studies going?"

I wanted to scream. We didn't have time to talk about Lucas's studies, not with Crispin counting down the seconds.

"They're going well," Lucas said. "I'm planning to study engineering once the war is over."

I gaped at Lucas. We had never talked about school or anything like that. Engineering? I had a hard time even imagining Lucas sitting still in a classroom.

Lucas's father nodded. "Good." He took his glasses off again, and again he polished them. I held my breath, waiting for his next words. He put them back on and said, "I will."

A huge feeling of relief washed over me. One hurdle crossed.

When we went outside, the body of the soldier was gone. Crispin was leaning against the wall, cleaning underneath his fingernails with his knife. It just added one more aspect of unreality to the situation. My sophisticated brother who always looked and dressed perfectly was standing outside a German barn cleaning under his fingernails with a knife he had just used to slit someone's throat. I felt a bit of hysterical laughter bubbling up.

I took a breath and shut it off. "Crispin, Lucas's father has agreed to go."

"Good," he said, nodding at Herr Mueller. I noticed that he didn't put away his knife.

"Wait, there's something else we need to discuss. We've got a problem," Lucas said to Crispin. "Since you can count, I'm sure you realize what it is."

"What?" I said. "I can count too."

Crispin looked back and forth between Lucas and me. "Oh, no . . ."

"Do you know how to fly a plane?" Lucas asked him.

"Barely," Crispin said. "I had enough lessons to solo, but no practice after that. I know everything about how to build them, but that's not much use. I don't think I'm good enough." He ran his hand through his hair. "This is a nightmare. Why me and not you?"

"It may be our only option," Lucas said. "For Mina's sake, it's better if you go and I stay here with her. I have dual citizenship, American and German, because of my father."

I wondered if I was in the middle of a bad dream taking a bizarre twist. I had no idea why Lucas and Crispin were talking about me staying in Germany. "Will you stop talking as if I'm not right here? What is going on?" I didn't see what Lucas's citizenship had to do with me.

"My mother became a German citizen when she married my father. If Mina marries me, she'll get German citizenship and that will keep her safe until the war ends. And since she speaks German so well, no one has to know she's English," Lucas said.

"Wait! Stop! Why are we talking about marriage?" I asked.

"Mina, the plan was for me to fly my father out of here," Lucas said.

"That makes sense, with all the time you spent practicing at Cranwell. I still don't understand the problem." I stopped, thinking of Andrew and Lucas in the plane. "Oh." I felt like someone had hit me in the stomach. Aeroplanes only held two people. There were four of us. "But what about Andrew? He was supposed to be here instead of me. How was he going to get out?"

"He wasn't, not right away. He was going to stay behind with me. We had another mission planned," Crispin said.

I tried to think up a brilliant idea of my own. "Why can't we go back the way Lucas and I came? We can catch a train and go back to Brussels. The family there will help us." If they hadn't been arrested. My stomach tightened at the thought of putting them back in danger.

Lucas and Crispin looked at each other. "That might work," Lucas said.

"No," I said, shooting down my own idea. "Even if we make it there and then on to the coast, we don't have any way to get back to England. And it's a hard journey to get there." But I couldn't come up with any more ideas. "So only two people get out of here," I said. "And one of them has to be Herr Mueller."

"Yes," Crispin said. "The Germans have the borders very tightly sewn up. They've had far too many prisoners of war escape, and they've tightened inspections on everything leaving. There was someone who managed to get out by swimming down the Rhine and over the border into France, but he nearly drowned. It's a hard swim."

"How were you and Andrew going to get out once you'd finished whatever it was? Why can't Lucas and I go that way?"

Crispin looked down at the ground. "We were going to swim." He held up his hand. "And before you tell me that was a bad idea, it really wasn't. Both Andrew and I are strong swimmers, and we're both healthy at the moment, at least since my leg healed." He looked up at me. "I don't think you have the strength, Mina. If you practiced, maybe, but it's very, very risky. And they guard the river there, shining lights on it at night."

He was right. I was only a fair swimmer at the best of times.

Crispin came over to me and took me by the shoulders. "I can't believe you are here." He let go of me. "There's no time," he said, almost as if to himself. He closed his eyes briefly. When he opened them, he said. "We'll have to carry through with Lucas's plan. Herr Mueller has to go, even if it means you have to stay." He turned to Lucas. "I'm counting on you to take care of my little sister."

Andrew's voice popped into my head—Andrew at dinner talking about the Australian pilots and how they gave people rides on the wings of their aeroplanes. Could that be done? Or was I just grasping for anything to get us away?

"We have another problem too," Crispin said. "There are soldiers in the village. I don't know if they are searching for us or someone else. We can't wait until they are gone. It's going to be daylight soon. We are going to have to be as quiet as possible. The aeroplane is in another barn. I'll show you."

Crispin led us down a lane. We didn't see anyone. When we came to the other barn and Crispin and Lucas pulled open the doors, all I could think to say was "Does it actually fly?"

The aeroplane in front of us didn't even look sturdy enough to hold together where it stood. There were rips in the canvas on its wings that had been patched with what looked like strips of an old quilt.

"What did you expect?" Crispin said. "The Germans don't leave perfectly good aeroplanes standing around unused. We had to find one no one wanted anymore. It's an old reconnaissance plane that has been replaced by a newer model. But the engine has been completely overhauled. It's supposed to fly just fine."

Now was the time to tell them about my plan. "I have an idea." I explained about what Andrew had said at dinner. "If the Australians can do it, we can too."

The three men looked at me as if I was speaking gibberish.

"That would never work," Crispin said. "We'll stick to the original plan. Let's get the plane out of here."

I looked over at Lucas. His eyes were narrowed as he stared at the plane. I knew he'd want to try it. He wouldn't turn down a challenge.

"Let's talk about it when we get it out in the field," he said. "If it's still holding together then, Mina might have just solved our problem."

"We're sticking to the original plan," Crispin snarled. "Now, push."

"Okay, we'll push," Lucas said. He winked at me. I took it to mean he wasn't going to abandon my idea. We all worked to push the plane out and onto the field beyond the barn. As we got the plane into position, I heard shouts from the village.

"What are they saying?" Lucas asked. All of us held perfectly still, trying to hear.

"They are on to us," Crispin said.

"Get in the plane, Father," Lucas ordered. "I'll get the prop going. Crispin, Mina's idea will work. I know it will. I'll fly the plane and you and Mina can ride on the wings."

"No," Crispin said.

"Stop!" A German soldier came running toward us, his rifle and bayonet pointed at Crispin.

CHAPTER TWENTY-TWO

CRISPIN PUSHED ME behind him. I could tell he was trying to decide whether or not to go for the gun he had.

"All of you, move over to the side of the barn," the soldier ordered.

Crispin hesitated and then motioned with his head for Lucas and me to obey the soldier. I purposely did not look at the plane. I thought the soldier might not be able to see Herr Mueller in the early morning light. I wondered what the soldier would do. Would he call for help? This one was far older than the one Lucas and I had met in the forest. He didn't look scared. He looked pleased.

"I think I will save our firing squad some ammunition," he said. "Filthy spies die anyway." He trained his sight on Crispin. "You look like the ringleader."

"My sister isn't a spy," Crispin yelled. "Let her go, please."

"No!" A voice came from right behind the soldier just as the man pulled the trigger. Crispin let out a cry of pain and collapsed. The soldier swung around as Oscar came around the side of the cottage, holding a large branch above his head. I couldn't believe it was him. Had he followed us all the way from the abbey? I remembered thinking that I had seen someone in the woods. Or had he just decided to come back to the village after Sister Ann was taken away?

Oscar brought it down on the soldier's head and then stopped, an expression of surprise on his face. The soldier dropped to the ground.

I could see Oscar then. He stood still, his mouth open, gazing down at the soldier's bayonet embedded in his chest. Oscar looked back up at me and then down again at the weapon, as if he didn't understand. He put one hand on it and then fell against the side of the cottage. Lucas ran toward the two, his revolver in hand.

"Mina, help me," Crispin gasped. There was blood on his leg, seeping through his trousers. Lucas's father was there before I could regain my senses. He grabbed Crispin under the arms and struggled to raise him, but couldn't get him far enough off the ground. I knelt down to help, getting on one side of him and putting his arm over my shoulder.

Lucas ran over to us. "Oscar is dead," he said. "I think the bayonet went right into his heart. I don't know about the soldier."

I felt so light-headed that I thought I was going to faint.

"The sound of the shot is going to bring people here. I don't know how many soldiers are out there, but we need to move," Crispin said. "You're going to have to fly the plane, Lucas. I can't."

"We can't just leave Oscar here," I said.

"We don't have a choice," Lucas said.

"Perhaps I should stay," Herr Mueller said. Lucas gave his father a sharp look. "I want you to go, Lucas. I haven't been much of a father to you, but I can't just go and leave you here."

"No," Crispin said. "You're not staying here."

"We're all going," I said. I was getting tired of Crispin's stubbornness. "Let's stop arguing. Why not take the best chance we have?"

"Even if Lucas could fly the plane with wing riders, the extra weight would make us burn too much fuel. We'd never make it to England."

"Why do we have to go to England?" I said. "We've got an aeroplane. We can fly it in any direction we choose. We just need to get out of Germany and German-occupied territory."

"She's right. If we made it to France or Switzerland, we'd have help to get back to England," Lucas said.

"Switzerland is too far," Herr Mueller spoke up. "The border with France is much closer."

"Except there are about two million German soldiers between

us and the British line in France, all of whom might be inclined to shoot at an aeroplane carrying people on the wings," Crispin pointed out. "You're better off with as few people as possible."

I couldn't take any more. "I'm tired of all your stupid bravery and nobility," I said. "Haven't you done your part? There are other people who care about you."

We heard a motorcar approaching. "I don't know who that is, but I suggest we leave," Lucas said.

I held my breath, waiting to see what Crispin was going to do.

Crispin looked at the aeroplane and then back toward the village. "All right, I'll go, but I suspect I'm dooming all of us. This plane is not going to get all of us out of here."

"Let me worry about flying," Lucas said. He held out the revolver to his father. "How good are you with this?" he asked him.

"I was considered quite a marksman in my youth," Herr Mueller said, taking the gun.

Crispin pulled out his own revolver. "Mina, I know Father taught you how to use his. If anyone gets close to us, just shoot in the general direction."

I took it. It was heavier than the one I'd learned with. "What about you?" I asked. "I'm sure you are a better shot than me."

"I have one." He pulled out the one he had taken off the soldier he had killed.

We were all speaking so calmly, as if we were just making plans to go on a grouse shoot. I tried to swallow, but my mouth was so dry that I couldn't manage. I took the gun even though I didn't really want it, and I forced myself to climb up onto the spot on the lower of the two wings. I sat down and pulled my knees up close to my chest, gripping the braces tightly.

"The engine is going to get hot," Lucas said, "so don't lean against the plane." He smiled at me. "I was hoping the first time you flew with me, it would be a little different from this."

I tried to give him a weak smile in return, but my stomach was churning. I heard shouts.

"That's our signal to go," Lucas said. The engine started and I looked over to see soldiers coming toward us.

"I thought we were going!" Crispin yelled. "We're not moving."

"The engine has to warm up," Lucas said. Herr Mueller aimed the revolver at the approaching men and let off a shot. One man yelled and grabbed his arm.

"I fear I am out of practice," Herr Mueller said to us. "I was aiming for his heart."

I stared at the man. So Herr Mueller was a bit more than a bookish scientist. He was a little frightening. I suspected he'd get exactly what he wanted once he reached England.

The plane began to move, picking up speed. The remaining men ran after us, shooting, so Crispin and Herr Mueller shot back. I realized I couldn't shoot my own gun and hold on at the same time. The field was too bumpy. I didn't know how Crispin was able to manage. I decided just to concentrate on not falling off.

The aeroplane lifted off the ground, but the engine was struggling and I knew all our weight was a problem. It climbed so slowly that I didn't know if we would clear the trees at the end of the field. We did, just barely, and Lucas yelled, "We're going to have to stay low. It will be bumpy."

I didn't care as long as we left the soldiers behind. The ride actually wasn't as bad as our trip on the train had been, though I wished I had goggles. I kept my eyes closed some of the time, but occasionally opened them to look at the land below. As we flew south, the terrain changed from spring green to more and more gray mud, and I knew we were getting close to the front lines. After only a few more minutes, I could see an entire waste-land with nothing growing in it, just mud and dead trees. Tents and trenches and huts for thousands of German troops covered it.

I tightened my grip on the braces, fearing that someone would start shooting at us. It was so early that there weren't many men out. The ones that were did look up, many of them pointing at us, but there was no gunfire. Some of them started to wave, and then it hit me: We were in an aeroplane clearly marked as German. I waved back, feeling huge relief. We were low enough that I could see them shouting and pointing.

Lucas yelled to me, "They're not used to seeing a girl on an aeroplane wing!"

There were miles and miles of troop encampments, all in a gray, muddy landscape. I thought it looked like something out of a nightmare, so bleak and desolate that it was as if all hope had disappeared from the Earth. There were a few houses, but no signs of growing things or animals, or even of anyone but sol-diers. Then the landscape emptied of even soldiers and I couldn't figure out why until I saw up ahead that the encampments started again. We had crossed the front lines and were almost over the Allied troops. In a German aeroplane flying low to the ground.

Lucas realized what it meant too. He yelled, "I'm going to try to get higher," but the aeroplane could only climb a little way. The first weapons were fired at us and flak exploded all around. A shot whistled by my ear.

"Go lower!" I yelled. "So they can see us."

Lucas's eyes were wide. I nodded and then took my hair out of its plait so that it began whipping around in the wind. They'd have to see that I was a girl.

He turned the nose down. I positioned myself so I had one arm wrapped tightly around the brace and the other free to wave with. As we went lower, men began to come out of tents and huts to see what was going on. I waved and shouted hello and smiled, though I had no idea if they could see my expressions or hear my words. Crispin caught on and did the same from the other side. I couldn't see him, but I could hear him. The men waved back, pointing at me.

"Hold on!" Lucas yelled. "I'm going to wiggle the wings." I tightened my grip and Lucas tipped the plane from side to side.

I tried to see a place where Lucas could land, but there weren't enough clear areas. There had to be an airfield somewhere, but without knowing where, we could fly around for a long time without finding one. Another burst of gunfire shocked me. Someone had decided we were still suspicious enough to shoot at. The gunfire continued and I just hoped we could get past the guns before we were hit. The aeroplane had to be an easy target. Then there was an awful jolt that almost made me lose my grip, and the machine started to shake and quiver like jelly. I could see Lucas fighting the controls.

"Oil pressure's gone!" he yelled.

Behind us, I could see a stream of black oil leaking out. A shot had hit us. The engine quit. For a moment I thought my heart had quit with it.

The aeroplane immediately began to descend. Ahead of us, I still saw just rows and rows of tents. I wanted to crouch down and close my eyes, but I made myself stand up so I could see better. Slightly to our left, I saw a field with a stack of building materials piled at one end. It looked as if it was a site for a building yet to go up.

"Over there!" I shouted. I had no idea how he did it, but Lucas managed to get the machine turned in the right direction. We were gliding in, going lower and lower, and slowing at the same time. I bit my lip hard as I imagined the jolt that would happen when we hit. I closed my eyes.

"Brace yourself!" Lucas yelled.

I crouched down just in time. The aeroplane touched the ground, but there was no bounce like I expected. Instead it came to a sudden halt. Mud sprayed up as the wheels sank. The plane tipped forward and I slid off onto the ground in between the upper and lower wings, hitting my head hard on one of the supports. Through the pain I saw Lucas reaching for me. I took his hand and then there were soldiers running toward us and noise and shouting.

It was hours before everything was all straightened out. We

had to repeat our story over and over, first to the officer where we landed, and then again to another officer at a field hospital we were taken to. I still felt so shaky I could hardly stand. A nurse took me into a small room with a hip bath and left me a clean nurse's uniform to put on. My own clothes were taken away, I guessed to be thrown away.

When I emerged, feeling a little better, I saw Crispin in a bed down the ward. He had been cleaned up and his leg was bandaged. He smiled when he saw me.

"Where are Lucas and his father?" I asked.

"They are off talking to more officers. Our story seems a little hard to believe. I don't even believe it. I'm sure there are wires being sent back and forth. It will all be straightened out, though. I can't believe I'm going back to England. It's been a long time."

I felt a rush of anger. "I've spent a long time thinking you were dead. Do you know how miserable I've been? Why couldn't someone have told me? It wasn't like I'd have told anyone who would have gotten word to the Germans."

"I'm sorry, Mina. Father made the decision, and I'm sure he thought it the safest. You know how cautious he is. He didn't tell Margaret either, only Mother, and of course the people in the Foreign Office who needed to know. It wasn't you in particular who weren't told."

That made me feel a little better. Now, it was time to tell Crispin what he needed to know. "You'll find some changes at home," I said. "Major changes."

"Like what? I've heard about the bombings in London. But they are already rebuilding, aren't they?"

"Yes, it's not buildings." I paused. I had to tell him now. "I met a girl you knew. Her name is Gwendolyn Slade."

He tried to sit up. "How did you meet her? Is she all right?"

I didn't know the best way to give him the news, so I just went ahead and said it. "Gwendolyn has a son—your son. A little boy named Gordon who looks just like you. I haven't seen him, but I saw his picture."

Crispin lay back on the pillow and stared up at the ceiling. "A son?" he croaked.

"Yes."

He sat up again. "I didn't know she was going to have a baby. I never would have volunteered for this if I had known."

"She told me that. She's nice. She's a friend of Margaret's."

"Does Margaret know?"

"No one knows except me. Not even Father."

"Father!" Crispin groaned. "This is going to be a shock for him."

That was an understatement.

He grimaced. "And Gwendolyn's parents. I'm sure they despise me."

"I don't know. She didn't say anything about them, except that they are keeping the baby for her while she's at Hallington visiting Margaret."

"A son!" he said to himself.

A doctor came over to us. "Captain Tretheway, you and your party are being moved farther away from the front lines. An ambulance will drive you. How is the pain?"

"Not too bad," Crispin said.

269

"I'll give you something for the ride. The jolting is going to make it worse," the doctor said.

That whole day and night we were on the move, by ambulance and car and lorry and ship. I didn't have a chance to see Lucas alone, and I was so tired, I just let people lead me to places and tell me what to do.

Once on the ship, I kept Crispin company as best I could, helping him with sips of water and wiping his face. He had begun to run a fever. A nurse told me infection had set in. "Is Gwen really all right?" he asked for about the hundredth time. "She doesn't hate me, does she?"

"No, of course not. And the baby is adorable, just like you were."

"We're going straight to Hallington, aren't we?" he asked. "And she's still there?"

"We are, and she is, as far as I know." I patted his hand. "You should sleep now. It will help you get better."

I sat with him and watched him sleep. I knew I should sleep too, but I couldn't stop thinking about Sister Ann and Oscar. I pictured Oscar cradling the pigeon. Who would take care of the birds with him gone? Would they miss him? It wasn't fair. None of it was fair. I wiped away a tear. Tears wouldn't help Oscar now.

I decided that after the war, I would ask my father to find out what had happened to Sister Ann. If I could find her, I could tell her how brave Oscar was. It might not help much, but it was better than the nun not knowing.

Crispin woke up and asked for another sip of water. I gave it to him.

"Mina." I heard Lucas's voice in the doorway. "We're almost there," he said. "You can see the coast. Come up with me for a minute."

Crispin waved me away. "Go," he said. "You've been sitting with me long enough."

We went up to the top deck. I leaned on the railing, breathing in the fresh air, trying to forget the smell of the sick bay for a little while. "I've never been so happy to see the cliffs of Dover," I said. I glanced over at Lucas, expecting to see him grinning. He wasn't.

"What's wrong?" I leaned closer so our shoulders were touching. "Aren't you happy we're going home? I can't wait to get back to Hallington. I didn't have a chance to properly show you around. Spring in Lincolnshire is lovely, and I'm sure Mrs. Brickles would make us a picnic so we could spend all day out and about—"

He interrupted me. "I can't go to Hallington, Mina. I'm going to London."

I gripped the railing. "Why?" I asked.

"My father wants me there until all the details about his laboratory are settled. He doesn't trust the British. I'm not sure what he thinks I can do, but he's asked and I've said yes. After that," he said, shrugging, "it will be up to the American military."

I stared out at the waves. He put his arm around me. "I'm sorry about keeping things from you. I misjudged you all along. I won't do that again. We made a good team."

"I thought we'd have some time together." I tried not to cry. I knew that in wartime no one made plans, but I hadn't wanted long-term plans. I'd wanted a few days. That hadn't seemed like too much to ask.

"We have now," he said. "We'll find a way to see each other again. I'm good at getting what I want." He grinned. "That is, if you want to see me again."

I didn't answer. A worried look crossed his face. I looked around. No one was paying any attention to us. I leaned over and kissed him. "There's your answer," I said.

For a moment he stared at me, and then he put his arms around me and pulled me so close I could barely breathe. I didn't care. "I didn't think someone like your ladyshipness was allowed to kiss in public," he whispered.

I was feeling a little dizzy. "Her ladyshipness has decreed that she is allowed," I said. The next kiss went on for a long time. I'd have been happy if it never stopped, but I heard someone clearing their throat behind us.

Lucas loosened his hold on me, but I didn't let go of him. I wasn't sure I could stand on my own.

I twisted around to see a sailor standing a few feet away. "Um, excuse me, Lady Thomasina. I have a telegram from your father. I was supposed to deliver it right away, but I couldn't find you earlier."

"Thank you," I said, taking the envelope. Then I turned back to Lucas so he would kiss me some more.

"Aren't you going to open it?" Lucas asked.

"Should I?" At the moment I was more interested in Lucas than in what I was sure was a furious telegram from my father about what I'd done.

"You should."

I sighed. "All right. Don't go anywhere." I ripped it open.

Come to London. I have a job for you.

I showed it to Lucas. "We have some time after all. Now, kiss me again. I don't want to waste any of it."

AUTHOR'S NOTE

The story itself is of course fiction, and all of the characters are fictional, except for Prince Albert, though his relationship with Margaret is imaginary. However, the real Prince Albert, who later became King George VI, was actually at Cranwell Airbase in Lincolnshire in the spring of 1918. He did serve under the alias of Albert Smith, and it was a rather open secret among the locals that he was there.

The Arnold Cipher is an actual cipher used by John André and Benedict Arnold when Arnold was attempting to surrender West

Point to the British in 1780. It's a very useful cipher because it is very secure as long as only the sender and the recipient know which book is used.

The raid on Ostend and Zeebrugge did occur, and was one of the most daring operations of World War I, though it is rarely mentioned in history books any longer.

There was a cat named Unsinkable Sam, though he lived during World War II rather than World War I. Ships during both wars usually had cats on board to control the mice and rats, so it's not too far-fetched to think there was more than one unsinkable cat.

The White Lady underground operation did exist in occupied Belgium during the war, and many of the details of Lucas and Mina's adventures took inspiration from accounts of the participants.

ACKNOWLEDGMENTS

Since I was one of those children who practically haunted my small town's library, it seems appropriate now to thank the librarians of the Public Library of Cincinnati and Hamilton County who helped me find the resources I needed to write this story. And with the librarians, I'd also like to thank the taxpayers who are willing to fund such a fabulous library. How many libraries are able to keep an assortment of frivolous novels set in England and published in 1918 and 1919? Having access to those helped me with the language and the small details of everyday life so important to a work of historical fiction. It's really a dream come true for me to have a good reason to spend so much time in this particular library.

I'd also like to thank my family, who always contribute to the making of all my books: my husband, Dean, who patiently talks out plot problems with me when I'm sure he'd rather be doing other things; to my daughter, Hope, who proofreads for clarity and accuracy; and my son, Garret, who, while my harshest critic, is always willing to brainstorm at a moment's notice. In a way, this book was more a family activity than most of my other books. It was inspired by the Downton Abbey series, which our whole family watched, debating whether or not we liked Matthew (split two and two on that), who Lady Mary should marry, and what happened to Lady Edith's beau. I'll always keep that memory of us all together as my children get older and move out into the world.

Thanks to Chris Bruch who offered his expertise on World War I aircraft and to Liva Pfuhler for her German translations.

I'd also like to thank the Swoon team for all their hard work getting this book into print: Kat Brzozowski, Holly West, Lauren Scobell, Mandy Veloso, Liz Dresner, Kim Waymer, Emily Settle, and Connie Gabbert.

And finally thanks to all the writers out there who have supported me, whether through commiserations, suggestions, boosting my books, or just passing the time with me while I procrastinate.

Check out more books chosen for publication by readers like you.

DID YOU KNOW...

readers like you helped to get this book published?

Join our book-obsessed community and help us discover awesome new writing talent.

1 **Write it.**
Share your original YA manuscript.

2 **Read it.**
Discover bright new bookish talent.

3 **Share it.**
Discuss, rate, and share your faves.

4 **Love it.**
Help us publish the books you love.

Share your own manuscript or dive between the pages at **swoonreads.com** or by downloading the **Swoon Reads app.**